Death on the Green
a Detective Hooper Mystery

Roy Ingamells

Copyright © 2023 Roy Ingamells
All rights reserved.

ISBN: 9798861695435

E-MAIL: royingamellswriter@gmail.com

Available in print and E-book from
www.amazon.co.uk and Amazon worldwide

For more information, visit **www.zen2books.com**

DEDICATION

*For my daughter Ruth
With eternal thanks for her unfailing
support and encouragement*

DEATH ON THE GREEN

ACKNOWLEDGEMENT

My thanks and best wishes to Louise of Zen2 Books without whom this book would never have seen the light of day

DEATH ON THE GREEN

ABOUT THE AUTHOR

Roy Ingamells was born in 1933 in the quaint village of Thurnscoe Yorkshire. The son of a miner, he was an inveterate reader, frequenting the local library from the age of 7. He left school at the age of 15, became an apprentice painter and decorator and served an indentured apprenticeship for six years. A small foot deformity prevented him from being called for National Service in the armed forces which greatly disappointed him because he always wanted to be a pilot.

At age 23 he started a small painting/decorating contracting business and later began a house letting/cleaning service. When he was 63 he trained as a glider pilot and fulfilled his childhood dream of being an aviator. He pursued that hobby into his eighties, and retired from business when he was 83.

In his early twenties a correspondence course enabled him to get his first story published in a London evening paper and throughout his life he continued to write stories. *Hooper* is his first novel. When he is not writing, he regularly plays bowls and table tennis. Roy has one daughter, one grandson, and one brother twenty years his junior.

Roy now lives in Hampshire, calling himself a Yorkshire immigrant to Hampshire. His Detective Hooper was born in Hampshire and it is here that he will continue to live his fictional life.

Chapter 1

The sun was streaming through a crack in the curtains and glinted on the buttons of Hooper's police uniform. The wife, he thought, is at her sister's for the weekend and I have a day off. Today I am going to trounce that know it all, king of the bowling green, Ray Stacey. Ha! Ha! The club president out in the first round. That'll be something. He slipped on his white club shirt and grey flannels, the uniform for bowls matches, mentally preparing for battle.

The bright early morning sunshine would prove excellent for bowling, and a good bacon and egg breakfast will set me up nicely for the match he thought. Ray Stacey didn't know it but today, Ray Stacey, would get his comeuppance.

Hooper strapped his bowls bag onto its trolley and set off on the short walk up the hill to the club. He crossed the High Street and up through the long passage that led to the church. The closed door of the Bell pub stifled his desire to sink a glass of bitter before the match. He strode over the ancient gravestones of the ancient church and on to the path up towards the club. The stone flagged causeway twisted through a dank tunnel of trees and shrubs always giving Hooper goose pimples and a shiver down his spine. A great place for a murder.

Today he shrugged the feeling off, today, his priority lay in the trouncing of the club president, bowling him off the green, sending him home in total ignominy. He was also sure Ray had other ideas.

The club carpark lay at the top of the path and as he reached it, he thought only one car. 'So' he muttered to himself, 'he's here already, trying to steal a march with some extra practice.'

He'll be up there with his flat cap perched forward like a horse trainer at Epsom, his self-satisfied smile oozing over-confidence. But it won't do him any good this morning, Hooper paused and looked at the car. That's strange, he thought, there ought to be two cars we need a skip to adjudicate, but perhaps he's brought Pete Livsey with him.

The long lane from the car park to the bowling club also served the tennis club and the croquet club which although grouped together, was not associated, except that the other two sometimes used the bowling club clubhouse for functions.

Hooper reached the gate and noticed the padlock had been removed and put in its safe place. He looked across the green where something seemed to have been dumped in the middle. No, it was a person. He ran across. Why was Ray lying down in the middle of the green?

"Hey!" Hooper shouted, "Ray come on, it's not time to sleep now."

Ray didn't move.

A cold shiver trickled the back of Hooper's neck as he reached Ray.

Stacey's dead eyes gazed at the sun filled sky as he lay staked to the grass. A Croquet hoop pinioned his wrists and ankles like massive staples, while his head had been battered into a bloody soup, with a bowl, carefully placed beside it; while, into what remained of his mouth, had been forced, a pale-yellow tennis ball.

Hooper's day off had just ended.

He staggered backwards to the edge of the green slumped down and sat with his feet in the ditch and pulled out his mobile pressing the office button.

"Basingham police station Sargent Trench speaking."

"Hooper here," he gasped, "Get someone out to Odsham bowling club; there's been a murder. Oh and get Prune out here too."

"It's her day off sir."

"Was, Sergeant. Was."

Prunella Prune, perched on the tips of her toes on the edge of the high diving board, her pointed fingers stretching to the sky, enhancing an already tall body, with an hourglass slim figure, and savage red hair, that peeked out of her cap. She was savouring her first dive of the day when she heard the ring tone of her mobile phone,

"She'll be coming round the mountains when she comes,
She'll be coming round the mountains when she comes,
She'll be coming round the mountains, coming round the mountains,
Coming round the mountains, when she comes.
Singing, Hi Hi Yippee, Yippee Yey
Singing Hi Hi Yippee, Yippee Yeh,
Singing Hi Hi Yippee,
Hi Hi Yippee,
Hi Hi Yippee Yippee Yey."

The ringing phone was far below and she ignored it, "Sod off," she thought, "I'll bet that's daddy wanting to use the pool in my time." Rising higher on her toes she did a backflip out into the air of the silent pool, curled into a double somersault, and cut into the water without a splash.

She surfaced, but "Hi Hi Yippee" was still blaring from her mobile phone, glorious in its new pink flowered cover and lying in her Tom Taylor bag hanging on a clothes rack at the other side of the pool. Turning onto her back, Prunella slowly backstroked to the edge and hauled herself out.

"This had better be damn good," she muttered "on my day off."

The mobile told her it was the office. "Chuff me!" Prunella pressed call back.

"Ah Prunella. DCI Hooker wants you at his bowls club ASAP and that means yesterday. There's been a murder," said Sergeant Trench.

"Who?"

"His club president, Ray Stacey."

"Christ! Ten minutes."

The bowling club car park was full; staff cars from the adjacent school. "That's a problem," thought

Prune, "we'll have to seal it off. How many staff? How many kids?"

Blue flashing lights filled the car park, blocking the hundred metres of lane leading to the club entrance. Police constables were in every adjacent garden, questioning old ladies from the elderly people's bungalows.

Prunella pushed her way through the throng, running where she could, pushing people out of the way where she couldn't. She could see that the club gate, standing in the chain link perimeter fence, was open. She made a beeline for it, shouting "'Police, Police, move."

Herb Hooper, his shoulders sagging, his head hanging, was sitting on the edge of the green with his feet in the ditch when Pru came through the gate. She put her hand on his shoulder. He looked at her with a weak smile.

"Hi Pru. You'd better go and take a look at him. The Doc's with him."

Prunella walked across the green and knelt down beside the doctor.

"Dead," observed the doctor.

Prunella didn't reply. The doctor looked at her

again. "Are you OK? You're as white as a sheet."

"Doctor, look whose name is on that bowl."

The doctor looked closely, "Hooper," he said.

"And the tennis ball is mine. Look I marked it with a marker pen."

She looked back at Hooper, and standing up began to walk unsteadily towards him. Hooper unhooked his feet from the ditch, launched himself clumsily on to the green as Prunella reached him and sat down abruptly.

"Pru, what the hell's the matter? You look like death."

"Herb, your wood, was used to bash his head in," she said. "and, it's my tennis ball that's stuffed in his mouth. We're being set up Herb. We're being set up."

"No!"

"We are Herb."

"But why? Who?"

"I don't know. Why would someone do this?" A little colour began to creep back into her cheeks. Pru shrugged her shoulders helplessly.

"Hooper, Prune, what's going on here?"

They turned at Assistant Chief Constable Sampson's sharp voice.

Hooper pointed, "Take a look Sir."

Sampson strode across the green and paused looking down at the remains of Stacey for a few moments. "Bad do, Doctor," he whispered.

"Yes Sir."

"He was my cousin, Doctor." He spun on his heel and marched back across the green.

Hooper and Prune stood up smartly as Samson reached them.

"Right, I'll see you both in my office in the morning. You know this means suspension from duty."

"But Sir!" Hooper began.

"Office in the morning," he said and left. Hooper and Pru looked at each other dejectedly.

Hooper looked across the green to where a group of officers were being marshalled to start a fingertip search. He nudged Pru's arm.

"Come on Prune. Home. See you tomorrow."

Prune nodded. "Yes," she replied wearily.

Hooper opened the gate to let Prune out and was faced by a small boy.

"Oh! Can I help you lad?"

The boy held out his hand. It was a lapel badge in the shape of a Buffalo's head. "The man dropped it," he said

"Which man?"

"The man who ran out of the bowling green."

"Here, Pru listen to this." "Did you see him? Can you describe him?" asked Hooper urgently.

"Nah"

"Why?"

"He 'ad one of them big white hats on wiv a net down the front."

"You mean a beekeeper's hat?" asked Pru.

"Yeh, you see em on telly, but I couldn't see 'is face, the net was too thick."

Hooper slipped the object in his pocket and patted the boy on the head. "What's your name lad?"

"Jimmy Knolles. Are you going to give that to the police mister? It's a nice badge; it's got gold on it."

"I am the police, Jimmy. Detective Chief Inspector Hooper."

Jimmy looked from Hooper to Prune. "Will there be a reward?" he asked.

Hooper dug into his pocket and then flipped a fifty pence piece into the air which the boy caught at his eye level. 'Ta. I'll be off then.'

Hooper put his arm around the boy's shoulder preventing him from running down the lane. "Jimmy, did this man see you?"

"Silly bugger knocked me over. I gave 'im a mouthful I can tell you. Look, I grazed my knee."

Hooper bent down and pulled Jimmy towards him and looked straight into his eyes.

"Jimmy, he said 'look at me. Do you live in the village?" The boy nodded. "I want you to go straight home. Don't stop to talk to anyone. Don't tell anyone you were here, for now, not even your mum, and nobody at school. Can you do that? Can you keep a secret?"

Jimmy nodded slowly, then broke away from

Hooper and ran off down the lane shouting. "Yes Mister, I can keep a secret."

Prune dropped her head on Herb's shoulder. "Do you think he's in danger?"

Patting her on the back he said, "No doubt, he saw a killer. And tomorrow you and I will be suspended."

"Are you going to give the buffalo badge to the search team?" She motioned to where a line of police stretched across the green.

He shook his head. "I think I'll hold on to this for now."

....

Hooper pulled his black Jag into the police station car park. The building was looking its age. A 1960's building, its curtain polished wood and glass frame and front door looked across a flight of worn pseudo stone steps which in turn, led down into Churchfield. Churchfield was a listed site of an ancient church, the remains of which still stood in a scattering of trees.

"'God it's full and I'm early," muttered Hooper, "why are there so many people here?"

He pushed through the door letting it bang behind

him, and walked through into the front office. The large room in front of the enquiry desk was packed with constables and top brass, everybody was there. Assistant Chief Constable Sampson had positioned himself beside Trench, the Desk Sergeant, where he could see everyone.

Hooper saw Prune across at the far end of the room and signalled to her. He struggled and pushed his way through the crowd towards her.

"What's going off Pru?"

"That boy Jimmy Knolles didn't get home last night," muttered Pru.

Hooper looked across to the sergeant's desk where Sampson and the Chief Constable were in deep conversation. They looked up simultaneously, looking directly at him and dropped their eyes immediately.

"Pru, we ought to have taken him home."

Pru looked at Hooper. "Why?"

"We should have made sure he got home and not sent him off by himself."

"But we didn't know he wouldn't get there," Pru replied.

"I agree, but I think you and me are going to

be blamed for it."

....

Sarah Hooper sat in front of her dressing table polishing her nails. Today she had to look her best, today she had a date. Ever since Herb had made Detective Chief Inspector she hadn't had to work, in fact he had insisted she didn't. Sarah had joined the "ladies who lunch group". This collection of well-off local ladies, who met twice a week for lunch and gossip, included Janice Sampson the Assistant Chief Constables' wife, and Helen Wilkinson, the Chief Constable's wife.

Sarah smiled at herself. Curly blonde hair, dark blue eyes, cultivated eye lashes, an oval face leading to round chin and dimples when she smiled. Just a touch of make-up; she usually didn't need make up but today was different. Today she wasn't going to lunch with the ladies. Today she had a date.

She suddenly tingled with excitement and anticipation, her body quivering; she squeezed her body together, every fibre vibrating. He was a dangerous bastard but that was part of the attraction.

....

Sarah entered the restaurant and was greeted by the head waiter. She shook her head and looked around. He was there, at a quiet corner table. Good choice she thought. She caught his eye, waved and pointed to the restroom. She hung up the old coat, her jacket, and her bag - she didn't want any accidents with that. She sauntered over to the mirror, adjusted her hair, no point in being in a hurry, admired her bright yellow sweater, her slim fitting, sharp creased slacks, they made her look tall. She slowly eased her sweater down into a prominent profile. Satisfied, she headed for the door.

Entrance she thought. She paused at the top of steps leading into the restaurant. Moving into her best model pose she looked slowly round the room, her eyes resting on him last. Sarah walked slowly across the highly polished floor, her eyes never leaving his. As she reached him, a slow smile crossed her face. He stood up and kissed her cheek whispering, 'You look fantastic." His eyes black and steely caught hers.

Inside Sarah shivered. "Thank you, darling."

He passed her a menu. "What shall we eat Sarah darling? Steak perhaps? I can recommend it underdone. That is when the blood flows, Sarah."

Sarah looked at him, her mouth dry, her throat unable to swallow. "Sometimes I think he is too brutal and he's gone insane," she thought. "I'll have the salmon."

He looked at her with cold eyes, "Something fishy there Sarah."

Sarah spread her napkin on her knee and glanced up at him with a nervous smile. They ate in silence.

He sat back and looked at her steadily without a smile. "That was a lovely meal Sarah, we should do it again."

"Yes we should," she smiled.

"Why don't we complete our afternoon and visit our secret boudoir; it's the most comfortable bed I know."

"No, no, I can't," she protested, 'Herb will be home soon.'

He began to chuckle. "He will be incarcerated very shortly along with that prig of a sergeant of his. Charged with Stacey's and the boy's murder."

Sarah stood up sharply, the chair toppled over behind her. "I'm leaving."

He grabbed her wrist. "No, we are going for our

afternoon rendezvous."

He pulled her tightly to him and marched her to the restroom and shoved her inside. "Get your coat. Fast."

The restaurant manager rushed across to him, "Sir, the bill, I'll call the police if you ….."

He pushed fifty pounds in the manager's face and flashed a card at him.

The manager staggered back, "Police," he gasped.

"Yes and I've just arrested her; go and pull her out of that restroom."

"There's an outside entrance sir."

He pushed the man away and raced for the exit.

Sarah was just getting into a taxi.

……..

Hooper gazed around the officers, all busy chattering about the missing boy.

"Quiet!" Sampson's voice rang around the room.

The rabble of voices chopped off in mid-sentence. The Chief Constable scanned the silent room.

"As you all know, a young boy, Jimmy Knowles has gone missing. We have to find this young boy, and we have to find him quickly, or you know the consequences. If he isn't found within forty-eight hours he'll be dead." He said. "Assistant Chief Constable Sampson has worked out a search schedule and you should get your orders from the Sergeant. Every nook and cranny gentlemen; don't fail me."

The Chief Constable caught Hooper's eye, and with a quick double jab of his finger mouthed 'my office'.

"Come on Pru, here we go."

They watched him climb the stairs two at a time and enter his office, and then followed him at a slightly slower pace.

Hooper knocked on the door firmly. A sharp 'come in' rapped out. They entered. The Chief Constable glanced up. "Sit," he said and went on with his papers.

Hooper and Pru fidgeted in their chairs. The time seemed like eternity as he continued to shuffle through the papers.

Suddenly the Chief Constable's head jerked up.

"Looks like you two are likely to be charged

with murder and you are suspended right now. Give me your cards."

Hooper struggled with his wallet and placed his card on the desk. Prune fumbled with her bag and did the same. They started to rise from their chairs.

"I haven't said you can go," he said.

They sat down and looked at him expectantly. He returned their gaze silently.

He came to, as though startled out of a trance.

"Hooper, you didn't kill Stacey did you?"

"No sir."

"I believe there is something strange going off at this station. Things aren't normal. I can feel a tension, but I can't put my finger on it."

"But what can we do? We're suspended," said Prune.

"That is the point, Prune. You have no authority; you can't be suspected of being the police, but you have the skills, and I want you to go on the streets and use them."

Hooper and Prune stirred uneasily in their chairs and looked at each other. Hooper nodded at

Prune, she nodded back.

"Right, you're on sir."

"Good. I want you out there observing, asking discreet questions, because someone knows; someone knows something. People don't disappear."

Prune coughed and the chief looked at her expectantly. "I don't suppose you could arrange us some finance sir?"

The chief smiled, "I'll see what I can do Prune."

They got up and left the office.

"You're a cheeky bugger," said Hooper.

"Ask and it shall be opened unto you," Pru smiled.

They tripped down the stairs and stopped, Sampson was waiting for them with a smile on his face. "Out on the street Hooper?"

"You could say that sir."

The phone rang on the Sergeant's desk, they all turned towards it. Sergeant Trench said "God no." He handed the phone to Sampson.

"I don't know how you organised this Hooper, but I'm sure you did. Christopher

Woodley, the bowling club Vice President has been found dead, staked out just like Stacey."

"You can't hang this one on me sir."

"We'll see." Sampson turned back to Trench.

Hooper and Pru walked past them and out onto the steps. Hooper looked around, sniffed the air, "I think we'll have some rain soon. Clear the air, don't you think Pru?"

"Where do we start Herb?"

"The bowling club's first stop I think. My car."

They set off walking rapidly towards the Jag. A voice bellowed behind them. The Chief Constable was standing at the top of the steps.

"Hooper, Prune, get back here."

They stopped in their tracks and spun round, paused, and then raced back to the station.

"Right Hooper. Get to the club and interview that lady, Mrs. Gardner, she lives next to the club. We know what happens to people who see this bloke." muttered the Chief.

"Sir," said Hooper with a nod.

Hooper and Prune sprinted back to the car. Only ten minutes separated the station and the bowls club. They made it in eight.

....

Hooper parked in the club car park and rushed up the lane to Mrs. Gardner's bungalow. The garden gate was standing open. They raced down the garden path and knocked sharply on the door. No reply.

"She's not in," called a voice.

A face appeared between the bed sheets drying on a line in the next garden. Pru walked over to her while Herb inspected the outside of the building.

"Who are you?" Pru asked.

"Mrs. Lomas."

"Did you see Mrs. Gardner leave?"

"Yes, about half an hour ago. A man called and they went off together."

"Can you describe him?"

"Not really, I was tangled up in all this washing."

"Didn't you notice anything?"

She waddled her head and pursed her lips. "I think

he had blonde hair."

"OK Mrs. Lomas; thanks for your help."

Herb came round the corner. "Did you get anything?" he asked.

"She thought the man who called for Mrs. Gardener had blonde hair."

"That's a start."

They walked briskly across the green. Christopher Woodley was lying on his back, his legs and arms spread-eagled, and fixed to the green with croquet hoops; his torso parallel with the ditch; the sole of his feet facing the clubhouse. His head had been battered in with another of Hooper's bowls and another tennis ball belonging to Prune had been pushed into his mouth.

Hooper circled the body. Prune stood gaping at the scene.

"What is this nut case up to?" Hooper asked.

"Boss, Herb, do you think he's got a grudge against the club members?"

"That's a thought Pru."

Hooper dropped to his knees on the green and began to scratch in the grass with his fingernails.

"Look here Pru."

Prune kneeled beside him. Pressed into the green was a Buffalo lapel pin. "So, is someone leaving us a calling card?"

"It looks like it. Pru, you go home and search your laptop for Buffalo organisations. I don't want anybody looking over your shoulder."

"Ok, it should only take me a couple of hours."

"Ring me if you find anything urgent, otherwise I'll see you in the morning."

....

Pru slowed and turned into the front gates of her end terrace house, pulled across the front of the house and parked. When she bought the house she had pulled down part of the front wall to allow her easy parking, but also to allow visitors to park in the backyard.

She slipped her latch key into the lock and let herself into the hall. She stood for a moment and thought "it seems awfully quiet." Pru hung up her coat and walked through into the kitchen, placed her laptop on the large deal topped table and thought "Coffee."

She filled the kettle and plugged it in, fished in the cupboard for vegetables for dinner; celery, swede, sprouts. She looked through the window, "No, something's wrong." She gazed around uneasily. Where's the cat? Where's Macilroy? That's it. Macilroy always greets her when she comes in.

Pru walked across to the back door and opened it and stepped on to the top step overlooking the yard.

"Maccie" she called. "Maccie, puss puss, Maccie"

There was no response. She looked around the yard to see if she was hiding in any corners.

"She'll come back when she's ready," muttered Pru. Her eyes fell on a strange car parked at the bottom of the steps. Next door must have visitors, she thought. Out of habit she glanced at the number: GFE69 0ZH. She stepped back into the house and closed the door.

At that moment two huge blows hit her on the shoulders, she staggered and fell on to her back, her head hitting the door.

Through bleary eyes she looked up; her attacker was standing over her. She could barely see him through the tears, he was a black smudge. As her eyes cleared, a black clad figure was standing over her, his arm raised.

"Don't speak a word or you're dead," his voice muffled by the black hood covering his face.

"Kill a police woman would you?"

He replied with a savage blow across her mouth with the back of his hand. Pru sank further to the floor.

"On your feet" he snarled.

Pru didn't move. He grabbed her hair and pulled her up hitting her in the stomach, she folded over like a closing book. He picked her up and threw her on to the long kitchen table, fastening a rope around her wrist he dragged her full length across it and tied the other end to the table leg. He grabbed the other wrist and tied that to the other leg.

Pru kicked and squirmed and tried to hit him. He struck the back of her neck with the edge of his hand and she slumped, dazed, her head spinning. Slowly she regained her senses and tried to move. She wriggled but her arms and legs were securely tied to each corner of the table and a blindfold was placed over her eyes. When she raised her head and squinted through the bottom of her blindfold, she could just make out a black clad figure was standing in front of her. He was tall, that fitted she thought, that's what young Jimmy had said.

"Aren't you the lucky one? You are splayed out like the losers on the green, but I'm not going to kill you this time."

"No, the next time we meet I'll be cuffing you," Pru gasped.

"Wishful thinking Prunella. At some point your boss is going to come looking for you, and I want you to give him a message."

"Oh yes?"

"Tell him to keep out of my business or you will both end up in the middle of the bowling green."

Chapter 2

The next morning Herb drove up to the bowling club and parked. Then he strode purposely along the lane to the green to take another look at the murder sites. They had been carefully marked out. He circled them both, carefully searching for any further evidence which they might have missed. He didn't think that much more evidence would be gleaned from there. The bowling green had revealed all its secrets.

He looked at his watch. Pru should be here by now he muttered to himself. Herb let himself out of the green, carefully locking the gate behind him and walked down the lane to his car. Still no sign of Pru.

He dialled the station. "Hi Trench. Is that you?"

"Yes Hooper, as always at this time in the morning."

"Is Pru there?"

"No, and she hasn't called in."

"OK, I'll give her mobile a ring."

Hooper switched off and dialled Pru's home number. The phone rang for six rings and then switched to an answerphone. 'Hi, this is Pru, so sorry I'm not in, please leave a message, Herb clicked off. He dialled her mobile number but it went straight to voicemail. He ended the call.

"Where can she be?" he muttered to himself, "She surely hasn't gone to the pool when she knew she had to meet me. She might have slept in. Maybe I'd better go down to her place."

A car pulled in beside him, it was the club secretary Valerie Evans.

"Good morning Herb, you're early,"

"More to the point Valerie, what are you doing here? This is still a murder site and you shouldn't be crossing the tapes."

"I have to collect some info for the committee meeting."

Hooper nodded and watched her walk up the lane to the gate. She let herself in, walked across the green and entered the clubhouse. He decided to wait and see when she left. Fifteen minutes later she came out and relocked the door. Herb thought "Rather a long time to collect some papers for a meeting, also she wasn't carrying anything." Herb took out his pocketbook and made a note.

Hooper started the car, let in the gear and set off to find Pru. The weather was turning grey again as he slowly rolled down the narrow lane away from the club. Two or three curtains flicked as inquisitive neighbours checked to see who was around. Herb mused to himself, Pru wasn't usually difficult to contact. He decided to start with home. It seemed the obvious place. He depressed the accelerator. Five minutes later he pulled into Pru's house. "Ah," he thought, "her car is here. She slept in." He made his way up the front steps and knocked loudly. No answer. He knocked again. A window opened in the house next door, and a woman who was cleaning the windows leaned out.

"I think she's in. Her car's been here since yesterday."

"Nosey neighbours," thought Herb. "Pity there weren't more like this lot at the bowling club." He waved to the neighbor. "Thanks I'll try the back door."

Herb scurried to the back of the house. Up the steps; the door was unlocked. He pushed it open. "Security needs to be improved, Pru," he muttered moving into the hall.

"Pru!" he shouted. "Pru!"

Uneasy now, he moved cautiously into the kitchen and he stopped dead. He pressed the emergency button on his phone "Man down man down."

He strode quickly to the table relaxing as he realised she was gagged but apparently uninjured. He walked around the table. A smile broadened his face until she could see him. "You're in a bit of a pickle there Pru." He started to chuckle as he removed the gag.

"Come on you long streak of shit, unfasten me!"

"Oh the boys will be here in a sec, I think I'll leave you for a bit. Finish making this coffee shall I?"

"You bastard!"

Herb began to unfasten the ropes on her wrists which was a mistake because she immediately shot out her fist and hit him in his crotch. Herb doubled up at the waist and started laughing and gave her hair a hard tug.

"You wait!"

"No, Pru, seriously now. What happened?"

"He left you a message."

"A message for me?"

"To keep your nose out of his business or both you and I will end up in the middle of the bowling green."

"So Pru, there we have a threat and a challenge. What are we going to do about it?"

"Take it. I told him I'd cuff him the next time I met him."

"Good. I still think the club is where we start."

"I'm not so sure about that. This man knew me well. He called me both Prunella and Pru. Maybe we should start at the station, even though the boss told us to look at the street."

"You think he's a Policeman?"

"The thought had occurred to me." replied Pru. "It's someone who knows us, including where we live."

Pru rolled off the kitchen table rubbing her sore wrists. "Let's have that coffee," she said.

"I'll make it," said Herb. "Tell me what happened."

"Sounds like someone you knew," said Herb thoughtfully, as Pru described the attack. "I don't suppose you recognised the voice."

"Muffled," replied Pru. "Sounded a bit familiar." She shrugged.

Herb slumped into an easy chair as a police car siren sounded outside. "Get out a couple of extra mugs Pru, the gang has arrived."

A draught of air slithered into the sitting room as two constables came into the room.

"This looks nice and cosy Detective Chief Inspector; we were sent to an emergency here."

"It's over. Your coffee is on the table. You can have a quick drink before you reconnoitre the scene."

Pru pulled out a kitchen chair and dropped on it rather heavily.

"Herb, if our man wants you to keep out of his business. I wonder what his business is?" said Pru.

"We might ask ourselves, what was Stacey's business; he was the first to die." replied Herb.

Herb and Pru sat looking at each other.

"It's nothing to do with me Detective Chief Inspector," said one of the constables, sipping his coffee "but there's a Stacey Transport down in town if that's any help."

Herb startled out of his thoughts said, "Is there now constable? Well that's where we'll start."

"They are tucked away a bit sir, down by the old canal docks. Can we get off now sir?"

"Yes, get about your business."

"Will Sergeant Prune be giving her statement about the attack down at the station, Sir?"

"Yeah, don't worry about it; I will sort it out," said Herb with a nod.

Herb stood up and looked around the kitchen. "A bit minimalist here Pru, but the coffee's good."

"And what's it to you? The bedroom's the same."

Herb raised his eyebrows inquiringly.

"Sod off," she snapped.

Herb laughed, "Come on we'd better go and investigate. Did the boss ever give us the cash you asked him for?"

"Not in my bank account."

"Nor mine," he said with a sigh. "Looks like we're picking up the tab for now."

"How do you feel about being a tourist Pru and going down to the local tourist scene, the canal docks?"

"Yea, I'll put a pair of hip hugging slacks on, a tight sweater, and link your arm," she said with a laugh.

....

Herb drove slowly along the canal side. In front of him was a large building, quite smartly painted, with huge roller doors and Stacey Transport written across them. One side of the building was built tightly onto the canal side, and protruding out at right angles was a short crane. Herb pointed at it.

"Look there, ideal for hoisting stuff from a canal boat."

The yard in front of the doors was laid in solid concrete, ideal for the huge trucks to be manoeuvred. They got out of the car and Pru linked Herb's arm and dropped her head on his shoulder. They wandered towards the canal edge.

"Look at that, there must be twenty Stacey trailers and containers over there and a load of caravans. I wonder what they want all those for?" murmured Pru.

"Big business. Look at those containers on the ground, there seems to be ventilators on the top," observed Herb.

An office door opened and a burly man appeared, he walked a few yards towards them.

"Private property mate, you're not allowed down here," He then started walking towards them again.

"We're tourists; we were told we could visit the old docks" explained Hooper.

"Not this bit; now scarper before I throw you off.'

Herb looked the man in the eye without any animosity. "Ok mate, no sweat."

He turned away and then turned back again. "It's just, I was reading the local paper, and it said a bloke called Stacey had been murdered."

The man clenched his fists. "The boss. What's it to you?"

"Well, you know what people are; you could get a lot of folks nosing around."

"They'll get the same treatment as you," promised the man,

"Who are you anyway?" asked Pru, her voice raised in protest.

"His brother lady," he replied angrily. "Now get lost, both of you."

"You own the place now?" she asked cheekily, pushing it a bit further.

The man began to walk towards them, his face turning puce with rage, and his fists akin to soccer balls clenching and unclenching. "I have told you, and I won't tell you again, get lost."

Pru turned away from him and tugged on Herb's arm, "Come on darling, let's go." And wiggling her shapely hips she dragged Herb towards the car.

Herb depressed the accelerator and sped back the way he had come. As they drove Hooper said, "You were pushing our luck there Prune. I don't think I could have taken him."

"Hooper, you can take anybody."

"Optimist."

"That reception makes you wonder what sort of business Ray Stacey and his brother conducted down here," he said, slowly driving across the garage forecourt, and leaving the figure of Stacey's brother watching them, standing solidly like a monument, his feet wide apart, his whole posture oozing aggression.

"Stop," Pru said abruptly. "Now just look at what is drawing into the dock."

A narrow longboat with Stacey Transport written on the side was easing to a stop at the unloading bay.

"Yep, Pru, but there's no law against Ray Stacey owning trucks and boats; it's what's inside them that counts."

He gazed at the boat coming into the dock. The burly figure of Stacey's brother slipped his hand inside his bomber jacket and a gun appeared in his hand.

"I think we'd better go Pru. This man means business."

Herb depressed the accelerator and sped away the way he had come.

....

Hooper drove back into town. "I'll drop you off at your place and then head off home and see what is happening there. I'm going to have to break the news to Sarah and tell her she will have to drop Ladies who lunch. She won't be best pleased."

Pru giggled, "I don't suppose she will. You can always tell her you're job searching."

Herb pulled the car to a halt at Pru's front door and braked.

"Coffee? Assuming the dynamic duo has finished searching the place for clues."

"No, better get off. You need to get down to the station and give a statement as well. There is one other thing Pru."

"What's that?"

"We are going to need a Headquarters; we can hardly use my place with Sarah around."

Pru opened the car door and got out. She leaned back into the car. "We can always use here; it's out of the way and the neighbours will talk, when you start appearing regularly," she added.

"Yeah, they seem a bit on the nosey side. But as someone is targeting us that is not a bad thing."

Pru walked up the steps to the front door, Herb turned the car around and saw the neighbours net curtain flicker as he drove away.

·········

Once home Herb let himself into the house, he could hear Sarah fiddling about upstairs. He walked across the hall into the kitchen, no sign of dinner.

"Hi darling, what's to eat?"

"I thought you were taking me out?" Sarah tripped downstairs stacked high on four-inch heels and a pale blue dress, which crossed over low enough to expose a glimpse of her ample breasts.

Herb frowned and then smiled. "Sorry darling, not on to-night."

"Oh. Why?"

"I've been suspended without pay over young Jimmy's disappearance." Hooper filled her in briefly on the previous day's events.

"What? That's ridiculous. What shall we do?"

"I'll start job hunting tomorrow. Something temporary. Pru's out too."

"Not so bad for her."

"Why?"

"She's well off. Miss Money bags she is."

"She's my sergeant; she can't be that well off."

"That's what the ladies group says, including the Chief Constable's wife, so they can't be that far wrong."

Hooper headed for the kitchen. "Come on Sarah, we'd better rustle something up; we're not eating out tonight."

Sarah sulked her way to the kitchen and opened the freezer. "There are a couple of frozen meals in here," she said.

"OK."

Hooper munched his chicken in white wine, "I just don't see how that can be right about Pru having money. Pru's car is ready for the knackers' yard. I'll quiz her tomorrow though."

"Herb, you know the Basingham Estates?"

"What about them?"

"Isn't the bloke who owns them called Prune?"

"Yes, Gerald Prune, his name crops up at the station now and again."

"Well?" she said pointedly.

"You're nuts. Why would somebody belonging to him be a policewoman?"

Sarah spread her fingers out on the table and pretended to study them. "That's what Helen Wilkinson says."

"So what?"

"She's the Chief Constable's wife so she could know stuff we don't."

Herb stood up suddenly scraping the chair across the kitchen tiles. "Bugger it; I'm going for a pint. I know we're hard up but I think I could stretch to a G and T. Coming?"

"I'm a bit overdressed for the Odisham Arms but I'll not say no. And let me tell you something else, don't you go dragging the kitchen chairs over my new tiles."

Herb pulled into the Odisham Arms car park, "Sod it, the damn place is full," he said.

"Over there under the trees, there's a space."

Herb drove through the carpark to get to the space. He manoeuvred about until he could reverse into it. He put Sarah up against the hedge making it easy for him to get out and pushed the door open impatiently with his foot. The door shot open and stopped as it hit the adjacent car, "Hell" he muttered under his breath. He bent down to take a closer look.

"Dammit Sarah, I thought we were going to have a quiet night. This is Sampson's car. The last thing I need tonight is having to chat to the top brass."

Herb opened the pub door, "Find us a table darling" and headed for the bar.

Sarah looked around, there was a table by the far wall away from the bar but she had to pass Sampson to reach it. Sampson was busy talking to a heavy, thickset man. He had black hair dropping over his ears and eyebrows low over his eyes obscuring them, while his mouth seemed to be snarling his replies to Sampson. Sarah tried to give them a wide berth but as she passed them Sampson gave her a sly knowing smile. She tried to control the shudder that set her body quivering, but she couldn't. She knew this man.

Herb left the bar, a pint of beer in one hand, a G&T in the other and walked across to Sampson's table.

"Nice company you keep boss, even if he is your cousin."

"No business of yours," replied Sampson.

"We met earlier today but he didn't give me his name. Why don't you introduce us?" suggested Hooper.

The man stood up. "Buster" he said, "and it will give me great pleasure to bust your head in."

"Sit down Buster. Not in here," snapped Sampson.

"You should talk to him about what he carries in his inside pocket boss. He has interesting articles in there."

Hooper stared at Buster and laughed as he walked on, and across to Sarah.

Sampson clenched his fists and glared at his cousin, "Come on, let's get out of here."

"I'm not going to leave because of a blasted policeman."

"Don't be stupid; we can't talk here with Hooper within hearing distance," he whispered.

They rose from the table and made for the exit. Sampson raised his hand and Hooper nodded an acknowledgement.

Sampson pushed Buster towards the door, who turned to give him a warning look. Once outside Buster grabbed Sampson by the throat.

"Don't you go showing me up in public or I'll tear you apart."

Sampson pushed him away and then dragged him towards the car.

"Buster, first of all you don't go flashing that gun around. That is only to curb the people we bring in. Ray should have told you that."

"He did. He also told me you didn't get involved in running the business. So, are you trying to muscle in now that Ray's gone?"

Sampson pushed Buster towards the car, "Get in; we don't want to be overheard."

Buster rolled into the passenger seat and as Sampson closed the driver's door he drove his elbow into Sampson's stomach and bashed his head on to the steering wheel. "Now tell me who did for Ray. You?"

Sampson jerked up, his face covered in blood from his bleeding nose and lips. "Buster..."

"Who did for Ray?"

"How would I know?" said Sampson groping for a handkerchief.

"You're the policeman."

Sampson pulled the handkerchief from his pocket and began to staunch the blood flowing from his nose.

"Did you do it?" Buster asked.

"Me? Why would I do it?" snarled Sampson.

"You might not get your hands dirty, but you like the profits. Cutting him out of it and muscling in would be just like you."

Sampson started the car, let in the gear, and sped out of the car park into the lanes leading to the main road.

"Where are you going?'" shouted Buster.

Sampson didn't answer.

"Where are we going?" Buster rapped out punching Sampson on the shoulder causing the car to swerve across the lanes. Sampson pulled the car back into the fast lane and banged the accelerator to the floor. "Where do you think? I don't trust you within spitting distance."

"Damn you. Where are we going?" repeated Buster.

"To check on what arrived on the boat today," said Sampson grimly.

"To the canal?"

"Where else? Now Ray has gone I wouldn't put it past you to hive something off for yourself."

"You're crazy; it will be heaving with police looking through the paperwork. We have delayed the shipments until you lot have finished."

"Then they'll recognise me, won't they?"

The car wheels screamed to a halt as Sampson slammed the brake to the floor, jumped out, and began to run towards the garage.

"Stop!" yelled Buster grabbing Sampson's arm, "there's a light on in the boat."

"Why shouldn't there be?"

"What, at this time of night?" said Buster.

The light flickered and went out and then a tall figure emerged from the boat and jumped on to the canal side. He stood still looking at them, his face covered in darkness. "Who are you?" shouted Buster reaching into his pocket.

"Good evening Mr. Sampson sir. I thought I might find you here. You left us in such a hurry; I was worried about you."

"Hooper?"

Yes sir." He replied. "The boat staff has just given me a cup of tea. Everything seems quiet. Are you OK sir?"

"Yes, Hooper. You can get off now."

"What about you sir? It's not a place to hang about at this time of night."

"That applies to you, Hooper. I've told you before what I'd do if you didn't leave these premises," interjected Buster.

"Hmm, Bluster Buster," mocked Hooper.

"Leave Hooper," said Sampson, placing a warning hand on Buster's arm.

"Sir, while I'm here why don't you give me a conducted tour? After all, being on suspension I can't apply for a search warrant."

"I said leave Hooper," repeated Sampson. "I've got this under control. We are checking this area, given Stacey's death."

"OK Sir, see you around. Hey, maybe even in that posh garage there. Perhaps we may even find some illegal live species."

Sampson caught Buster's sleeve as he moved to cross Hooper's path. "No," he whispered.

Hooper crossed the forecourt keeping a smiling eye on the two cousins. He got in his Jag and opened the window.

Buster turned to Sampson, "Zeke won't be pleased to hear about this."

"Who is Zeke?" snapped Sampson.

"Oh, cousin, you are such an innocent," mocked Buster.

Hooper started the car and drove slowly out into the dark lanes. Yes, thought Hooper "I wonder who Zeke is?"

....

Hooper went back to the pub, looked around, and then walked across to the bar. The barman pulled him a pint. Hooper nodded at the place he'd been sitting.

"She left just after you," the barman said.

Hooper picked up his pint and walked across to his table. He dropped his chin to his chest in thought. Now what had Sarah been saying? Pru was possibly rich. She was connected to Gerald Prune who owned Basingham Estates. That could make her seriously rich. So why was she in the police? Hooper gravelled through the possibilities.

Old Prune was also very dodgy. No. She couldn't be handing police information to the scum of

Basingham. Why would she do that? Hooper dismissed the thought.

He picked up his glass, it was empty. He signalled the barman. A pint glass appeared on the table, a big white froth curling over the edges.

Several pint glasses later Pru dropped on the seat beside him. "I thought you and Sarah might be here?"

"She's gone."

Pru noticed Hooper's head sink down to his jacket.

"Herb I think you're tipsy, I'll get you home."

"I had a bit of a skirmish."

"Never mind, you can tell me tomorrow."

She heaved him up and they staggered to the door, waving at the barman as they left. The barman remarked "The trouble with Hooper is he can't hold his beer."

Once outside they tottered towards Pru's car.

"Sh- omebody's been telling me stories about you," he said, giving her a hefty shove. Pru fell to the ground under the force of his weight and rolled away from him. Pulling herself into a sitting position she asked. "What's that for then?"

Herb raised himself to his hands and knees and began to crawl towards the car and immediately collapsed on to his chest and face.

"You," he said, spitting out gravel, "are wealthy, you're worth millions, and you never told me, never said a word."

Pru, embarrassed, riddled around in the loose tarmac.

"Wellsh." He tried to shout, but the word only slurred out.

"I am not wealthy," she objected.

"Not swwhat my wife says,"

Pru raises herself up onto her feet, the sharp gravel digging into her fingers and palms. "Let's get you home."

"Ansher me."

"Tomorrow," she said.

Hooper let her bungle him into the passenger seat and immediately dropped to sleep. Pru drove to Hooper's house and pulled into the drive. Sarah opened the door at the first ring of the doorbell and stepped back in surprise.

"Come in," she said.

"No Sarah, he's in the car, help me get him in."

They pulled Hooper from the car and dragged him into the house. Struggling, they got him on to the settee, Sarah ran for a blanket and they wrapped it around him to make him comfortable.

"Thanks," said Sarah.

"No sweat," Pru said as she turned to leave.

On reaching the door she turned back to Sarah. "Sarah, I think you should know that I am not a rich young girl with money to burn. Goodnight."

Hooper wiped his wax sealed eyes and opened them, his head still feeling like a solid block. He threw off the blanket and tried to sit up, but slumped back on to the settee. "Oh god, why did you let me do it?"

"Don't blame me; I'd come home. Pru brought you back," said Sarah crossly.

"But if you hadn't left I wouldn't have done…"

"Herb, you know you have a booze problem; control it."

Hooper sat up. "Mind making me a coffee?" he asked.

"Black?" she asked.

"Blacker the better."

·········

By next morning Hooper's hangover had cleared and "never again" was his waking thought. He could hear Sarah clattering about in the kitchen so he picked up his phone and texted Pru, "I am setting off in a few minutes. I will call you about our next move."

"OK" came bouncing back.

"Want some breakfast?" Sarah shouted as she heard him stirring.

"Bacon and egg," he replied, "Two eggs."

"Hm! You must be back to normal."

He dropped into a chair at the table, showered, and fully dressed with a smart shirt and tie.

"Going somewhere?" asked Sarah.

"Job hunting."

"What sort of job will you get?" she sneered. "You're a policeman."

"Security, or in private investigation perhaps; just something temporary while this thing is cleared up."

"Yes, I suppose," she replied, thinking I'll pass that on; it would be a nice way to make things up.

As he left, Herb banged the door and Sarah sighed with relief, but tension tightened her body as it immediately reopened.

"Is my car still at the pub?"

"Yes. Shall I run you down?"

When Sarah got back she picked up her phone, she looked at it, 'dare she' she wondered. He was angry the last time they met, the time she'd run away from him in the restaurant. She was both scared and fascinated by him. She dialled. It rang. No answer. She put it down on the table. Herb's breakfast things were still sitting there. She supposed she'd better wash up.

The phone suddenly began to dance on the tabletop, vibrating like a mad Christmas Mickey Mouse. She grabbed it, and still hesitated; dare she answer?' She pressed the button.

"What do you want"' the voice was low and cold.

"I have something that might interest you."

"Tell me."

"No. At our favourite place."

"You think I have any further interest in you or your body?"

"But you will be interested in my info."

"Tell me!" His angry voice almost made the phone vibrate again.

"At the castle." She said, and rang off.

Sarah didn't bother to dress up. She removed her bra and then slipped on a dress that would unfasten easily and a light coat over that, because she knew the one thing he couldn't resist was her body. And the one thing she didn't want him to resist was her body.

Chapter 3

Sarah approached the castle cautiously; she paused at the top of the stairs. She thought she could hear a moan. Surely he had not brought another woman here? She went down the stairs, she reached for the light switch, and a vice-like hand gripped her wrist, crushing her bones, and her screaming mouth was stifled by a punch in the stomach, and her lungs collapsed from lack of air.

Sarah awoke slowly, her head rolling around trying to gain consciousness. She tried to sit up but couldn't move. She wriggled around and decided she must be in her comfortable feather bed in the castle, but she couldn't move her arms. They were stretched out above her, and her legs were stretched out below her all tied with rope to the Victorian iron bedstead she loved so much. She was stripped bare. A hand suddenly swept gently over her breast, lingering over the nipple.

"You like that, don't you Sarah?" a voice said.

"You sod!"

"Do you like to be splayed out like Stacey?"

"Unfasten me," she demanded.

"Why should I when you love this bed so much?"

"I'll be a very good girl for you."

"'But I can do whatever I like with you as you are."

"That's not the same as having me curled around you."

"True. I could just kill you, Sarah. I'd make it look just like Stacey. I'll steal one of Hooper's bowls. Then they would definitely think your husband had done it."

"You're insane."

"Say that again Sarah and I will kill you. I'll kill you with my bare hands."

Sarah began to scream and struggle. He slapped her hard across the face. "Be still you whore; that's what you've come for isn't it? To be raped?"

He walked to where she could see him and began to undress unhurriedly. Sarah watched him as he revealed his muscled body, never taking her wanton eyes off him. He came to her and she embraced him with kisses and heaved and writhed to the motions of his body until they lay exhausted.

"Why can't I like it warm and gentle?" thought Sarah.

He lay there at her side for just a few moments listening to her contented breathing and then rolling out of the bed he said. "There now, Sarah. All satisfied again? You can't get enough can you? I'm sure every man in the station could go through you and you still wouldn't be satisfied."

"You bastard," she screamed. "Don't leave me here."

"Don't worry darling, I'll be back."

. ...

Hooper closed the door and smiled to himself, "job hunting" and headed for his car. Once inside he zipped through Pru's number on his mobile, it was picked up on the second ring.

"Ready to go job hunting?" he asked.

"I assume that is what you told Sarah?"

"See you in the club car park."

Hooper pulled into the bowling green car park and settled down to wait. "What was he going to say to her?" he mused to himself. Was he going to come straight out with it? "Are you rich Pru," or say nothing and wait and see what she says?

He drummed the steering wheel with his fingers. Does it matter if she's got a few bob? He tapped the clutch with his foot. He looked up and he could see the club secretary, Valerie, disappearing up the lane to the clubhouse.

"Again," he muttered, "that place is supposed to be shuttered. No access. Where's the constable?"

A car turned in beside him. He opened his door, slammed it behind him and climbed into Pru's.

"Time you replaced this old banger, with all your money Pru."

Pru said nothing and stared at him. Hooper looked straight ahead.

"Can't afford one."

"That's not what I've heard."

"What I can and can't afford is my business."

Pru crashed the gear lever into first. "If it wasn't for this banger you'd still be laid out on the pub floor."

"Why didn't you tell me you are just an old soak? Where are we going?"

"Why didn't you tell me you had money to burn?" he asked.

Pru didn't move. She just looked forward through the windscreen.

Hooper stayed silent for a few moments. They had been work partners for a year with never a wrong word.

"Turn off the engine Pru, and let's go and have another look at clubhouse."

The club's curtains were drawn. Hooper gently turned the doorknob. Door locked. "Let's try the rear door," he said.

The asphalt path ran all the way around the clubhouse. They hurried quietly to the rear exit, it stood open. Valerie Evans the club secretary had left.

Hooper stepped through the door and into the office, Pru shadowing him. The place was empty except for the chaos. The curtains were still drawn and the club was in darkness. The curtains rustled as a slight breeze wafted through the low hanging trees and through the open door. The club files were smashed open. The documents scattered over the green bowling mats, laid ready for the indoor season, and were being flicked around by the freshening turbulence.

Herb clicked on the lights. How could so much damage have been done in so short a time? Someone must have been in a frenzy. Had Valerie Evans done this and if so why? Hooper stepped through the open doorway surveying scene, he felt Pru standing very close beside him.

"I wonder what they were looking for," Pru said.

"Let's think Pru. What connects, the Police, the bowls club, Stacey Transport, the canal? I think it is you Pru."

"Me?"

"Yes, you Pru."

"Herb I don't have any connection to them," she cried.

Hooper lapsed into a morose silence. They stood in the ransacked building looking at each other, their trust slowly evaporating.

"What aren't you telling me Pru?"

They stood looking at each other silently, their eyes never wavering.

"Nothing here," Pru said, pointing at the chaos. "If there was, I bet it has been taken."

"Let's get back to the cars," Hooper said. "By the way, did you find anything on that buffalo lapel pin that Jimmy found here?"

"Not widely available, a company called Bespoke Badges makes them."

"Never heard of them," muttered Herb.

They walked back round to the front of the club and down the long path to the carpark, the only sound was their feet clicking on the asphalt. They reached the cars and made for their own car doors.

"No Sergeant, in here," Hooper said pointing to his passenger seat.

"Am I still your sergeant Herb?" Pru said softly.

"Yes, you are. But you puzzle me."

"If you come from a wealthy family, why are you in the Police?"

Pru sighed and shuffled uneasily in her seat. "Look Herb, I joined the Police because I wanted a career. It's as simple as that."

"I'm not sure I believe that. You can't need the money?"

"That's where you're wrong."

Hooper stared at her, then turned and looked out through the windscreen and began to drum on the steering wheel with the tips of his fingers.

"Why is that then?"

"Herb, it really is none of your business. I joined the Police and I'm your sergeant."

Hooper turned towards her, such pretty eyes he thought.

"I thought we were partners, mates. I thought we shared things?" he said.

Pru dropped her hands onto her knees and looked down so Herb couldn't see the tears forming and beginning to trickle down her cheeks.

Hooper reached across and patted her arm, "Come on, no need for tears."

"No. I left home because I had a disagreement with my father. Although it was nothing to do with me, I didn't like how he was operating the estate."

"He cut you off without a penny, as the saying goes."

Pru lifted her head and smiled at him. "Not quite, he gave me an allowance, small enough to exist, but I needed a job to make life worthwhile. Hence the Police. A career, a chance to progress, an increasing income. Security."

"But you didn't think that at some point someone might shoot at you?"

"No, I didn't think of that."

"Well, someone's got it in for us now."

"Do you think Wilkinson would issue us with firearms?"

Hooper laughed. "While we are suspended, can you shoot anyway?"

"I used to shoot pigeons on daddy's estate; started as soon as I was big enough to hold a gun."

"Underage I suppose?"

"Mmm, nobody to see me."

Typical, Hooper thought, one law for the rich another for the poor. He looked at her, so beautiful, so privileged, so mixed up. She came from a background of money, her own pony, maybe more than one; private schools, private tutor. He thought of Miss James at Station Road Junior School and the cane that lay across the top of her desk. One stroke for a cough, two strokes for a whisper, three strokes for a word which all the class could hear. Silence was Miss James's motto. Three strokes across your palm and it would be sore for a week, and when you got home your dad would want to know why you had got the stick, and then give you another licking for having got it.

Hooper came out of his reverie; well, he'd moved on since then, and perhaps his and Pru's reasons for joining the force weren't so far apart. Again the thought crossed his mind "I wonder why she really left home."

"We ought to get a move on Pru."

"Yes, but where to? We've been to the canal wharf and we know something isn't kosher there and we know something isn't above board here." Pru replied, nodding towards the club.

"We can always go back to the canal when Buster and his gun aren't likely to be there."

"When?"

"Tonight, eleven."

"Dark anorak?"

"Yes"

....

Hooper arrived home and let himself in. Dusk was falling and the house was dark. He shouted for Sarah but there was no reply. God out again, he thought, this woman is never in. She ought to be in at this time, I wonder where she is. He went upstairs and began to sort out his gear for tonight's expedition. A black anorak and trousers, there was a black shirt he used to wear when he was young, still hanging there if it still fitted, and a roll neck sweater together with dark trainers. That should keep him somewhat invisible even though the wharf was well lit. He dropped to his knees and rummaged in the bottom of the wardrobe to see if there was anything else he could usefully use. Ah, here was something he'd forgotten about, his old police baton. He placed it on his pile of clothes and wondered if he should take it. Well, Buster carries a gun.

At ten thirty he dressed and clipped his baton onto his belt. He glanced at the clock. Sarah is not back yet. The thought niggled him. Where could she be? No time to worry about it now. He closed the door quietly behind him and walked to his car some way down the street.

Pru was waiting for him in the shadow of her front door. She quickly crossed to the gate and into the car. Hooper saw the next door curtain flicker open and close again. So much for secrecy.

Hooper drove slowly down the street, and once into the main thoroughfare put his foot down heading for the canal.

"What's the plan Herb?" said Pru.

"First off, we park a good distance away."

"Yes, we don't want to get caught out like last time,"

"No."

"There's the path through the wood," suggested Pru.

"Do you know the way?"

"Yes, daddy used to bring me when he came here."

They entered the wood through a gate in the fence, a well-worn path traced its way through the trees, and they could see the moon glinting in the water of the canal basin.

"That's where the boats turn round," Pru whispered.

"Shush."

They walked in silence until Pru stopped and pointed. The Stacey garage was silhouetted in the moonlight.

"Damn, it could have been a bit darker," Hooper said.

"It's only twenty metres to the edge of the trees; what do we do then Herb?"

"First we take a look and see if there's anybody around."

They dropped to their knees and crept forward.

"We'd better enter under the hedge; coming out by the path will be a bit obvious." Hooper whispered. Pru nodded.

"Pru, you go to the right and round to the caravans we saw and listen for any activity in them. I'll go left and approach the garage along the canal side."

"You'll be very exposed there Herb."

"Let's hope there's no one around."

Slowly, Hooper edged his way to the canal side. The rough grass and broken, spiked, hawthorn branches lacerated his knees. Unnoticed he passed a nettle bed until his face flared with a sudden sting.

"Shit," he muttered.

He reached the canal; the Hawthorn hedge reached to the ground, he would have to go back. He shuffled back and found a small opening just big enough to squeeze through. It would be tight for his broad shoulders but manageable. He slid his head through, cheek to the ground gritting his teeth as fallen thorns bit into his skin. One arm and shoulder next and a push with his toes and he was through. He smiled to himself. Suddenly, he felt a hard round object against his neck. He froze, and then slowly turned his head.

"Ah, Mr. Hooper again. I thought I told you to keep away from here," said Buster.

"I don't have to do everything you say."

"Come through Mr. Hooper, but very slowly and stay on the ground."

Hooper dragged himself through and began to turn towards Buster.

"Face down Hooper. Make no mistake. I will shoot you where it will be very painful."

Hooper went on to his knees, and then lay out full stretch on the hard rubble of the garage yard, but didn't reply. He listened as acutely as he could for any sign of Pru. What could she be doing?

"What am I going to do with you Hooper?"

He didn't reply. He thought he heard running footsteps. Buster spun round at the noise. A stream of people was running from one of the caravans and into the woods.

"Stop, or I'll shoot," Buster screamed.

Hooper twisted on to his back and kicked Buster behind the knees bringing him down to the ground. He jumped to his feet, picked up the gun, and kicked Buster in the face, disabling him. Gun in hand, he ran across the yard towards the caravans where Pru was helping people out of the caravan on to the yard and they were fleeing into the woods. As he reached the caravan there was the sound of a shot and a bullet clipped the door above Pru's head.

"Down Pru," Hooper screamed. "Damn, I should have frisked him."

They dropped to the floor and scrambled behind the van. "You OK?" he asked.

"Yes. You?"

"I think we'd better get out of here, Buster will hurt somebody with that gun yet."

They ducked under the barbed wire fence and into the wood by some dense holly bushes, Hooper signalled Pru to crawl underneath them just as

Buster arrived at the van. He looked underneath the van and then walked round the back and looked over the fence and into wood, mumbling to himself.

Hooper could just see Buster through a space in the holly branches, and hoped he'd move on so that he could free himself from the sharp spikes of the holly leaves which were piercing his back from his neck to his posterior. He smiled at the thought of having to disentangle those prickly holly leaves from Pru's long red hair.

He clenched his teeth and breathed with shallow breaths to reduce his movements. He could hear Pru's gentle panting at the other side of the bush; he only hoped Buster couldn't hear them too.

Buster moved forward and back along the fence and reloaded his automatic rifle.

"I know you're out there Hooper," he called, "and I'll get you sooner or later."

He moved away from the fence and down to the caravan door. He climbed inside, blundered around, lifting up seats and looking in the toilet to make sure no one was hiding. Fifty scruffy illegals gone. There's going to be hell to pay for this, he muttered as he left the van and set off across the yard. He'd better ring the boss.

Hooper breathed a sigh of relief as he saw Buster ambling down towards his office. Once Buster was inside the office, he called softly to Pru. "It's time to go."

They wriggled out from under the bush and silently began to walk deeper into the wood and back towards the car. They drove back to Pru's in silence. There was no flicker of the neighbour's curtain.

"Coffee?" Pru asked.

He nodded. They walked up the front steps and Pru let them in and they walked across the polished floor of the hall into the kitchen. Hooper slumped down on to a kitchen chair and Pru filled the kettle.

"It won't be long," she said.

He looked up at her long red hair hanging down, lank, dirty and bedraggled, mud on her face and the front of her well-shaped sweater.

"You look a sight."

"You should see yourself," she countered.

"Dirt and scratches, they'll both cure."

Pru brought the coffee pot to the table, not instant, but strong black Brazilian coffee to warm their bones and lift their hearts, and sat down on the hard chair. Dried mud crumbled and fell to the floor and she brushed the remaining black dust of the woodland after it.

"You need a shower," she said.

"Mm, how did you manage it?"

"What?"

"To release those people."

"I picked the lock."

"You picked the lock?" repeated Hooper. "You never cease to amaze me. How did…"

Pru's laugh tinkled across the table and she swayed the chair back on its rear legs. "You should live on a farm with dozens of keys which you lose or forget, and you're a couple of miles from home.

He cut her off. "They'll be all over the countryside by now."

"God knows where they'll go," replied Pru.

They sat looking at each other, their eyes reflecting the hopelessness which the both felt, Hooper drumming the table with his fingers. "Maybe they'll head for London."

Pru fiddled with her hair and pulled out a holly leaf holding it up triumphantly.

"It wasn't such a successful night, was it?" Hooper said.

"Oh, I don't know. We gave Buster a shock and set some people free," Pru replied.

"I had better call it in. I'll have to come up with some reason why we were at the canal. I'd better tell the station there are illegal immigrants running around town."

"How do you think this fits with Stacey and Woodley's death?" Pru asked.

"Don't know, but you can bet it is linked."

Hooper gazed at his fingers as he drummed them on the table thoughtfully. Pru watched him with an indulgent smile spreading over her face. She began to mimic his drumming fingers; he looked at her and began to laugh. He swatted at her hands and for a moment their fingers entwined and they quickly released them, embarrassed by the intimacy.

"If they're illegals, someone will be looking for them."

Pru sat back in her chair dragging her fingers through her knotted hair. "You mean someone has lost a great deal of money now they have escaped."

"Exactly."

"And that someone will have us in mind too."

Hooper lifted his head and gazed at the beautiful bedraggled and mud strewn woman in front of him.

"Sorry I got you into this Pru."

She shrugged, thinking, "in for a penny, in for a pound."

Hooper stood up, "I should go."

He walked across the kitchen and over the polished parquet wood floor of the hall, reflecting the soft light from the wall lights and wondered if Pru did the polishing. Opening the front door, slowly, he turned and gave her a nod and a wan smile; he passed out into the early morning.

....

Buster came out of the caravan and stumbled across the broken tarmac of the yard and kicked open the office door. It was a large utilitarian room, with shelves lining one wall full of box files, all neatly labelled. A large desk dominated the room, and tucked away in one corner was a camp bed with a sleeping bag neatly rolled up at one end. The other three walls were windows giving him an uninterrupted view over the yard and the interior of the garage. He could see everything that was happening from his swivel chair.

He picked up the phone; he must call the boss immediately. Phone in hand, he stopped. What was he going to say? Zeke wouldn't be pleased. Thirty odd workers escaped into the woods, or worse, into town, the inside of a caravan totally wrecked. Zeke would be livid.

Buster put down the phone and swivelled the chair with the tips of his toes pondering over the position he was in. How could he mitigate the situation? He would have to pay in some way. If he was lucky it would be monetary, if he was unlucky it would be a beating, at worst it would be both. No, the worst would be the canal. They would treat him no better than the unwanted dogs that the Basingham people got rid of.

He sat at his desk pondering over the words which he knew would only bring swift retribution. He picked up the phone and began to dial.

………

Hooper arrived home and let himself in; he didn't want to disturb Sarah, by now she should be fast asleep. He walked across the hall in stockinged feet. It was 3 a.m.

He poured himself a Johnnie Walker and slumped into the easy chair. The events of the night began to run through his head. It had been a fiasco. They had released a load of illegals but had found out nothing to help them with Stacey's death other than Stacey Transport was dodgy

He was sure Sampson was involved somehow but he didn't think he was the boss. What was it Pru had said? She had been to Stacey's with her father, and she left home after a disagreement with him over how the estate was managed. Why did he go to Stacey's? Was there a connection between Prune's estate and Stacey Transport? Did Pru know what it was? Was it connected to why Pru had really left home? What should they do next? A further visit to Stacey transport seemed indicated but Buster seemed to be on watch twenty-four hours a day. When did he sleep?

The whisky was beginning to hit his sleepy head. The spare room, he thought. Don't disturb Sarah. He struggled to the stairs and began to climb, his toes clipping the edge of each tread he fell forward onto his hands, his feet slipped back on to the lower tread and he fell face down on the hard oak stairs.

Through bleary eyes he could see the banister rail, he reached out and grabbed a baluster and heaved himself up. He was aching all over, his head, his chest, his thighs, and knees which collapsed as he tried to put his weight on them. At the top of the stairs he decided to look in on Sarah and quietly opened the door. The bed was empty. She wasn't there. He tumbled into the room and over to the bed. "Sarah" he called. No answer. He fell on to the duvet padding with his hands, sure she was there. But she wasn't.

His tiredness and whisky blurred head were whirling around. He fell on the bed and sank into the soft springs and oblivion.

Chapter 4

He awoke next morning, his head throbbing like a bass drum, his mouth dry and putrid with stale whisky. He rolled over and pushed his head into the pillow, his hands holding the back of his neck as he tried to force himself from his stupor. The crisp whiteness of the clean duvet coaxed him to sleep again. He forced his head up and the early morning sunshine felt like a spear on his retinas.

"Never again," sifted through his hazy brain, succeeded by, "where have I heard that before, followed by, "I must ring Pru."

Hooper rolled over to the edge of the bed and dropped his feet to the floor and pushed himself up onto unsteady legs. He looked round the room, still no sign of Sarah, He called her name, still no response. He couldn't find his mobile phone, probably dropped it he thought. God, not in that wood last night.

There was a phone on the bedside table; he picked it up and dialled Pru's number. She answered on the second ring.

"Prunella Prune," she said, sunshine gleaming in her voice. "Who's speaking please?"

"What have you got to be so bright and breezy about?" Hooper growled.

"Herb Hooper, you've been drinking again."

"Uug."

"I'll cook you breakfast if you like."

Hooper ignored the comment, his head in an alcoholic whirl. His knees sagged and he slumped on to the edge of the bed. His head told him to lie down but he knew he couldn't. Something was wrong. Sarah never stayed out all night.

"Pru, Sarah isn't here, and she wasn't here when I got home last night."

"Oh."

"There's no reason for her not to be here."

"What are you going to do? Why don't you come here and we can talk it over?" she said, her voice subdued.

"Give me an hour."

Hooper limped to the shower holding on to any piece of furniture within reach. He turned it to scorching and stepped in. The jet of heat hit him like the thrust of a jet engine; he cried out and twisted the knob to cold. He gasped at the contrast. Now, wide awake, he tumbled out and grabbed a towel. For a moment the house was silent, and then he heard the click of the front door closing.

"Sarah," he called. No reply. "Must be mistaken," he thought. He walked to the bedroom door and out onto the hall landing. He stopped dead.

"Sampson!" he exclaimed, "How…?"

Sampson swung the club he was carrying and hit Hooper on the waist, Hooper heard his rib crack. He fell against the banister and then the club hit his head and he fell to the carpet.

"That's for interfering in my affairs," Sampson said to deaf ears. "Stay away from the canal and my family's business. You and that sergeant of yours have been sticking your noses in my business since I arrived. You're supposed to obey your superior's orders."

Hooper came to his senses with the phone ringing in the bedroom. He began to move but a spear of pain shot through his side and he screamed out into the silence of the house. The phone stopped. He moved an inch and the pain zipped across his side. He clenched his teeth muttering, "I have to get to that phone." And inch by inch he began edging his way towards it, knowing that no one heard his piercing scream with each move.

The phone rang again, and again, each time stopping at six rings. Hooper checked the time on the hall clock; it was an hour since he had spoken to Pru. He continued to pull himself painfully toward the phone, at this rate he thought it would be another hour before he reached it.

Sequentially, inch by inch, he scraped his way over the thick pile of the carpet until the phone stood above him, but still out of reach.

It peeled out again, strong and harsh on his ears. It wanted to talk to him and he couldn't reach it. He could just reach the cord. He pulled it and it crashed to the floor, the handset disappearing under the bed. He could hear Pru's voice, muttering something about cold breakfast.

"Pru!" he shouted. "For God's sake get over here."

He thought he heard the phone click and he tried to relax. He told himself to relax but a wave of pain seemed to roll through him with each thought. He closed his eyes and blanked out his brain, thought of nothing, it seemed the only way to dull the pain.

Hooper heard the door open again; I hope it's not Sampson and his bat.

"Herb! You are not supposed to sleep on the floor."

Hooper opened one eye; her tall shapely figure towered above him, her laughing green eyes gazed down at his prone figure. Pru stretched out her hand, "Come on let's have you up."

Hooper shook his head. "Get some help Pru. I think I've broken some ribs."

Her smile widened into a chuckle. "That is very painful." Her smile faded as she realised Hooper was in serious pain. "What happened? You still over the limit?"

She tripped around the room in a search for the paracetamol. Hooper briefly considered telling her the truth. But where would that get them? We would surely want to do things by the book. Storming down to the station and demanding an inquiry into Sampson, the guy who had suspended them. Would anyone believe them? They would point out that the Chief super could just have Hooper arrested for interfering in an investigation; he didn't need to beat him up, which was a good point. Why had Sampson reacted like this? He must be hiding something big. Even so it was madness for him to have attacked him. Had he attacked Pru as well? If he reported him, how much danger would be putting Pru in? He needed to figure out how Sampson was linked to all this and get some evidence before he waded in. It must be something big if he was prepared to risk his career to this extent.

"Yeah, something like that." he responded, trying to look sheepish.

Pru gave him a hard look but decided not to press the point. She bent down and pulled the phone from under the bed and put it back in its cradle.

"Pru, do something; don't just stand there like an ivory statue."

Pru placed her shapely posterior on the edge of the bed and looked down at him again. "Just what would you like me to do?"

"Get somebody to help."

"You do realise if I phone the hospital they will inform the police. I wonder who would turn up?'" she said, watching Hooper carefully.

Hooper dropped his eyes as the implication of her words struck him like a jack hammer.

"Herb, there is also another little problem."

"What's that?"

"There is no treatment for broken ribs."

"No?"

"No, you will have to sit in a chair for six weeks until they heal."

Herb Hooper raised his eyes to his red-haired, green-eyed partner and said "We'd better get on with it then."

Pru slipped off the bed and knelt down beside him. "We have to get you off the floor," she said.

Hooper moaned and said "I suppose so."

He clenched his teeth together as Pru gently eased him away from the bed, and then placing her hands beneath his arms, began to lift him. He grimaced with pain, but put out his arm to take some of his weight, and lowered himself onto the bed.

Pru leaned over him and gently pressed his body where the club had hit him. "With a bit of luck it will only be bruised," she said.

"I'm OK if I don't move."

Pru looked around the room. "Do you have any spare sheets? You look quite fetching there all starkers, but I think I had better cover you up."

"You mean in case Sarah comes in?"

"I mean you will get cold."

"So solicitous. I'm feeling very tired now."

Pru found some bed sheets and covered him up and gently tucked them around him. "Now, some soup and then sleep."

"Yes ma'am."

Pru tripped down the stairs and found her way to the kitchen. She began poking around in all the cupboards, very conscious that it wasn't her kitchen she was searching but Sarah's until she found some tinned soup. She heated it on the gas stove and walked steadily upstairs. He was lying where she had left him, his eyes closed and he looked relaxed.

"Come on, sit up and eat this soup."

"Can't move."

"You are just one big baby."

Pru put down the bowl on the bedside table and pulled a dressing table stool over to the bed. She picked up the bowl and spoon and said, "Open."

Hooper opened his eyes.

"Mouth, idiot."

He smiled and dropped his jaw open. She began to spoon feed him, slowly one spoonful at a time.

"You are enjoying yourself aren't you?"

"Mm, I could get used to this," he replied.

"Well don't, because I'm off in a minute before Sarah comes in."

Hooper opened his eyes again and said, "It's very strange her not being here."

Pru stood up and taking the bowl said, "I will wash this up and then I'm off. If you're fit, give me a ring in the morning."

Hooper watched her all the way across the room until she closed the door behind her.

……..

Hooper woke up slowly, his eyes focusing on the lamp shade above him. "Blue," he thought, "why does Sarah like blue lamp shades; they are all over the house."

"Sarah, I wonder if she is home." He shouted, but it came out in a hoarse whisper. His throat was dry. Lips parched. He tried to reach for the water Pru had left on the bedside table but a pain shot through his side. He stopped. Sleepiness began to clear from his mind, and he started to remember what had happened. He turned his head but bright sunlight shattered his vision. He winced. Turning his head away from the bright light he realised he was still tightly bound by the sheets that Pru had efficiently wrapped him in. Damn the woman. He needed some pain killers. Sarah! Where was Sarah? He had to get out of these blasted sheets. He wriggled his feet around. Humph, no pain. He tried again. The sheets round his feet began to loosen. Slowly he worked his feet around, and then his knees, until his mummifying wrappings began to unravel. He pulled at the sheets with his hands until they no longer felt like some gigantic roller bandage. He was free. Slowly he eased the sheets over to the side of the bed. He slid over to the edge of the bed, lowering his feet towards the floor, but the pain zigzagged through his side.

He lay flat again. He relaxed his body, slowly working up from his toes in yoga fashion. Pain or no, he said to himself I have to get up.

Rolling slowly onto his front, pausing on every zig, and every zag of pain in his side, he moved his feet and legs to the bedside. Gradually, he lowered his feet to the floor. All he had to do now was stand up. With his toes on the floor he tried to raise his body upright. The jagging, twisting knife in his side cut through his back, his ribs, and his stomach. He thought of the Paracetamol sitting on the kitchen worktop and pushed himself up.

Sarah's cheval dressing mirror was facing him. He looked at his reflection in the mirror. Not the sort of image it's used to reflecting he mused. Normally, in a masculine sort of way he could compete with Sarah - Six feet one to her five feet eight. Hair as black as Whitby jet, to her corn cob blonde, which surrounded an oval face and cornflower eyes, and rolled down to her shoulders like the sunset glinting on ocean waves.

The image faded. He looked at reality. The broad muscled shoulders, the weight trained biceps, the hard treadmill thighs; a lacerated temple where Sampson's baseball bat had used his head for a ball. The spreading yellow blemish blighted his rugged handsomeness from his eyes to his chin. His torso still sang in protest with every movement, but he knew he must get pain killers. "Not much of a specimen to show Sarah now," he thought. "Or Pru."

"I wonder how many times he hit me. He must have hit me more than once," he thought.

The urge for several pain killers drove him away from the mirror, forward across the landing, down the stairs, and into the kitchen. How many of these can I take? Sod it; four? No six! He gulped them down. What now? Phone Pru. Sarah's mobile phone was sitting on the worktop. Sarah, where is she? She never goes out without her phone. She must have left in a hurry. He picked up the phone and prodded in Pru's number. The phone was picked up on the forth vibe.

"Prunella Prune, who is speaking please."

"It's me."

"Herb. Are you ok?"

"You mean apart from being black, yellow and blue from head to toes?"

"I wonder what colour those would make if you mixed them together," Pru bantered.

"A mucky green," he hissed. "Pru, that's not the point. Sarah still isn't here, and this is her phone."

"Oh, where do you think she could be?"

"Pru listen! I don't want you going out on the street, but could you ring around her friends. You know the lunch club lot, and see if anyone's seen her?"

"Yes, OK."

"I'll have to sit down. Talk later."

The phone clicked off and he slowly slithered his way across the kitchen and into the lounge and lowered himself into his favourite chair. Perhaps the pain isn't so bad, he thought. He closed his eyes and sleep began to steal over him.

....

Sampson stood over Hooper and thought, "God, I hope I haven't killed him." He gave the prone Hooper a kick. Better be gone. He bounced down the stairs and out of the front door. The streetlamp was out. He'd parked his car three hundred metres down the road. He stopped. No point in running. An easy walk. Don't attract attention. Damn, I'm still carrying the baseball bat. He pushed it between a garden hedge and a low wall and just kept walking.

Sampson let himself into his car, whipped the engine into life, and breathed a sigh of relief as he headed for home.

The pungent smell of stale curry assailed his nostrils. Four take away trays sat on the worktop; she couldn't even be bothered to put them in the bin. He slid the bin lid open and dropped them in. Better to think of curry than Hooper lying on the hard floor of his landing. Should I phone an ambulance? No, that would identify him. He looked at the coffee pot and decided on whisky. He put whisky on the coffee table and dropped on to the soft cushions of the lounge settee. Someone will find the bat! Did I have gloves on? No. Idiot! God, what a mess. Why did I do it? I couldn't help myself.

Hate the man. Won't have him interfering in my affairs. Bed now. Ring the chief in the morning.

The following morning, Sampson drove to the police headquarters knowing that Hooper would not be contacting the Chief Constable with his report on the murder of Stacey or the missing ten-year-old Jimmy. He glanced at the castle as he pulled into the carpark. The old woodland obscured the entrance and the locked iron gate but he still wondered if he dared have the area taped off to discourage the occasional nosey visitors. But he knew others in the station would ask why.

He ran up the steps into the station and nodded at the desk sergeant. "Sir."

He turned to face the sergeant. 'Yes?'

'The Chief wants to see you urgently.'

He entered the office, boldly labelled C Wilkinson, Chief Constable. It was a large office with a large desk in the middle of the room, with an even larger man sitting behind it. Wilkinson looked up from the document he was writing and nodded at the chair. His hair was ruffled. He constantly ran his fingers nervously over his scalp, which he did as Sampson sat down opposite him without any deference to seniority.

"My opposite number in Yorkshire has phoned me and asked if everything is OK down here."

Sampson lifted his head and gazed steadily at his superior officer. "What a weak berk he is," he thought; he wanted the money and no trouble. Fat chance.

"Why do you think he did that?" said Sampson.

Wilkinson shrugged his shoulders and lifted his eyebrows. "I don't know. But worse, he wants to come on an official visit."

"How long can we delay that?"

Wilkinson stood up and crossed the room to the maps and the ongoing investigations pinned up on the wall. There were three major incidents, all murders, including Stacey's he noted.

"We might put him off for six months, claiming workload."

Sampson walked across to him and pointed at the case of the murdered Stacey. "That's the one we need off the list before anyone comes nosing around."

They walked back to the table and sat looking at each other in silence,

"That is the most difficult," said Wilkinson. "Don't forget we set Hooper on to get to the bottom of this and deflect attention from us."

Sampson began to chuckle which slowly increased to outright laughter and then a hysterical, maniacal laughter that echoed from the office walls.

"Hooper! If you could see him now you wouldn't give him a second thought."

....

Hooper stirred back to consciousness. What time is it? Why am I here? Then he started to remember. The mirror. The noise on the landing. Sampson standing there with a baseball bat. The hard edge of the bat striking his forehead. Oblivion.

He had promised to phone Pru, that was it. He was going to phone Pru. Could he manage that now? He was going to have to get back into the bedroom where the phone was. He tried to stand up, but the pain was excruciating, and he knew that wasn't an option. He tried to move, pains sliced through his ribs, and his head began to spin. He lay back down, he would have to crawl, or slide himself across the floor. The distance to the bedside table seemed an impossible task. The fifteen feet seemed interminable; I've done this once before today he thought, with a low laugh.

He pulled the phone down onto the floor and dialled.

"Why are you phoning me at this hour?"

"Uug! What time is it?"

"Six a.m., I thought you'd be in bed all day recovering," she replied.

"Get over here Pru, if you can."

"What about Sarah? Any news?"

"Still not here. Did you find anything from the ladies who lunch crowd?"

"Nothing. OK, I will be there in fifteen."

The phone clicked off and he tried to replace it on the cradle but missed and slid out of bed onto the floor. "Shit!" He closed his eyes and tried to think of nothing.

Hooper heard the outer door open and the footsteps tripping up the stairs and then Pru was at the door looking at him. "Hooper! Why do I always find you lazing around the floor?"

He opened one eye and drummed his fingers impatiently.

"Why does it always take you so long to get here when I need a hand?"

Pru put her hands under Hooper's armpits and lifted; he winced and squirmed but eased himself on to the bed. "Make that coffee I was after," he said.

Pru sat on the edge of the bed, "So where is Sarah?"

Hooper closed his eyes and didn't reply. He mentally ran over the events since he had left to meet Pru the previous evening at eleven. Crawling through the woods, his confrontation with Buster, Pru releasing some people locked in a caravan, Buster shooting at them, Sampson turning up here. He didn't answer. How did Sampson know to come here? Why should he know where he lived?

"I don't know," he said, "What I do know is I haven't seen her since we left for the canal."

Pru leaned forward and flicked his hair from his forehead, "I'll get that coffee."

She pulled some sheets loosely over him and went downstairs to the kitchen. There was Nescafe in the cupboard but no ground coffee to make black. She loaded four heaped teaspoons into a mug and went back upstairs.

Hooper opened his eyes as she came in. Pru's a good looker," he thought.

She put the mugs on the bedside table. "Come on ease up and drink this," she said putting her hand behind his head.

"What we need…"

"What you, and I, need to do is sleep. We will talk about 'need to do' in the morning."

The morning sunlight woke Hopper up with the trace of a headache gently throbbing across his forehead.

"Shit'" He thought, "some more painkillers before I can think."

The door opened and Pru came in with a steaming mug. "Tea this time," she said

"It'll do."

"Such gracious thanks."

Hooper chuckled.

"That sounds more cheerful."

They sat in a comfortable silence, each absorbed in their own thoughts. The sunshine playing through the wafting curtains from the open window.

"I never thought I would be sitting at your sick bed Herb."

He jerked up. "Sick bed? You're not. I'm outta here in a minute. We've got to plan."

He took hold of the bed sheet to remove it and then stopped, and looked at Pru. "I'm starkers under here."

"I know. I covered you up."

"You get out of here while I get dressed," pretending to pull the sheet further under his chin.

"Prude," she replied, and turned to leave the room laughing, "Give me a shout if you can't get your pants on."

....

Hooper gently eased his shirt over his sore shoulders, wincing as the cotton fabric touched his skin and as he twisted his waist with his arm movements. Bloody hell and I've got to get my pants and jeans on next, he muttered to himself.

The phone rang. He let it ring. It rang off. He relaxed. If someone wants me, and it's more likely to be Sarah they'll ring back. It rang again. He picked up.

"Yes?"

"Is that Detective Chief Inspector Hooper?"

"Yes. Well, was."

"Ah, didn't recognise you sir, It's Trench here; the CC wants a word with you. You don't sound like yourself sir."

"That's because somebody hit me in the teeth with a baseball bat, Trench. You'd better put him on."

Pantless, Hooper looked at his jeans lying on the floor. Maybe he was going to need Pru's assistance to get them on. Why had he let Sarah talk him into buying narrow legs?

The soft voice of the CC broke his attention. "Hooper, I hear from Trench you've been in the wars."

"A little sir."

"Sure you don't need a trip to Hospital? Baseball bats aren't the nicest things to get in front of."

"I'm OK. Somebody broke in; I don't know what they expected to find - a wide screen telly or something."

Hooper tried wiggling his toes wondering what was coming next. Well, he thought they work ok so there's nothing broken.

"Well you must report it, Hooper. Come into the station and give a proper statement." Wilkinson paused for a moment. "About our little investigation Hooper."

Ah yes, about that Hooper mused.

"You haven't brought in a report lately'"

Hooper eased himself forward on the duvet and tried to reach his jeans with his toes. They were just out of reach. "Damn" he muttered.

"Did you say something Hooper?"

"Err, no sir. But?" he reached a little further but his ribs ground out an objection, and he sat up sharply. "I think sir, we shall find there have been some irregularities down at Stacey's place on the canal."

"So you think the murder is related to his business dealings," said the CC reflectively. "Interesting."

"Possibly sir, I..."

Hooper could hear some shuffling at the other end and he was certain that Wilkinson was talking to someone. He coughed into the handset.

"Ah, are you still there Hooper?"

"Yes sir, about to go back to bed again sir."

"Ah, Yes. Well, keep me informed Hooper."

"Yes sir."

The phone went dead. "Pillock," muttered Hooper to himself as he braced himself for another attempt to retrieve his jeans.

How did Wilkinson know about the baseball bat, he thought. Trench must have mentioned it, he concluded.

He heard the door handle turn and Pru came in.

"I heard all that," she said. "He didn't seem that interested did he?"

"Humph," as he stretched out his foot again.

"Do you know sir; I really believe you need a hand with getting those pants on."

Herb collapsed on the bed. "Not 'til I've drunk that tea Pru."

They sat in silence sipping the hot tea; the only sound was some distant traffic on the road outside.

"Any thoughts Pru?" asked Hooper drumming on the edge of his mug with his fingers.

"I sense you think there is some sort of conspiracy going on at the station," she replied.

"Why do you think that Pru?"

"You're concerned about Chief Super Sampson's link to Buster. You're worried about my background and how that might fit into all this. You were less than forthcoming with the CC and there is definitely something you are not telling me about these attacks on you. Why didn't you just call 999?"

Hooper chose to avoid a direct response. "The Chief Constable was definitely talking to someone on the side."

"Sampson you think?"

Hooper turned his face to her, lovely hair he thought but with a smile playing on his lips said, "It could mean Wilkinson's also involved in what's going off at Stacey Transport."

Pru pulled a face. "A bit of a stretch based on the evidence." She caught the smile creasing Hooper's face.

"What are you thinking now Boss?"

"Nothing," he said innocently.

"As I said, you are a poor liar, Herbert Hooper."

Hooper laughed and said, "OK, let's take stock of what we know."

"Precious little."

'We know Stacey was murdered, Jimmy and Mrs. Gardner are missing. The clubhouse is wrecked; it may have been the club secretary went searching the office for something. There is something going off at Stacey Transport. Why are people locked in caravans down there? Why does Buster give us a hot reception every time we go there? My guess is they are involved with illegal migrants but it could be something else."

"Don't forget Christopher Woodley," Pru said.

"No, we'll not forget him. He might be the link. Are they all connected? It doesn't seem likely. On the other hand, Woodley's murder can hardly be a coincidence, given the bowling and tennis balls. But was Woodley connected to Stacey Transport?"

They dropped into silence again. Pru picked up the cups and walked towards the door. Hooper admired the swing of her hips, at the door she turned round and caught the look on his face.

"Boss!" she stopped and returned his gaze.

"Yes?"

Pru didn't say anything but stood and looked at him for a few seconds.

"Do you think that every one of these, Jimmy and Mrs. Gardener have actually seen him or know who killed Stacey and Woodley?" she asked.

Hooper's smile faded and he lay back down on the bed and closed his eyes.

"Herb this is no time for sleeping!"

"I'm not. I'm thinking."

"Good excuse."

"The bad news Pru, if that's the case, they could both be dead."

"And Sarah? asked Pru quietly.

"I don't know Pru. I am just hoping her disappearance is for a completely different reason."

"Are you going to report her missing?" inquired Pru.

"A grown woman, my wife, missing less than 48 hours. The lads would laugh me out of the door of the station," replied Herb.

....

Sampson left Wilkinson's office, fuming with frustration. The man was an imbecile. He wanted everything. He wanted to give the orders, he wanted a larger share of the profits and he wanted no risk to himself.

His mobile phone vibrated in his pocket. The screen told him it was Zeke. Buster had warned him he might call. He pressed the answer button. No image appeared. Zeke didn't allow you to see his face.

"Sampson. Second call in two days. Not a good introduction to the business. Buster tells me we have lost some people."

Sampson trembled as the ice cold tone pierced his ear drums, and his hand seemed to freeze to the phone. He started to speak but his terror tied his tongue to his throat like a hanging icicle. Somehow, he muttered trying to get control of his vocal cords "It wasn't my fault...."

"I don't want to know whose fault it was. Buster has already paid for his incompetence, and you will pay for yours if you don't get them back."

"How can..."

"You command a police force, don't you? Use it!"

The phone went dead. Sampson's legs buckled him into a chair. Just what punishment, he began to wonder, had been meted out to Buster for last night's fiasco.

Worse, what might be his fate? If he had known about Zeke and his people he would never have gotten into all this. Trust Ray not to have filled him in on the whole picture.

Sampson stirred himself. No use sitting wondering about his fate, he had to do something about it. Where would all those people be now? How many were wandering around the town? They would be easy enough to find. No way was he involving the force in this. He was starting to think Buster was right: Zeke was out of his mind. Buster, he needed Buster.

He left his office and out through the station foyer, waving a goodbye to Trench on the desk. Better if no one knows where I am, he thought. He headed for his own car. He flung his hat on the back seat, he would be less recognisable without a police officers' hat on. It was a fifteen-minute drive to the canal.

There was no sign of life about the yard. A canal boat was sitting in the dock, but no sign of anything being unloaded. He sat in the car for a few minutes pondering his next move. Was Buster in the office?

Sampson left his car and walked quickly across the yard and into the office. No one was there. He heard a low moaning. He listened carefully and decided it was coming from the garage. He went through the connecting door and gasped.

Buster was splayed out on the side of one of the trucks. His arms and legs nailed to the wooden side of the truck. His body was a mass of blood; he had been crucified. He lifted his head slightly and looked briefly at Sampson and then his head dropped to his chest. Now I know what Buster's punishment was. Sampson rang 999.

"Please send an ambulance to Stacy's garage at the canal docks there's been a terrible accident."

"Your name sir?"

Sampson clicked off. He ran across the yard to his car and drove away as quickly as he dared. He reached home and let himself in and rushed to the toilet and wrenched the boiling bile from his stomach. His wife stood over him and watched coldly, wishing she dared push his head into the stinking water.

"Bed for you I think."

Sampson looked up at her and nodded. "Ring the office and tell them I'm sick," he replied, wondering if Zeke had his home address. He had no desire to end up like Buster. A weak smile played on his lips,

Janice helped her husband out of the bathroom and into bed. "I'll bring you some tea and ring the office for you," she said.

Janice put the kettle on and picked up her mobile phone. The phone rang and rang and as she was about to click off a female voice answered, "Yes?"

"Oh, I thought this was…"

"Hooper's phone?" said Pru, "Yes, it is; this is Pru. Is that Janice?"

"Err, yes Pru," she said.

There was a pause and then Pru said, "I can give him a message."

"Well, err, never mind, it can wait."

Janice put the phone down; her suspicions could wait.

....

Pru went back into the bedroom and sat on the bed, "That was a strange call. It was Janice Sampson. She wanted to talk to you, but she wouldn't say what about."

"Which means," said Hooper, "She either wants something or she wants to tell us something."

Hooper drummed his fingers on their counterpane covering his bed. "What would it be best to do next?"

"We let those people out of one van, but there are more vans in the woods," Pru said.

"Do you think you could drive us down there again?"

"Herb, I don't think you should…"

"We'll just go and see what we can see from the car."

Pru helped him to dress and then supported him as he limped downstairs. When they reached the hall Hooper stopped and looked around. "It's very strange Sarah being out so long. I think something must have happened to her."

Pru put her shoulder under his arm to take his weight.

"Come on let's get to the car if you insist on going. You will have to give some thought to how you will find her."

Pru drove slowly down towards the canal with Hooper slumped in the passenger seat. She turned into the lane which led down to the canal dock and drove even more slowly towards the canal and Stacey's garage wondering if Buster and his gun were lurking around the yard. Pru glanced across at Hooper; he was still fast asleep, his head resting on the door and window.

"Herb," she whispered, her eyes on the dark, tree lined road. There was no reaction.

"Herb," she said, raising her voice.

In her dimmed headlights, she saw the next sharp bend. She turned into it and stopped the car. Through the leafless trees, lights were flashing. She leaned forward towards the windscreen, and strained to see what they were. Blue, blue flashing lights. Police! The police were at Stacey's garage. "Why?"

Pru leaned across the car and pulled at Hooper's coat sleeve. "Herb," she said urgently, "Wake up."

Hooper slowly stirred into life. Pru pummelled him again. "Herb, wake up!"

"What?" he said sleepily.

"Wake up! The Police are at the garage."

Hooper struggled to sit up. "Ugg," he groaned as a pain shot through his ribs.

"What?"

Pru pointed towards the garage and he struggled up to look. They both looked through the trees at the flashing blue beacons in the distance. There was a flurry of activity around the huge garage doors as they were eased open and the stutter of an engine broke the silence of the night.

Hooper and Pru slid down in their seats to dashboard level as the vehicles in the yard began to move. The first to approach the bend was an ambulance followed by two traffic police cars. They put their heads together like a courting couple until the screaming vehicles had passed.

"Ambulance!" exclaimed Pru.

"Yes, I wonder what's happened there," Hooper replied.

They heaved themselves into sitting positions. Hooper nodded towards the garage.

"I don't suppose there's anyone..."

"Don't even think about it," said Pru. "You have had a look and that is all you get for tonight."

"But it's ideal. Buster won't be..."

"No," said Pru, "back to bed for you."

Hooper looked at Pru's determined face and relaxed his head on to the headrest. "OK, Boss." He muttered.

Pru did a three-point turn and set off the way they had come.

....

Pru drove up the lamp-less lane to the major road into Basingham. The traffic was light through the city and she made good progress towards home. Hooper dropped to sleep again.

She pulled onto the car space in front her house and looked at the sleeping figure. How was she going to get him into the house?

She opened the car door and swung her legs out on to the patio flagstones, heaved herself up, and crossed to her front door. Opening it, she paused, listening carefully for any sounds, remembering what had happened once before. There was only silence; even Macilroy didn't come to greet her so she was still missing.

Pru walked back to the car and saw Hooper was still asleep. She opened the car door and she caught him as he began to slide out. He stirred, and moaned.

"Sit up Herb," she whispered, helping him into a sitting position.

"Where am I?" he said.

"At my place," she replied.

"Why?"

"It doesn't matter why," she answered.

He glanced up at her through water blurred eyes and sank onto the car cushions. Pru bent down and put her hands under his armpits.

"Come on Herb, help me; you can't stay out here all night."

Hooper eased himself up while Pru took his weight, and they limped to the door and into the house. "It's the bed settee tonight, Herb. We will see about the spare bedroom tomorrow."

Pru settled Hooper down and wearily climbed the stairs to her bedroom.

Chapter 5

The clunking rattle of mugs assaulted Hooper's ears like a kettle drum in a Boy Scout band, while the familiar smell of frying bacon twitched his nose. He lifted the corner of the duvet and peeked out. He could see Pru in the kitchen. "A good smell out there," he called.

"Oh, you are alive then?"

"I seem to be in one piece. I'm even dressed."

"One egg or two?"

"Need you ask?"

"Well, you are not getting it in bed so you had better move."

"Cruel woman."

Hooper swung his legs off the bed settee and tested his feet on the floor and stood up. "Not so sore. I think we should make another call on the garage while it's unattended."

"Unless the police are there," replied Pru. "Come along, breakfast is ready."

They sat down facing each other, eating in a comfortable silence. The blue tablecloth stretched between them like a great ocean that had no end. Their eyes met, and the sea dissolved. Words are an intrusion. The moment, a lifetime. Like all moments, it passed. Hooper looked towards the door.

"Shall we try again?" he asked.

Pru sat up straight in her chair. "If you feel up to it."

"Yes, but you drive."

....

The yard in front of Stacey's garage was deserted. There was no sign of any narrow boats in the lock or basin. Pru parked in the middle of the yard and they sat looking around for any reaction.

"I can't see anyone in the office," Pru said.

"Don't bank on it," Hooper replied.

"Same tactic as last time?" asked Pru.

Hooper nodded. They got out of the car and stood by the open doors ready to slide back in if anyone with guns appeared. Nothing happened. It was quiet. Too quiet. They looked across at each other over the roof of the car.

Hooper smiled and raised an eyebrow. He closed the car door and walked around the car to Pru. Pru closed her door and took his arm. They began sauntering toward the canal and from side of the office a tall slim man appeared. They stopped and faced towards him smiling.

"Good morning," said Hooper. "The tourist office said we could look around the old canal docks."

"This section is private sir. We do have very large trucks turning round, and that makes it very dangerous."

"I don't see any; couldn't we just take a look?"

"All the trucks have left for the day, but we do have lorries floating in and out. So, no, sir."

"Ah, that's a disappointment. Isn't it Pru?"

"Mm, yes, I thought we might find boat tours."

"I believe you might find those further down the canal by the locks."

"Shall we go there Herb?"

"It might be a pleasant way to spend the morning."

"If you get the right tour, you'll be able to have lunch."

"Thank you. My name's Hooper, yours?"

"Just Joe, sir. Now I'll have to ask you to leave before the yard gets busy again."

"Yes, OK," Hooper said and turned away towards the car.

Pru drove out of the yard, up the lane towards the city and pulled into a carpark. A portable refreshment van was just setting up; Pru nodded towards it. "Fancy a cup Herb?" asked Pru. Hooper nodded his reply.

Pru trotted across to the van and came back with two black coffees. She handed one to Hooper and sat down.

"You could have brought me a bacon butty."

"You didn't...."

There was a tap on the window; they both turned to look. There was a short, broad-shouldered man, looking at them, with dark eyes which didn't reveal their colour, and heavy eyebrows which almost hid them. His face, like his body, was stocky, broad and flat, his nose looked as though he had been punched at birth and it had never recovered. He looked eastern European. He had a slight smile which almost reached his eyes.

"Daddy!" gasped Pru, opening her door. He leaned in and gave her a peck on her nose.

Hooper slumped back in his seat, shocked. He could hardly relate the elegant Pru to this ape-looking figure in front of him. Although he knew of the man, he had never met him.

"And who is this, Pru?" he asked. His upper-class, cut-glass English accent belied his appearance.

"Daddy, meet Herbert Hooper, my boss."

He reached into the car to shake Hooper's hand.

"Herb," said Hooper.

"My friends call me Zeke," he replied.

"Ah," thought Hooper, "So this is Zeke."

"Pleased to meet you, Mr. Prune," he said politely.

"What are you doing down here at this time in the morning Daddy, and all dressed to go riding?" asked Pru.

"Just some business. I was called away as I was about to go out. What about you two, isn't this police time?"

"Didn't you know Daddy? We have both been suspended until the murderer of Ray Stacey has been found?"

"Why?"

Pru explained about the bowling and tennis ball.

"You might need a lawyer. I will talk to my guys and get one of them to call you."

"Daddy don't fuss, Hooper and I will solve the case."

Hooper watched Zeke's eyes flicker as his smile remained unchanged. "You should come home and do some riding."

Pru looked down at Hooper who was still sitting in the car. "I don't think Herb rides, do you?"

Hooper shook his head and took a sip of his coffee.

Zeke Prune looked at his daughter and said, "You are welcome anytime. Both of you."

With a nod of his head he turned about and although he was short he marched with a solid determined gait across the carpark to his classic E-type Jag.

....

Zeke climbed into the car and headed for the carpark entrance. Damn the girl he thought, too much like her mother. Too much of the red-haired colleen in her. Blasted Irish. Too much Irish and not enough Estonian. I should have sent her back there when she was born, but those Russian Oligarchs or the KBG, would probably have murdered her in my place.

But she's just as beautiful as her mother was. He laughed to himself; she's got her mother's temper too. Best of luck to the guy who marries her.

His eyes narrowed. Someone was trying to frame his daughter. That was not cool. He would be having a 'word' with someone when he found out who it was. He had suspected Buster but from what he had got out of him during his 'punishment' he decided it probably wasn't him.

He pulled to a stop at the estate gates and waited for them to open, activated by the cameras recognising his profile and allowing him through. He drove up to the front door of the ancient Basingham mansion, derelict when the Oligarch bought it, and restored in every detail to its ancient magnificence.

And all for money. What they didn't know was how much he had creamed off for himself; how many illegal cut and uncut diamonds were lodged in his safe deposit box; how much cash was in his Swiss Bank Account, just waiting for the day when he opted out. They thought he was their pawn, but it was they who were the unwitting pawns. When he disappeared, they would have egg on their faces to face their KGB masters.

Zeke drove to the back of the house, the garage doors opened and he drove in. His English butler was already waiting and opened the door for him. He nodded a greeting but didn't speak; he couldn't because Zeke had cut his tongue out thirty years ago when he had first arrived in Britain, tying him to his service forever. He planned to kill him when he decided to get out.

"Thank you, James", he said and looked into his eyes where he saw the hate behind his smile. James nodded and used sign language to say food and drink were ready.

Zeke was expecting someone to meet him at the estate when he first arrived; what he didn't expect was a gorilla of a man recruited from East End gangs of London. After a few days, he drugged him, bound him, and relieved him of his tongue. When he awoke, he put a gun to his head and told him exactly what he expected of him. James had been compliant ever since, but Zeke always slept with his bedroom door locked, especially since Pru had left.

They walked towards the house, "That was a good job you did on Buster" Zeke said, "I think it deserves a bonus. Would a thousand do?"

James signed his acceptance.

Zeke retired to his study and sat down at his desk. He pondered his next move. The new Manager, at the docks, Joe Black should be perfectly reliable, if his last employers were to be believed and would do whatever was required of him. He would be going down to meet him shortly.

The main problem was the released immigrants. How would he get them back, and how could he prevent this situation happening again?

He took out a piece of paper and began to write out the present system. He stopped. The system was perfect. It worked with digital precision, or it had until Woodley and Stacey had been killed. How the hell had that happened? Which idiot had thought it made sense to draw attention to the operation in that way and try to frame his daughter? His major problem was who was his enemy? Until he knew this, he couldn't make plans with certainty. He had the police force from the Chief Constable down corrupted with their own greed; all looking for the big payoff. None of them knew of the Russian oligarch who pulled the marionettes strings. They were in for a shock. So, who was his opponent, who could cut the marionettes? When he figured that out, he would know where to send his faithful butler next.

He walked across the room to the bar and picked up the whisky decanter and pulled out the glass stopper. He poured a generous measure of Glenfiddich, his preferred thinking liquid, into his favourite cut glass tumbler and savoured the golden fluid. He smiled; the liquid seems to stimulate logical thought he murmured to himself. Lowering himself into the deep cushions of his armchair he sipped the Oligarch's gift slowly, his eyes closed but he didn't sleep. He analysed his position. Could Hooper be his most dangerous opponent? If so, he would have to be eliminated, and by default that meant his daughter too.

"God no," he muttered and suddenly the whisky was like ash in his mouth.

....

Zeke stood up and walked across to the window. The view stretched for miles across his green acres; all the villages which the estate would have originally owned were scattered all around him and, on the horizon, Basingham, where his pastimes were located. It was also where Wilkinson, the Chief Constable, was located.

That would have to be his next move: contact Wilkinson. Perhaps he could move Pru out of the way; send her on a course somewhere, or get her transferred for a time and let him deal with that interfering Hooper. James would take care of Hooper, and the estate was large enough to have him tucked away. He chuckled at the thought; he had just agreed with the local authority to extend Blackdown Woods. Ideal, Ideal. The thought cheered him up and strode across the room and poured himself a fresh whisky. He picked up the phone and dialled.

....

Hooper looked at Pru over his coffee with a twinkle in his eye.

"So. That's papa?" he said.

"Mm, this coffee is a mite bitter."

Hooper shuffled in his seat. "You make better coffee than this," agreed Hooper. "We should have gone to your place."

"I keep telling you, you'll have the neighbours talking."

"Do you care?"

"Not much."

They dropped into silence and sipped their coffee as the minutes ticked by.

"The point is what is our next move?" Pru muttered into her plastic coffee carton.

"That's what coffee's for; mulling things over, but not when it's as bitter as this."

"You don't know."

"It's not obvious."

He scrunched his plastic cup but it just flicked back to its' normal shape. "You done?" he asked.

Pru handed him her cup and pulled a face. "My percolator does better than that."

Hooper smiled and took the container from her and eased himself out of the car. He walked slowly over to the waste bin by the side of the mobile coffee stall and dropped the cartons in. He looked up at the title across the top. "Coffee Old Bean." He grinned at the double meaning, "Natty name for your stall," he said to the vendor.

"Not my idea, I only serve the coffee."

"That guy we were talking to, does he come into this carpark often?"

"Yep, he owns the place."

"Does he!" Hooper exclaimed. "He's my friend's father."

"Lucky girl, this is a franchise; there are stalls like this all over the country and he owns the lot."

"Whew! That'll surprise my friend. Does he visit you often?"

"Sometimes it's another bloke, but he's dumb. They come when a package has been left."

"Is that so; are they large packages?"

"No, you can hold them in one hand."

"Where are you from, you're not English?"

"Estonia, we stay in caravans until we can find something better."

"Have you been here long?"

"About a year."

"Is this a busy car park?"

"Packed most days. He must make a fortune."

"I'll tell his daughter," Hooper grinned again.

The man paused looking down at Hooper suspiciously. Hooper returned the look still smiling.

"I think I tell you too much."

Hooper dropped his smile, "I thought my friend, you know, Mr. Prune's daughter, would be interested.'"

"I think she should ask him."

He turned away and began to tidy his cupboards and shelves. Hooper walked back to the car. He opened the door and dropped into his seat.

"That took you long enough."

Hooper began drumming his fingers on his knees.

"Interesting though."

"Really?"

"Did you know that Papa owns that coffee van and a string of them across the country?"

Pru turned to face him. "You are joking!'" she exclaimed.

"No," he said.

"Well, he sells rotten coffee."

"Did you know he picks packages up there?"

Pru began to drum her fingers on the dashboard.

"Don't do that."

"Why?"

"It irritates me."

"You do it all the time!"

"Do I?" he asked in a surprised voice.

"Yes, you do and it irritates me."

Hooper looked down at his feet stretched out in front of him and began to tap them on the floor of the car. Pru glanced across at him but said nothing.

"Let's go and get a decent cup of coffee," he said, "and think of our next move. I should really report that packages are being delivered; could be drugs."

Pru let in the clutch and moved off. Hooper's mobile phone rang; he flicked the on button and looked at the screen. The Chief Constable.

"Yes sir?"

"Have you got anything for me?"

"There's no sign of Jimmy sir," Hooper said.

"Where are you now?"

"We have just called at Stacey's place again. There's a new chap in charge down there."

"Is Prune with you?"

"Yes sir, she's driving. We have just met Mr. Prune from the Basingham Estates."

"Oh yes. He comes into the station sometimes; usually to complain."

"Did you know, sir, that he is DS Prune's father?"

Hooper heard a shuffling of a chair at the other end, followed by a long pause.

"No Hooper, I didn't know that. That is very interesting. Although we have probably got it on file somewhere."

"Yes sir," he replied.

"Hooper, I must have some progress reports on the Stacey case and the disappearances. The Chief Constable of West Yorkshire is angling for a visit and I want this tidying up before he gets here."

"When is that sir?"

"I'm putting him off as long as possible so get on with it."

"How is the official investigation going; are you making any progress?" inquired Hooper hoping to subtly remind Wilkinson.

"Slowly," snarled Wilkinson. "You and Prune are still in the frame, so I would get a move on and make some progress if you want your truncheons back."

"Yes sir." "Hypocrite," Hooper muttered as he ended the call.

Pru began to brake, and as she pulled into the parking space in front of her house, the curtains next door quickly opened and closed again.

"Brazilian?" Pru asked

"And some of your walnut cake."

"That should improve your temper. And your waistline," she added.

....

Sampson didn't sleep. The thought of Buster spun around his brain; imaginary pictures of that gigantic torso beaten and broken, crucified on the side of a Stacey truck and then lying on a stretcher swirled and tortured his mind.

"Janice," he called, his voice wavering.

There was no reply. He was certain he could hear her downstairs and he shouted again, his voice stronger.

"Janice!"

Sampson heard her footsteps on the stairs and the bedroom door opened. She looked at her terrified husband. "Yes?"

"I think I'd better go to the station."

"I thought you were ill?"

"You would be ill if you saw what I saw yesterday."

"And what was that?"

"Janice, in police work you see many brutal things, but I've never seen a man crucified before."

Janice grasped the edge of the door and then staggered over to the bed and sat down.

"Who?"

"No one you know, a man who works for Stacey Transport. He was nailed to one of their wagons. Crucified."

"My God," she whispered. "What's going on? First, Ray and now this. What's going on? Are they connected?"

Sampson pulled himself into a sitting position and took his wife's hand in his.

"I think it was perpetrated by a man called Zeke Prune." He paused. "And I think I might be next."

Janice sat down heavily on the bed. "Why?" she whispered.

"I can't tell you Janice."

They sat together on the bed and Janice pulled her hand away from his. He turned his head and looked at her.

Janice kept her eyes down and said. "Is he her husband Paul?"

"Whose husband?"

"The woman you're having an affair with."

Sampson grabbed her arm again. "I'm not having…"

Janice gave a short laugh. "Don't lie to me, I know you are. Is it this man's wife? Is this why you're so frightened of him?"

Sampson stood up and walked to the window and looked down on to the street through the net curtains. He spun round and looked at her still sitting on the bed.

"You're deluded Janice. There is no affair. The crucifixion thing has nothing to do with any woman.

In future you mind your own business and keep your nose out of mine."

"Then why tell me about the crucifixion?"

Sampson paused, "I want you to be on your guard."

Her eyes widened. She looked at him defiantly,

"I want to know what's going on. I'm your…"

She stopped as she saw a look in his eyes which she had never seen before. It was cold, hard and deadly.

"I'm going to the station now; I don't know when I'll be back."

Janice watched him cross the room to the door. She went to the window and watched as he climbed into his car and drove off down the street.

"That is not the man I married," she muttered to herself. She walked back to the bed and sat down. Looking around her, her eyes fell on the bedside phone, which over the years had woken her in the early hours of the morning, dragging her husband to some emergency or other.

She looked at the phone for a long time, feelings of guilt pulsing through her. She picked up the handset and dialled Herb Hooper's number again.

....

Sampson drove like a man on auto pilot - his hands on the wheel, his feet on the pedals, his eyes vaguely registering the traffic around him.

He parked in his allotted place. Shaking his head, he brought his mind back into focus. It was early; would Wilkinson even be here yet? Probably not. Why had he come? What would he say? God, it was a mess.

He opened the car door and got out and leaned against the car savouring the morning air. Mrs. Gardner filtered into his brain, Jimmy, Sarah, what was he going to do with them. He couldn't leave them very long or they would die anyway. Should he release them? No, not until this was over, there was too much at stake, too much money. He had to be free and clear before the Chief Constable from Yorkshire came nosing around. He wouldn't have his eyes shut or his ears closed.

He slammed the door and headed for his office and the coffee pot. It would be at least two hours before Wilkinson shewed. He was wrong. He passed Trench who was sitting behind the desk.

"Don't you ever go home?" he said.

"Overtime," he replied. "Sir" he added as an afterthought.

Wilkinson was standing at the top of the staircase, a steaming mug in his hand.

"Coffee?" asked Sampson, hoping the pot was already on.

"Tea. Strong and black."

Sampson pulled a face.

"Can't you sleep?" he asked.

"No more than you can, obviously."

Sampson spooned coffee and sugar into a mug and poured on the water.

"Rot your teeth, that lot," observed Wilkinson. "'You want to take better care of your health…"

Sampson smiled a humourless smile. He glanced round. "Have you heard about Buster?" he asked quietly.

"Zeke Prune's work I should think," Wilkinson replied bluntly.

"What are we going to do about it?"

"Thank the lord he didn't put one through his forehead."

"Can you prove it was Prune?"

"No. Besides, he's in the set up with us; let's not rile him."

Wilkinson stood up straight, drawing himself up to his six feet three inches. He turned to go and then looked back at Sampson.

"I would never have got involved if I had known Prune was the backer," said Wilkinson quietly. "He's unhinged. You should have told me."

"I didn't know. Not until after Ray died. I have never been involved in the details. Safer that way."

....

Pru picked up the phone. "Hello. Pru here; who is speaking please?"

"Janice Sampson, Pru. We met at the Christmas party. I wanted to speak to DCI Hooper, although," Janice paused, "it might be better if I spoke to you."

"Hi Janice," she said brightly, she mouthed silently to Hooper 'Janice Sampson'. "What can I do for you?"

"I need to have a word with you."

"Why don't you come down here for a coffee?"

"Yes, I'll do that. Will we be on our own?"

"Herb will be here."

The phone went silent. Pru waited. The silence dragged on.

"Janice," Pru said, "Why don't you come down here now? You sound very worried and nothing you say to us will go any further."

Janice didn't say anything for a few moments, but Pru could hear a quiet sobbing.

"Are you crying Janice?" she asked softly.

"I'm alright," she said. "When shall I come?"

Pru smiled into the phone trying to make her voice as light as possible. "Come now Janice. Stop whatever you are doing; get in your car and come."

"Yes. Yes, I will," her voice, more determined; the phone clicked off.

Pru clicked off her phone, walked across the room to the window and pulled open the curtain. The day was changing, a thin drizzle was casting a curtain over the street.

"She'll be here in a few minutes Herb. What shall we say to her?"

Hooper stirred on the bed. "I told you earlier she had something to tell us. Go and have the coffee on for when she arrives, and just let her talk. Don't ask her anything."

"What about you?"

Hooper drummed quietly on the bed clothes with his fingers ticking over the previous conversation, Pru pulled a face which he didn't see.

"Given she decided to talk to you, she may not be comfortable with having me around, so I'll stay here. You give me a shout if you need me."

Pru grimaced and headed for the door. Hooper slid down further into the bed.

The kettle began to boil as Pru heard the doorbell ring. She walked across the hall, her slippers hissing as they skimmed the hardwood floor. She looked through the door viewer; she had no desire to be taken by surprise even if Hooper was upstairs. It was Janice. She turned the doorknob and the latch together and let the door open the length of the security chain.

"Janice," she said, "you on your own?"

Janice nodded. Pru opened the door.

"Come in, let me take your coat," Pru said fussily, helping Janice out of her jacket and hanging it up. Taking Janice's arm she said, "Let's sit in the sitting room; I'll get the coffee."

Pru scuttled into the kitchen and returned with a tray of steaming mugs, plates and biscuits. She sat down opposite Janice and smiled, "Help yourself Janice."

Pru looked at Janice as she relaxed into the easy chair, her face still puffy with crying.

"Thanks," she said.

Pru picked up the other mug, remembering what Herb had said, and leaned back into the cushions. Janice sipped her coffee and looked down avoiding Pru's eyes.

She suddenly looked up at Pru. "Why were you suspended? Paul told me it had happened but not why."

Pru shrugged her shoulders but didn't reply, wondering where this was going.

"Hooper's been suspended as well. Is this something to do with Ray Stacey's death?"

Pru let a small silence ensue and then said, "You know I can't give you details of an investigation. I don't think you came to talk about our problems did you Janice?"

Janice shook her head, her eyes bleak and terrified; she clasped her hands, twisting the rings on her fingers. "Where do I start?"

"Say whatever it is that has put you in this state," said Pru.

Janice looked down at her hands. "It's Paul." She stopped and looked up. Pru nodded encouragingly. He came home yesterday and he was frightened," she stopped again.

"Go on," Pru said.

"He was so frightened he went to bed and begged me to say he wasn't at home if anyone called. At times he seems unhinged, talking to himself, mumbling…"

Pru watched her with a steady gaze but didn't say anything.

"He didn't get up until this morning," Janice stopped speaking again and began wringing her hands.

"And?" Pru said.

"He told me about his cousin Buster, what someone had done to him. Have you heard?"

Pru shook her head.

"Someone nailed him to one of Stacey's trucks. He was crucified," she whispered.

Pru gasped, "Oh my god!"

"He was terrified they would do the same to him."

"But who?"

Janice shook her head. "But that's not all. He was rambling and talking in his sleep about that missing boy and that woman as though he knew where they were."

Pru intervened, "Do you know Herb's wife Sarah is missing too?"

Tears filled Janice's eyes and start to flow down her cheeks; shaking her head she met Pru's gaze.

"And that's another thing," she said.

"What?"

Janice began shaking her head in despair. "I think he is having an affair."

"With whom?" Pru asked through barely moving lips.

"Sarah Hooper," whispered Janice.

Pru sagged into her chair. "We will have to tell Herb."

"No need," said a voice. "I heard." Hooper was standing in the doorway leaning against the door frame, his face ashen. He strode across the room and dropped to his knees in front of her. "And, do you know where she is too?" he asked gently.

She fell back in her chair, the tears welling up in her eyes. "No, no. I'm not even certain it is her'" she whispered.

Hooper collapsed onto the floor and sat looking straight at Janice.

"Sarah's been missing for 48 hours. Even if what you say is true I am concerned because it doesn't sound like she is with your husband, given your description of the last 24 hours."

He paused and rubbed his chin. "Janice, you must know something more. Think, Janice. Anything."

Janice looked at him woefully and shook her head.

Hooper hobbled on to his feet, wincing as his ribs let him know they were moving in the wrong places. He reached an easy chair and Pru supported his arm as he lowered himself into it.

"We had better get our heads together, three heads are better than two."

He looked at them in turn. Pru nodded.

"Do you agree Janice? It's your husband who may be at risk."

They stared at each other for a few moments, and then Janice nodded. "He isn't the man I married. I think he may have turned into a monster."

Hooper gave a deep sigh and said, "We had better review what we know which isn't much."

They moved to the dining table and sat down, Hooper brought out a notebook and pencil.

"We think Stacey's death may have been linked to his business. We know that illegal immigrants are brought to the canal docks. And we know they are sleeping in the caravans in the woods."

"We also know that the police, or at least your husband," Pru said, glancing at Janice, "are ignoring the fact too."

Janice looked thoughtful, "Does that mean Paul knows about them?"

Hooper nodded, "He must also know they are shipped out to work every morning."

"You know Janice, they have been making money out of them," said Pru.

"Slave labour! Oh heavens." Her voice cracked as she struggled to prevent the tears filling her eyes from rolling down her cheeks. "How could he?"

Hooper stood up and began to pace the room. "What else do we know?"

"I don't know if it's significant," Janice said, "but he's been saying he and Chris Wilkinson are thinking of early retirement."

Hooper stopped, "To do what?"

"Well, he said, 'buy an ocean-going yacht and sail the world for a year.'"

"That would cost a fortune, more than a little extra income from illegals doing some farming work."

They looked at each other, Janice's face brightening into a smile. "I wonder how much money he has?" she asked.

Hooper sat down at the table again, his face glowing in anticipation. "Can you find out?"

Janice reached for her handbag and pulled out her phone and clicked the buttons. "Our current account has a thousand in."

"That won't get you far," said Hooper.

"Building Society accounts?" asked Pru.

Janice fiddled with phone buttons. "Mmm, short term accounts five thousand, long term account ten thousand."

"That also won't get you very far on an ocean-going yacht," he said.

Janice kept on clicking; suddenly a wide smile cracked her face, "Well now. There is a folder called Overseas Investments. I didn't know about that."

"Interesting," commented Hooper.

"Damn, its password protected."

"He doesn't want you to know what he's got." said Pru.

"Except I know the passwords he uses on the internet, unless he's created a special one for this."

Janice continued to push the buttons, "No," she said, "That can't be. I don't believe it."

Janice handed the phone to Hooper. He took the phone and gazed at the screen.

"Phew! That'll help," he said and handed the phone to Pru.

"Ten million pounds!" she gasped. "But where did he get that?"

Hooper stood up and began pacing the room. He took the phone from Janice and had a quick look at the account before passing it to Pru.

"More to the point," he said, "How did he get it?"

Janice leant back in her chair. "I have not the faintest idea. After our wedding he had fifty pounds left in his account."

Hooper crisscrossed the room, his agitation visible in his long face, his teeth grinding together like iron clad clogs on cobbled streets. He stopped by the table and sat down; he was sure Janice wasn't telling them everything she knew. "Janice, what aren't you telling us?" banging the table with his fist on every word.

Janice jumped. "I don't know anything else; he doesn't tell me anything."

"What has he said about Zeke, or Wilkinson?"

Janice crashed her head on to the table, covering her ears with her arms. "I don't know," she wailed.

Hooper drummed his fingers on the tabletop. "Janice, he must have let something slip."

Janice raised her head, her brimming eyes on the point of tears. "He has become very secretive during the last few months."

Hooper tipped his chair back and raised his eyebrows at Pru and the question hung in the air between them. Pru shook her head.

"Janice, we are both police trained and we know when someone is not telling us everything."

Janice pushed back her chair and stood up. "If you think that, if you think I am lying, you are no help to me. I think I should go home."

Herb shrugged. "Well, that's that. I don't think we will get much more out of her."

"I don't think we need to." said Pru. "One of the entries on that account was a payment to Bespoke Badges."

Herb stared at her blankly.

"The firm that makes the buffalo badges," Pru explained softly.

....

Sampson and Christopher Wilkinson's eyes locked across Wilkinson's desk.

"You fool, you stupid fool! You stupid unadulterated fool!" Sampson's frenzied voice ricocheted around the room. "And what do we do now?"

"Shut up! It may not have been my best idea. Indeed, almost as stupid as killing Stacey and Woodley," Wilkinson replied, his voice quiet and quivering. "We get out now."

"And to think you two are senior police officers and bickering like schoolgirls.'"

They lifted their heads to the new voice in the room. Trench was standing in the doorway.

"Thinking of leaving me to take the rap? Oh no you don't." he said.

"Then what do we do to get out of this pea soup we're in?"

Sergeant Trench walked further into the Chief Constable's office and without being invited, sat down by his desk. He sat there for a few moments, his eyes flicking from on to the other.

"The answer," he said, "is simple."

"Simple?" asked Sampson. "Simple?"

"Yes, and don't shout at me," he replied, his voice rising.

"How?" Sampson dropped his voice to a whimper.

A slow smile trickled across Trench's face and slowly he licked his lips. He began to laugh, his laugh increasing in volume until his shoulders were shaking, and he was rocking back and forth like the rocking horse in his kids bedroom.

"I have it. I have it, I have the perfect answer!"

"Then tell us," snarled Wilkinson.

He stopped shaking and stood up. "We are all on the same level now," he said, "and whichever of you two sorted Stacey, you should do the same to this girl and her fancy man, Hooper".

The room went silent. The two men shuffled their feet.

"Murder, not me," said Wilkinson.

"Nor me," said Sampson. "'and these two are not Stacey: they are aware, they know what's going on. And, I've already had one go at Hooper."

"What was the point of that?" asked Wilkinson. "I hope he didn't see your face."

"I'm sure he didn't," lied Sampson.

"Good," snapped Wilkinson. "However, it is a bit worrying that he didn't report it, not even to me."

Trench leaned towards them, "Well something has to be done before that Yorkshireman gets here. He won't tolerate any nonsense."

Wilkinson slumped down on to a chair, followed by Sampson. Wilkinson began to chuckle, the other two looked at him questioningly.

"Three thief catchers trying to be thieves," he said, "That's a joke, that's a good joke." He gave a humourless laugh. The others just looked at him.

"You're insane," said Trench, "You're both insane."

No one said anything. Trench rose from his chair and said, "I suppose I'd better get back to the desk. Somebody may come in to report a murder."

Sampson and Wilkinson stood looking at each other.

"We both had better give this some serious thought," said Wilkinson, resuming command.

Sampson nodded and walked slowly from the office, down the passage to his own office and sat down, his head in his hands. "It was going so well," he thought.

He looked up at the map of Basingham on the wall and his eyes picked out the castle. He smiled a self-indulgent smile, thinking at least I have that; perhaps that is my refuge against Zeke, and turned on his coffee pot.

Christopher Wilkinson watched Sampson go and sat down in the little used easy chair, reserved for VIP visitors. His chin dropped to his chest, and he thought of his wife.

How would she cope with being a prison visitor? How would he cope with being a Chief Constable in prison? It must not; it will not come to that.

…………..

Hooper drummed his fingers on the table.

"Every drum a sparkling thought?" said Pru imitating him.

A smile broadened his face and broke into a laugh, he stopped. "No, but we got something from her."

"Not much. We are not going to persuade anyone to arrest him on the strength of a few mutterings in his sleep and a purchase from a badge company."

Pru sidled off into the kitchen. "Another coffee?" she suggested. "It is much better for thinking than drumming your fingers."

"Mmm, OK, Yes," he replied, standing up and walking to the kitchen door. "You know Pru this whole problem revolves around the long boats and the garage."

"Stacey could have been killed for reasons unrelated to the business. What about his wife, children?"

Hooper shook his head. "Wife's dead. They never had any children. No, it has to be the business. Also, Buster's crucifixion is just too much of a coincidence. It is not surprising Sampson's worried if he is involved in the family business."

Pru filled the mugs and said, "I wonder where the boats pick up the migrants?"

"I wonder what else they pick up. Sampson didn't get that bank balance from migrants," replied Hooper.

"I thought trafficking illegal immigrants was lucrative?"

"Not that lucrative," said Hooper drily.

Sipping her coffee, Pru, studied Hooper over the rim of the mug. "What about her suspicions about Sarah and her husband?" asked Pru hesitantly.

Herb shrugged, "If she'd any real proof she would have told her. And wherever Sarah is, it does not sound likes she is with Sampson at the moment."

"Did you have any suspicions?"

"That she was seeing someone?"

Pru nodded. "Not really. She has never mentioned Sampson. Shall we pay another visit to the clubhouse Herb, in daylight we might find something we couldn't see in the dark?"

Hooper went back into the dining room and sat down at the table on one of Pru's hard chairs, watching her, busy with kitchen things. She wore a green top tucked into pale red slacks, her golden red hair fell almost to her waist, and she stood at the sink in profile to him. He swallowed hard and turned away.

"We do need to do that Pru, but I still think the problem and the answer is at the canal. Why do we meet such heavy opposition at that place? I know they want to keep the immigrants a secret but they are being very heavy handed, almost attracting attention to themselves."

Pru came through into the dining room and sat beside him, and began drumming the table lightly with her fingers, and a laugh playing across her lips.

"Come on, decision maker. What are we going to do?"

Hooper thumped her arm with his elbow. "The clubhouse" he said, "and you're driving."

He pulled himself up and headed for the front door, "On your feet slowcoach, sitting drinking coffee gets us nowhere."

....

Pru and Hooper parked in the only space left in the car park adjacent to the school. Term had started and as usual it was almost full. Fortunately, the space was nearest to the club and they could see up to the club gates from the car.

"The police tapes are still up." Hooper said, "I wonder if anyone is on duty?"

They walked up the lane to the club gates. The padlock was in place so Hooper fiddled in his pocket for his keys and found the padlock key. They went through and walked round the path to the clubhouse. The curtains were still drawn and Pru said, "I wonder if anyone has been here since we were here last."

"'We'll find out in a minute."

They walked round the back of the building. The door was still open. Hooper stepped inside and Pru followed him. The clubhouse was still littered with paper, drawers pulled out of desks and cupboards, chairs overturned. Nothing had altered since Valerie's or whoever it had been frantic search.

"Whoever it was certainly made a mess," said Pru. "What could she be looking for?"

Hooper walked down to the men's changing room. The room was tidy, with members' clothing still on hooks, and bowls bags lying around on the floor. "I'd better lock up or some light fingers will have a very profitable half hour here. Can't see anything here," he called.

"Nor here," Pru replied, coming out of the women's changing room. "I'll try the kitchen."

Hooper walked slowly down the bowling hall, over the mats which had been laid for the coming indoor season. He walked from side to side doing a fingertip search without getting on his knees. He could hear Pru poking about in the kitchen cupboards; pans clattering, pots tinkling. Suddenly the noise stopped and Hooper looked towards the kitchen.

"'Herb, come here, I think I've found something."

Hooper walked quickly towards the kitchen. "What is it?"

Pru was standing there looking at the palm of her hand. "Do you think that is, what I think it is?" she asked.

Lying in her hand was a small, tiny object, about three millimetres across. Hooper picked it up, it looked slightly blue. "I think it's a blue diamond Pru. It must be worth a few thousand pounds. No wonder Valerie was going frantic if she's lost it."

Pru shook her head. "No Herb, I think she came to collect it."

Hooper rolled the diamond around in his hand with his finger. "I could have this put in a ring and give it to you for Christmas," he joked.

Pru laughed, "No Herb, a silver necklace, or better still, buy another to match and make me some earrings."

They laughed and Hooper said, "I knew you weren't cheap."

Pru clenched her fist and thumped him lightly in the chest.

"The real question is what do we do with it?" he said.

"Are you going to tell Wilkinson about it?"

"I think this is the connection between the club and the canal," he said. "So, no, I think we keep it quiet for the moment."

"Do you think there could be more of these?" Pru asked. "Could the club be a distribution centre?'"

"Pru you're brilliant! I think that's exactly what it is." He said leaning forward and kissing her lightly on the cheek.

"Herbert Hooper you are too forward for words."

Hooper handed the diamond back to Pru. "You look after that for now Pru."

"Do you think it is genuine?"

"I suppose so, why shouldn't it be?"

"So, Valerie's probably involved in this as well," observed Pru.

"Probably; explains Woodley's death as well," pointed out Hooper.

"He was involved?"

"In whatever this is, or found out about it," said Hooper thoughtfully

Hooper began to clear up the mess Valerie had made. He stacked the papers and files on the desk in the office; someone else would have to sort that lot out when the club committee could have access to the building again. Picking up the chairs which normally ranged down the sides of the mats, he sat down.

Pru came out of the kitchen with two steaming mugs, "I found some biscuits too."

"You're a treasure. The best sergeant I ever had."

"Pig," she said, throwing a biscuit at him.

Hooper caught it in his left hand. "Always was a good stumper."

Pru sat down beside him sipping her coffee thoughtfully. "If this diamond is as valuable as you think, where shall I keep it? It isn't mine, so technically we're stealing."

Hooper looked at her. "We are looking after it, keeping it safe. Pru, you must have a corner somewhere in that big house of yours to hide such a tiny object."

"I suppose," she said. "I...."

"I don't want to know where you hide it, otherwise it isn't hidden."

Pru took out her purse, fiddled in the bottom, and picked out the stone with fingers. "It is so tiny. You wouldn't think something so small could be worth so much."

"It's rare."

Pru sat silent contemplating the blue object in the palm of her hand. "Herb," she said as she rolled the stone around with her finger, "You don't think it could be a fake, or a sapphire?"

"Sapphire?"

"Well, sapphires are blue. Didn't Princess Di have one surrounded by tiny diamonds?"

"I don't know. We will need to get it looked at properly in due course."

They sat drinking their coffee and the stone sat in Pru's hand looking at them, shining and glinting as the light flashed through its facets, fascinating them. Just as it was supposed to do.

"It is unbelievable that murder could be committed for this," Pru mused.

"If that is a diamond, it could be worth thirty thousand pounds, and murder has been committed for far less than that."

Hooper got to his feet and looked around the club room, satisfied that they had done as much as they could for now. He wondered if a temporary chairman had been appointed to replace Stacey. He would have to ring round to find out. The thought flashed in his mind, were any more club members involved in this fiasco? If so, he would have to be careful what he said. One thing was certain. They wouldn't be meeting on the green for some time.

He walked across to the open double doors and started to close them. "We ought to go Pru. We shouldn't be here anyway."

She walked across to him and they left, this time locking the doors behind them, and setting off down the long lane to the carpark, leaving the scene of murder and theft behind them; the bright, innocent sounds of children playing at the school, echoing across the fields.

Chapter 6

Joe Black arrived at the Stacey Transport garage at 7 a.m. on the dot. He looked through the window and tried the office door. It was locked. He walked down to the canal side but he couldn't see any boats. He noticed that to his left the canal opened out into a big pool, widening the canal to seventy or eighty feet, and he pondered why that was there. He walked along the dock side as far as the fence to where the woods started, he supposed that's what it was, a dock, but it wasn't like the ones he'd visited in London. They were big.

Joe walked back across the yard to the office and looked through the window. There was a gun case on the wall; he smiled, there were plenty of those where he came from but not rifles, hand guns, and they weren't kept in cases, usually in somebody's waistband or pocket. The bloke in the pub who'd offered him a part time job, off the books to start with, had said some people lived in caravans in the woods and part of the job was to keep an eye on them. He sauntered to the other end of the garage where the yard wrapped around it to the rear, and here, there were a number of pan-technical tractors. Then he remembered, the bloke had asked him if he had a HG licence, and he had, and he could drive one of those monsters if he had to.

He laughed to himself when he remembered the day he had found illegals among his cargo, and he'd kicked them out at a transport caff on the A1. God knows what happened to them. He walked over to the fence that bordered the woodland on the other perimeter of the yard, and he could see the caravans scattered among the trees. He couldn't hear any sounds and assumed there was no one in them or they were asleep.

The crunch of wheels on the tarmac drew his attention. At last, and he turned towards it. The doors opened and two men got out of the large Daimler. The driver was a large well-muscled man well over six feet, the other short and broad and solid. Two toughs, he thought, could have come from the east end. He walked over.

"You're early. Good," the short man said. The big man said nothing but his face seemed to radiate menace.

"Joe Black, Mr. Prune?" he asked.

"Yes," he nodded at the big man, "James." He said, "You may see a lot of him." He smiled and continued, "He can't speak; he had a little accident for speaking too much."

Joe looked at the scowling giant and saw hatred in his eyes.

"Oh,'" he said. "I'm sorry."

"Don't be. Just do your job and keep your mouth shut, and then your tongue will be quite safe."

"Right. Yes, Ok." Thinking, if I didn't need the cash I'd be hoofing it out of here.

Prune turned on his short legs and marched towards the office, taking out his keys and letting them in, He pointed at the gun case. "Have you got a licence?"

Joe Black shook his head.

"Can you use it?"

Black nodded. "Army," he said.

"From today this whole place is your responsibility - the garage and its contents, the caravans and their contents. You have to take control of the 'merchandise' that arrives on the boats, house it in the vans and move it on each morning according to the schedule given to you by James. The boats will arrive once, sometimes twice each week; you won't have to drive, just make sure the wagons are loaded for when the drivers arrive.

That's why you need that," he pointed at the gun case. "One last thing, from time to time a very small package will arrive and will be handed to you by the captain of the long boat. Don't open it. Phone James immediately and he will come to collect it. He doesn't speak so just say the package has arrived."

Prune handed Joe Black a set of keys. "Have you got that?"

"Yes, Mr. Prune."

"You will also live on site. It's an easy job but it's twenty four hours. That's why the pay is high."

There's always a catch thought Joe.

"Yes, Ok, thanks Mr. Prune."

The two men got in the Daimler, the big man behind the steering wheel. The large car looked almost too small to contain him. The small, squat man, like a potentate, sat in the back, the long limousine seemed to smother him, and Joe Black sat behind his new desk and watched them go. What shall I do first he thought and spotted the kettle on a side table.

Joe liked his coffee hot and black. He sipped it slowly and looked around him, the charts on the walls referring to various farms around the country, each referenced to a location on the map. Behind him was a mattress and sleeping bag on the floor. "I hope that's not my permanent bed," he muttered to himself. He opened the door in the back wall and entered the garage. The large space was filled with trailers which, no doubt hooked on to the tractors he'd seen at the back of the garage.

To his right was a staircase which led up to a mezzanine floor occupying one corner of the roof space. Joe walked up the stairs. The door at the top was locked, so he tried his keys, one fitted. The door opened into a large airy living room. It was, he realized, an apartment built into the roof. The ceiling above him was all glass and provided the light. He quickly opened all the doors until he found the bedroom; this was more like it, he thought, a large double bed. "I'll get a good night's sleep in here," he thought. And then he remembered the mattress. Why was that there?

He went back into the living room; in one corner was a desk with a number of electronic monitors on it. He couldn't see a computer, so he turned knobs until they began to light up - all except one. As the monitors came into life he saw they surveyed the inside of the garage; he could watch what was going on. Suddenly the dead monitor began to light up, and Prune's face appeared.

"Ah, Mr. Black, so you have found your surveillance equipment, but as you can see, I can watch you. Just from time-to-time Mr. Black."

"Yes, Mr. Prune it's a good way to communicate."

The screen went blank. "Brilliant! I wonder if there's a camera in every room?"

Joe Black sat down on his leather sofa. "This is almost as bad as prison."

....

Hooper and Pru arrived at the carpark and Pru slid into the driver's seat and looked at Hooper for instructions.

"My place," he said, "We'd better find out if Sarah is back."

Pru let in the gear and drove out of the car park. The traffic was heavy and progress to the other side of the city was slow. Impatience welled through Hooper, his feet tapping to the beat of the engine.

"This place will be gridlocked before long," he muttered.

Pru ignored him, concentrating on the road. "We needn't rush." she said.

As they pulled into Hooper's street the road was parked up on both sides of the road, leaving a single one way track down the centre.

"Damn, why can't people park on their drives?" he moaned.

Pru squeezed between two cars encroaching on to Hooper's gateway. "I hope we don't need to leave fast."

Hooper let himself into the house but it felt silent and he knew Sarah wasn't at home. He walked across the hall glancing into the sitting room, and on into the dining room and kitchen calling her name. He ran up the stairs and into each bedroom, still no response. Hooper walked quickly back down into the hall and signalled Pru to come in.

"No sign?" she asked. He shook his head.

"I'm now beginning to think she's been abducted like Jimmy and Mrs. Gardner. When we find one, we find them all."

Pru went into the kitchen and put on the kettle and some coffee into mugs. "I'm not sure Sarah would be happy about me helping myself in her kitchen."

"It's my kitchen too."

She laughed and brought the hot mugs across to the table and placed one in front of him. Hooper stared at it, a puzzled frown cutting across his high forehead.

"What are our next steps and where do we start looking for Sarah?"

Pru shrugged. "Same problem or two different problems?" she asked.

Hooper shrugged "Don't know. Don't like coincidences. Any suggestions?"

"You're the boss."

"Some help."

"We could do a house-to-house search."

"What! The two of us? It would take months. And where would we search? "

"We have to start asking questions somewhere."

"True."

"Come on Herb, let's get a move on. We have to find a place for this beautiful blue stone as you won't have it made into earrings for me."

He grinned at her and stood up. "OK no point in hanging around here."

He gave her a gentle slap as she passed him. "Right. Let's get rid of that bit of rock and then go down to the station and see if Sampson's there. Maybe have a quiet word about all that money."

"Are you staying in the car while I find a place for this?" she asked as they arrived at her house.

He nodded and she let herself in and walked through to the kitchen. Hide in plain sight she thought. The drawer next to the cutlery drawer was an odds and ends drawer, in one corner was an old pomander, the scent long gone. She opened it, dropped in the stone, tied it up again and tucked it into the back of the drawer.

"As good as anywhere she thought, as long as I don't forget where I've put it."

Hooper watched her lock the door and smiled broadly as she slipped behind the wheel.

"What are you smiling at?"

"Nothing." He couldn't tell her his secret thoughts. "Burn up the gas sergeant. Let's see if we can find that Assistant Chief Constable."

Pru reversed out into the road, giving a wave to her neighbour as she saw the curtain flutter, and sped off up the road. Pru turned into the station and parked in her usual place. She nudged Hooper and nodded to where the Chiefs and his assistant's cars were parked. "They're in."

Hooper and Pru walked into the station and across to the desk. Trench watched them all the way.

"Hooper," he said, nodding at Pru. "What can I do for you?"

"The Brass in?"

Trench nodded, "They've just been rowing so the atmosphere up there is a bit strained."

Hooper made for the stairs.

"You can't go up there."

"Why not?"

"You're suspended. Wait in the waiting room. I'll tell them you're here."

Hooper stopped mid tread on the bottom step. He turned towards Trench and then without a word walked over to the waiting room, Pru following close behind him, and let himself in. The room was less appealing than his former office; painted pale cream with a line running around the middle in a dark green. Posters were blue tacked all over them giving out information on how to stay safe, or mug-shots on people who were missing, or people whom the police would like to interview.

They sat down on cushion less chairs. "All the years I've worked at this place and I've never been here before," whispered Pru.

"No need to whisper Pru; it's not a church."

"But isn't it bleak?"

"It's better than the cells. Folk who come in here aren't likely to stay overnight."

"Yes, I've seen the cells a few times, from the outside of course."

The door opened and Trench came in. "They say they're too busy to see you." He turned to leave.

"Trench, just a minute," snapped Hooper.

Sergeant Trench spun round his eyes flashing and his face flushing red with aggravation, "Sergeant Trench to you Hooper. You don't have any influence around here any longer, so I suggest you go about your business before I find an excuse to lock you both up."

Hooper and Pru followed Trench out of the room and headed for the front door and the carpark. Pru flicked off the car locks as they headed towards the car. She held out the keys to him, he shook his head and Pru sat behind the wheel and waited. Hooper slumped down beside her.

"That didn't get us very far," he said.

"No, so what next?"

Hooper pondered the question, his eyes closed, his fingers drumming silently on his knees. He looked up and across at her. "Thinking time, your place I think."

Pru let in the first gear and slowly headed for the exit. Neither of them saw Sampson watching them as they left.

…………..

Sampson walked back to his desk and sat down. Why had Hooper turned up at the station? To confront him or to report him? How much did he remember and why had he left without doing anything?

He knew now two things which he had to deal with. His boss, Wilkinson, couldn't be relied upon, and so he had to get his own funds topped up as quickly as possible and get out without sharing the payout. Even better if he could cut Prune out of the deal too; that would give him two million at a stroke. He banged his head on the hard mahogany desk, but the risk; Zeke Prune and Hooper, they were the risk. Prune was the most dangerous.

He would have to find somewhere where Prune wouldn't find him, and he would have to get rid of Hooper. What if he could get rid of them both? And Hooper's partner, what would he do with her? Could he get her into the castle? He laughed, as he thought, a partner for Mrs. Gardner. Prune, could he get him into the castle without that dumb giant of his?

A helter-skelter of thoughts whirled around his head until he felt it would burst. It is all too much, if only Wilkinson would take some of the load. And then he thought of his wife, when faced with the reality of what was happening would she help? Perhaps she would lure Prune's daughter to the castle, if she thought it would be leading to a sun-drenched life in the Caribbean.

Sampson raised his head. He pulled a sheet of paper from the computer printer and placed it in front of him. A list, a plan, he must have a plan. Who to deal with first. Sarah? His wife? Could he get her to comply? Would she see sense? Sarah, dare he let her go? Would she go home and blurt it all out to Hooper? Hooper would certainly want to know where she had been for the last few days. He wrote, Wife, Sarah, on the paper and put it in his desk drawer. He would deal with those two problems first.

Sampson locked his office door behind him and went across to Wilkinson's. The door was closed so he knocked, he heard a chair move but there was no reply. He knocked again. A tired voice said "Come in."

Sampson opened the door and stepped inside. Wilkinson didn't turn around. He was sitting facing the window, his shoulders hunched forward, his chin in the palm of his hand. "Yes Sampson?"

Sampson remained silent, and after a few moments Wilkinson turned his head towards him. "Yes?" he asked again.

"I'm going home. I'll be back in later."

"Tell whoever is on the desk."

"Trench?"

Wilkinson nodded, and pushed back his chair and walked across to the window. The view across the city was broad. He could see the cathedral standing high above every other building. The lush green of Basingham Park stood out against grey roofs of the terrace streets of town houses. Over to his right, the spacious buildings of the white-collar professionals, and to his left, the two up and two down of the blue collar brigade. Each sector had its share of decent law-abiding citizens, and each had its share of criminal minds. This is my city, he thought, and I used to know my place in it, I wonder where I fit now. "We've got ourselves into a sticky situation."

Sampson moved about agitatedly, anxious to be on his way. "It's sortable. That's what I'm going to start doing now."

He didn't say he was going to sort it only for himself and leave his boss to stew in whatever mess he was in. Sampson left Wilkinson looking at his favourite view and strode downstairs, lifted his arm in goodbye to Trench and walked briskly to his car.

He let himself into the house and went into the kitchen and leaned against the door frame watching his wife at the sink.

"I want to talk to you."

She didn't respond.

"Come into the sitting room."

She didn't move; she went on with what she was doing. He walked over to her and grabbed her arm.

"I said I want to talk to you."

She tried to struggle out of his grasp but he pulled her across the kitchen and into the sitting room, flinging her into the settee and sitting down beside her. They sat side by side, he, looking at the profile of her drooping head, she fixedly at her knees

"Well," she said. "Now that you've got me here, what do you want?"

"What is your favourite holiday resort?"

Her head snapped up in surprise. Warily she sat up straighter on the soft cushions, puzzlement slowly addressing her face. Violence, then this sudden discussion about holidays; my husband really is going strange, she thought. "Holiday resort, why, are we going somewhere?"

"Just answer."

"The Caribbean Islands; you already know that."

"How long would you like to go for?"

"What is this?"

"Answer, damn you!"

Janice moved further into the corner of the settee, trying to put distance between them, as if distance could separate her from the frightening glow of her husband's eyes.

"Well?"

"I, I don't know; a month would be nice I suppose.'

A strange cackle of a laugh burst from his throat and resounded around the room. He jumped to his feet and pulled her up and began dancing her around shouting her name.

Janice thrust out her arms and pushed him; he stumbled backwards and fell back into the settee. He stopped singing. She looked down at him. He looked suddenly frightened, a nervous twitch twisting his mouth. His eyes lifeless.

"Janice, would you like to live there?"

His voice no longer a savage roar, just whispered through his twisted lips.

"Live there?"

"I need to get away Janice, Chris, Zeke Prune, and that giant of his."

"Why? How, how shall we live? What about your job?"

"It's over Janice."

"Have we enough money?"

"That's where I need your help."

A little confidence seeped into his face; he hunched forward sliding to the edge of the settee cushion. He reached out and took hold of her hand.

"My help?"

Sampson gave his wife's hand a little tug and she sat down beside him.

"I have some money, but not enough without my pension."

"I know we must have some; we have always saved."

He looked at her sharply. So she must have broken into my account; perhaps there will only be me in the Caribbean, but he didn't reply, and then went on. "I think we would need another five million to live comfortably."

"Another five million, that's an awful lot of money Paul. Where would we get all that?"

"As I said, that's where I need your help."

Janice laid back into the cushions and looked around her sitting room; the expensive floor length curtains, what had they paid for those, eighty pounds a metre? The carpet; the pile so deep it felt like walking on air. What had that cost? Where did the money come from? Paul was a policeman.

Policemen were honest. But he couldn't spend like he did on his salary. So where did it come from?

"Janice," the voice snapped her back to reality. "Are you listening to me?"

"Yes Paul, but how can I help you get all that money?"

"As you seem to know what's in my private account you probably know where I got it from."

"No, how could I?"

Sampson glanced at his wife and then through the windows, his eyes drawn to the garden outside but seeing nothing. Could he trust this woman? Could he trust this woman he had spent his life with? Or would her moral fervour make her betray him. Should he tell her?

"Janice, you know my cousin Buster worked for Ray as manager for Stacey Transport down at the canal docks?"

"Yes."

"Well, Chris Wilkinson, Trench, I, and Mr. Prune have an interest in it too."

"You're helping out with the transportation business?"

"In a way," agreed Sampson. "Every couple of weeks or so a package came for us on the longboats. Zeke Prune's man would collect it and then when the contents were sold, he would pay the rest of us."

"So, you are in business Paul? I thought policemen weren't supposed to have business interests?" She thought about telling him she knew about the illegal immigrants but decided against it.

"Never mind that. What I want you to do is to go to the canal and pick up the package and bring it back here."

"What about Mr. Prune's man?"

"You get there before him."

"Why can't you go, Paul?"

"The new manager wouldn't give the package to me."

Janice looked at her husband, doubt lining her face.

"Look, this will be easy for you. What I want you to do is go to the canal office and say you're Zeke's wife, and you've come to collect his package because James is ill."

"Are you going to share out the proceeds?"

"No, we will go and catch the first flight out of here."

"Where to?"

"Anywhere."

....

Hooper sat down on the hard chair in Pru's dining room and watched her in the kitchen. She had let down her hair and the rich golden red locks, streaming down to her waist, caught the shafts sunlight as she moved about.

"You really should get more comfortable chairs in here Pru; these are like rocks."

Pru walked in with a coffee pot. "Poor you. You got piles or something?"

She put down the pot and took the chair opposite him and filled his mug. "If we're here for a long session I thought we might as well have plenty."

"Have you any rum to put in this, it helps the thought process?"

"No Herb Hooper, I wouldn't give you any even if I had some."

Hooper pouted his faked displeasure and sipped the hot liquid. "At least it's strong," he said.

Hooper drummed on the table and looked at his partner, but she just concentrated on her mug.

"Now sergeant, any ideas?"

"You're the boss, I work on instructions."

"We've made some progress. We know what comes in on the longboats."

"Yes, Illegal immigrants, and possibly diamonds."

"We know the migrants are sent out to work."

"But we don't know where - farms, factories, city sweatshops."

"It could be book a bloke when you need one."

"How do you mean, Pru?"

"We know my father uses casual labour on the estate, I suspect he doesn't pay them, he just feeds them. I bet he's the driving force behind the enterprise."

"You can't prove it."

"No, we can't, but just think, if the local garage is extra busy that day, and he needs some help, he just rings Zeke Prune and, Hello, a man appears. He doesn't pay the man, he pays Daddy."

"Mmm, if that man was also a qualified mechanic as opposed to a labourer that would mean big money."

"Herb, but the really big money would come from the professions. Do you think he could be that well organised?"

"I don't know. Little pockets of mixed workers all over the country each guarded by the equivalent of Buster, all being hired out on demand; sounds a bit far-fetched to me."

"But possible."

"Yes possible. It will take more than you and me to tackle something like that."

"And you think Sampson is soaked through in this. Anyone else? Do you think Wilkinson suspects and that is why he has asked us to look into this?"

"I don't know. There has to be a risk Wilkinson himself is involved."

"Why?" Pru asked.

"Because if he isn't involved, the ACC is taking a hell of a risk," Hooper observed. "I wonder why they didn't try and rope you and me into this."

Pru filled up the mugs again. "They know you too well. The criminals' Rottweiler of Basingham."

Hooper laughed and stood up. He walked across to the window and looked out over the yard. It was surrounded by a high wall, on the left was a raised bed neatly planted with salad plants and vegetables. At strategic places there were Bonsai trees in decorative pots, but still leaving enough space to park the car. Suddenly, he saw a movement out of the corner of his eye, a cat was peeping from behind one of the pots. Hooper began to chuckle.

"What do you find so amusing about all this?'" Pru said, spinning round on her chair.

"You've got a great back garden Pru, but there's a cat in it."

Pru jumped up, her chair fell over; she rushed to the door. "Macci, Macci," she called.

Macci bounded across the yard and leaped up into her arms. She came back into the dining room nursing and stroking the cat. Hooper turned from the window towards her. Christ, he thought, she's got a bloody cat.

"I knew she would come back to me Herb. She's very thin, so I'm going to feed her."

Pru walked through and into the kitchen. Hooper heard the clank of a feeding bowl, and the sound of tins being opened.

"OK," he called, "But what about this top brass of ours; what shall we do about them?"

Pru came back into the dining room, picked up her chair and sat down. "When does that Chief Constable come from Yorkshire?"

"Wilkinson is trying to put him off."

"Couldn't you phone him?"

"I wouldn't get past the front desk."

"Has he got a personal email?"

"Don't know. Why?"

"If he has, and we send him a message, it will go into his email box and he'll definitely get it."

"Mmm, how do we find that out?"

"You're the detective."

Hooper raised his mug to his lips and then put it down again; he began to pace slowly around Pru's dining room. Pru sat at the table watching him. Macci jumped on her knee. Pru lifted the cat to her face and began to nuzzle her. Macci purred. The sound seemed to startle Hooper and he looked at them both and a smile trickled across his face.

"OK, but you're the computer wiz kid in this team, so let your fingers do some talking."

Pru put Macci down and pulled a mobile phone from her pocket. Hooper dropped into the chair beside her. "I thought you needed a laptop or something?"

"Get real Herb. Well?"

"The Yorkshire police will have a website won't they?"

"I expect so."

Pru's fingers piano the keyboard like a maestro. "Which part?"

"How do you mean?"

"Yorkshire is divided into four. North, South, East and West according to this."

"Do they have separate forces?"

"Mmm, it seems so."

"And they'll each have a Website?"

Hooper drummed on the tabletop for a few moments, his eyes closed, his head nodding. Pru was just going to tell him not to go to sleep when he opened his eyes and looked at her. "Pru, do we know the name of this Chief Constable?"

"Yes, Charlie Yates, or, to you, The Honourable Sir Charles Richard Yates, and don't let me hear you calling him Dickie."

"Levity doesn't become you. He'll be listed on one of those sites, won't he?"

"Should be."

"Then find him and see if his appointment schedule is listed."

Pru's fingers skidded over the keys, quickly zipping through the posted information, her flitting over the listings. "He's in North Yorkshire."

"Oh, he won't have much to do up there; they only have a few sheep, don't they?"

"Don't you be cheeky. There are some nice estates in North Yorkshire. I have some good friends up there."

"Yea, all green wellies and Land Rovers."

"He does have a personal email. Are we going to email him?"

Hooper shrugged his shoulders and raised his eyebrows. Pru looked at him in askance waiting for his reply.

"Well? It's easy enough to do."

"What does a suspended DCI say to a Chief Constable to raise his suspicions?"

They dropped quiet looking at each other. Pru poured herself some more coffee and held up the pot to him, he nodded. "Why not approach him as a concerned private citizen, instead of as a policeman?"

"He'd be dead chuffed when he finds out."

"What we need to do is excite his interest so he doesn't let Wilkinson put him off, don't you think?"

"You could get one of your green wellie friends to give him a ring."

"Now there's an idea. Who could I ring?"

"Perhaps you know the Master of the local hunt, or the Lord Lieutenant of the county?"

"As a matter of fact I do."

....

Chris Wilkinson watched his second in command leave to go to his own office. In spite of the fact that Samson thought he was being clever, he knew all about his dream of living it up on some Caribbean isle on secreted away money. It was a pied piper's fantasy. He was sure Sampson was going to double cross him but not if he got there first.

He sat up straighter in his chair. This had to stop now; he was the boss in this place; he would have to put his foot down and bring things under his control. His control. He picked up his phone and dialled Sampson's extension, no reply. He rang the switch board and asked to be put through to Sampson, he waited. After a couple of minutes the girl on the switchboard came back on the line. "He's not answering sir. I can ask the front desk if he's gone out, or try his mobile."

"Ring his mobile."

Wilkinson slumped his elbows on to his desk, one hand clamping the handset to his ear, and his chin resting in the palm of the other. His thoughts wandered, good job he hadn't said anything to his wife about his extra business activities, or it would have been all round the golf club by now. The girl's voice filled the handset. "He's not picking up sir."

"Will you ask the desk sergeant if he left a message as to his whereabouts?"

The line clicked off and Wilkinson waited, he twisted uneasily in his chair, rocking backwards and forwards, he stood up and then sat down again.

The switchboard girl spoke softly in his ear. "Sorry sir, he doesn't seem to be contactable."

"Right, thank you." He slammed the phone on its cradle. Sampson was avoiding him, plotting a quick exit probably.

What now? He told himself to relax and think. His first thought was of North Yorkshire and that Rottweiler of a Chief Constable. Could he use the visit to his advantage? He could invite him to come as soon as possible, and how glad he would be to make his acquaintance again after all these years.

Wilkinson picked up the phone. The switchboard operator clicked in, "Yes sir?"

"Get me the North Yorkshire Chief Constable."

"Right sir."

Wilkinson put down the phone and waited, impatiently tapping the floor with his feet. He walked across to the window, willing the phone to ring. He pirouetted around at the triple intermittent ring of the handset and quickly picked it up. The unhurried voice of the switchboard girl said, "Chief Constable Yates sir." and switched him through.

"Charlie, so glad I caught you."

"Hello Chris. It's been a long time since we had a chat. What can I do for you?"

"I've been thinking about that courtesy visit you proposed making. I think we should organise it as soon as possible."

"Well Chris, you have put it off so often I was beginning to think you were avoiding me."

"Not at all," he lied. "I've had a few problems down here but things are a little easier now. But I suppose sheep rustling is still a problem for you?"

"Ongoing Chris. I don't expect your probs are animal related?"

"Humans are animals Charlie and some of them have nasty bites. In fact, you may be able to help me while you're here."

Charlie Yates began to chuckle. "So you want to pick my brains while I'm there. And here's me thinking it would be a round of social events, dinner with the mayor and that sort of thing."

"I'm sure all that will be arranged, but on the side, I have a few nasty sheep which you just might help me to round up."

"Sounds interesting. I'll get my secretary to check the diary and be back in touch."

The phone went dead. Wilkinson muttered to himself, "At least I've primed him and he will know exactly what to do with Sampson."

He sat down at the desk again and looked at the notepad in front of him. He walked across to the coffee maker and switched it on, finding a mug he liked. He preferred his secretary bringing it in on a tray. It made him feel like the boss. While it heated, he went back to his desk. He picked up a pencil and began to doodle: he always thought best when he doodled. As he doodled a face began to appear on the page, Hooper, he doodled but all he had was Hooper. I wonder where he is, he thought. He picked the phone again and dialled the switchboard again.

"Yes sir?" the question hovered in the telephonist's voice.

"Put me through to records."

"Right sir. You do know you can dial directly, don't you sir?"

"Yes, I know, but your connections are logged, aren't they?"

"Yes sir."

"'Put me through please."

The phone burped intermittently in the records office, it was picked up immediately. "Yes," said a bored voice.

"Chief Constable here," said Wilkinson with briskness he did not feel.

"Oh, yes sir, how can I help?"

"Do you think you can find DI Hooper's details, address, phone number and so on?"

"Yes sir, I'll ring you back in a few moments."

Wilkinson thought he could probably have accessed the information himself, but he wanted the call logged and he wanted people to remember the request. And anyway, if you've got a dog, why wag your own tail.

He rang Hooper's landline but after six rings it went to voicemail and voicemail was full. He looked through the information records had sent him. Ah, mobile phone number. He dialled.

"Herb Hooper."

"Good morning Hooper. Have you got any further with that enquiry I sent on?"

"It's work in progress." He mouthed to Pru 'Wilkinson.'

"Can you let me have a report in writing? I have arranged a date for the Chief Constable of North Yorkshire's visit and I shall want to inform him about the business we have in hand. This is the most major case we have had in a long time Hooper."

"Yes sir, as soon as I can."

"Now Hooper," he instructed. "Keep me informed of what is happening."

"Yes sir."

Wilkinson put down the phone; he was pretty sure that Hooper would be in touch if Sampson turned up on his doorstep.

....

Hooper slipped his mobile back in his pocket.

"What was that about?" Pru asked.

"Wilkinson asking me for a report about the state of the inquiry. Obviously, he doesn't know I suspect him of being head over arse in corruption."

"Don't swear Herb. You think he is asking for the report to put you off the scent or is he really not involved in whatever this is?"

"Don't know. Anyway, let's get that email off to your posh mates in North Yorkshire."

Pru opened her laptop and clicked through to her email account. "What do you want me to say?"

"Just send her a chatty note, and then add you think your daddy might be involved in some smuggling, and the Chief Constable here, who's a friend of your daddy, might be involved too, and would she ask her daddy to talk to Charlie Yates about it."

"Mr. Yates?"

"Whatever; let's sow a few seeds and see what happens."

"I'll ask her if she's riding in the next county show."

"And when you've done that, send another to Yates, in a similar vein, from me."

"'And what do you think that will achieve?"

"Dunno. Just stir the pot until it boils and see what frogs jump out."

Hooper watched Pru's fingers skimming effortlessly over the keyboard. "You're pretty slick at that Pru. Where did you learn that?"

"It's another thing daddy sent me off to learn. I think he imagined me taking over the estate office."

"You could send one off to him too."

"What good will that do?"

"Who knows Pru; just keep the pot boiling. We know they are all involved so keep him informed. Step on his bunions and see if he yells, or worse."

"OK," she said and returned to the keyboard.

Pru pondered for a moment. Should she start 'Dear Daddy' or should she write it from Herb? She was fairly certain that he didn't like Hooper even if he had invited him to visit. It was a good job Herb didn't ride or there's no doubt he would try to arrange an accident. She dropped her hands from the keyboard to her knees, her head dropped and her chin rested on her chest. What was she thinking, how could she think such thoughts about her own father? Her eyes filled, and tears began to gently trickle down her cheeks. Herb was looking away from her and she quickly reached across the table for a tissue.

"Crying?"

"No Herb, I must have something in my eye."

"Tell me another. What's the problem?"

Pru silently began to weep openly. Herb stood and went to her and put his hands on her shoulders and bent down over her, his cheek touching her ears.

"Now, now, Pru what's the matter?"

She moved her head back and rested it against him "It's Daddy, I can't believe the things I'm thinking about him. My own father. Am I going to have to arrest him when this is all over?"

"I don't know Pru. I think someone else might do that."

She lowered her head and tears began to flood down her cheeks, her shoulders shaking as she sobbed with emotion. "Has he really done the things we think he has?"

"I believe so, Pru, or got someone to do it for him."

Pru's body heaved again as fresh tears filled her red puffed face. Hooper remained silent and drew her back towards him.

....

Yates, the Chief Constable of the North Yorkshire police put down his phone and walked thoughtfully over to his office window. The view across the historic town never failed to inspire him and concentrate his thinking. That phone call from the Lord Lieutenant certainly raised questions about what was going off in Wilkinson's patch and he would have to get it entered into the diary.

That was the second request he'd had to push forward his visit to Basingham. First Wilkinson implying he had problems he needed help in solving, and now the Lord Lieutenants' office suggesting that the senior leadership, and that might include Wilkinson himself, was involved in criminal activity.

That was going to need some nifty toe work. He buzzed through to his secretary. "Mary, check the calendar for a suitable date to visit Basingham. As soon as possible, move things around if you have to."

"Yes Sir."

What was it the Lord Lieutenant had said? His daughter had it on good authority that some of the senior officers were involved in diamond smuggling and helping illegal immigrants to get into the country? That all sounded a bit far fetched but it needed looking into, and it needed someone of his rank to do it. Did Wilkinson know, was he involved or did he only suspect there was a problem and simply wanted his help? He guessed he would find out when he got there. Should he make it official, or should he start with this courtesy visit and nose around when he got there?

Chapter 7

A couple of days later Yates set off for Basingham, his uniform carefully packed into his overnight bag, which was an exaggeration considering the number of social and official functions he was supposed to attend. If the information he had been given was correct it sounded more like being back on the beat. A one-man crusade against a whole crooked force.

The train pulled into Basingham station and, heaving his bag from the rack, he made his way to the entrance and hailed a taxi. "Metropole Hotel" he instructed the cabbie; he might as well have the best that Basingham can provide at his host's expense. He paid the cab off and looked up at the edifice in front of him. Well, it looked posh enough for a police chief. There were a number of people sitting around the foyer chatting, some drinking coffee, some had a glass in front of them. No one of interest he thought and smiled at the familiar phrase. He booked in.

"Top floor, Chief Constable Yates," said the receptionist. "Your reception tonight is on the first floor. Have a good evening."

"Thank you miss," he replied.

He took the lift which sped him to the top floor without a stop. His room 236, opposite the lift doors, was convenient. He slipped the key card into the slot and turned the door knob as the green light appeared. The room was large and spacious, and the ceiling to floor windows looked out over the town and had heavy drapes to keep out the night. He flung his bag on the bed, hung his jacket in the wardrobe and began to unpack. He'd better let his uniform hang for a while; he didn't want even a trace of a crease in it at tonight's reception.

There was a knock on the door. He paused, and looked at it. He wasn't expecting anyone. Reception perhaps. But they could have rung. The knock repeated; it seemed with a little more urgency. He walked across the room and opened the door. A tall man and a woman with brilliant red hair stood in front of him. "Yes?" he asked.

"DCI Hooper sir, may we come in?"

He stepped back and let the door swing open for them to enter. He looked meaningfully at the woman.

"Sergeant Prune, sir."

He nodded. "What can I do for you? I haven't even unpacked yet."

"It's a long story sir. May we sit down?"

"I have a reception this evening."

"I'll give you an overview sir."

Hooper started with the murder of Stacy and the disappearance of Jimmy Knowles and ended with the discovery of illegal immigrants and of what appeared to be blue diamonds. He also described the behaviour of ACC Sampson, his bank account, the Buffalo Badge and his suspicions about the Chief Constable.

"So, that was what Chief Constable Wilkinson meant when he said he had a few problems I might help him with."

"And us, sir, but we may be his main problem."

"Suspended you say, but only a pretend suspension?"

"Yes sir. We were supposed to find Stacey's killer from the streets. I don't know what he was really thinking as he was involved in it."

"It does seem like madness for Chris to ask you to investigate if he was involved," said Yates thoughtfully. "Right, Hooper, I'll get on now; let's keep in touch."

"Yes sir. Sir, you might keep an eye out for a chap called Prune, the sergeant's father. He's one of the persons of interest in this case."

"Do you really think she should be involved in this? There is a clear conflict of interest," pointed out Yates.

"That tennis ball had my name on it," said Pru.

"Yes, that makes it all so odd if your father is involved."

Yates turned towards his unpacking. Hooper nudged Pru and they walked over to the door. "Have a good evening, sir."

Yates didn't reply.

....

Wilkinson picked up the phone and dialled the Metropole Hotel and asked to be put through to room 236. It rang for a moment but was picked up on the sixth ring.

"Good afternoon Charlie. Did you have a good journey down? Chris Wilkinson here."

"Very comfortable, thank you." Should he tell him about Hooper and Prune's visit? No, he'd keep that to himself for now.

"And your room?"

"Excellent Chris, thank you."

"It's the best room in the place."

"Yes, I shall have a little lunch sent up in a while, not much, I expect you'll be feeding me up tonight."

"We won't eat until nine so don't starve."

"OK Chris. I want to rest this afternoon; I must be on the ball tonight."

Charlie put the phone down and continued with his unpacking, carefully hanging up his uniform. A long afternoon stretched ahead of him. A walk round the town might be useful, providing a little local colour to his speech. What about a visit to the canal? A walk along the towpath wouldn't come amiss. He could borrow a pair of binoculars and pretend to be bird watching. He rang Reception and asked if they had an ordnance survey map of the area.

"Yes sir, I'm sure we can find one for you."

When it arrived, together with his leek and potato soup, it was huge, two inches to the mile scale.

"Sorry sir. It was the only map Reception could find at such short notice."

The waiter came into the room and laid the small table by the window, placed his soup, brown roll, and napkin down, and the folded map beside it. Charlie wasn't sure whether to tip or not, so he didn't.

The soup was superb, and so was the map. He unfolded it and spread it out on the floor. He could see the canal quite clearly, and the basin, and Stacey's yard. At this scale the buildings were shewn individually, together with the yard in front of them, the woods surrounding them, and most importantly, the footpaths through the woods. He could also see that Stacey's truck garage was built along the canal side; there was no canal path through the property. An afternoon walk in the woods would stimulate his appetite for this evening's reception. Wilkinson had promised him a banquet to remember. Well, a walk might provide some local tidbits to include in his after dinner speech.

Yates picked up the phone and pressed nine. "Yes sir?" the polite receptionist's voice whispered in his ear.

"Thank you for the map you sent me, miss."

"That's alright sir, I hope it was what you wanted."

"Yes, it was. I'm thinking of going bird watching in the local woods this afternoon. Do you think you could rustle up a pair of binoculars too?"

The phone went silent, after a short pause the receptionist said, "I'll send someone out to ask the camera shop across the road if they will loan us a pair."

"'Your initiative is spectacular miss; we should recruit you into the police force."

She laughed. "Thank you sir, but I'm quite happy where I am."

Yates took the stairs down to the reception desk and as he approached the receptionist produced a pair of Zeiss binoculars.

"Superb," he said.

"'I have also taken the liberty to call a taxi to take you to that part of town, it's quite a walk."

"Indispensable. Miss…?" he raised his head questioningly.

"Merson, Julia Merson."

"Thank you, Miss Merson," Yates walked across the foyer to the exit thinking, this girl could be useful.

....

Hooper and Pru left the hotel and headed for Pru's car. Hooper ground in through the gears as though manufacturing face powder (which Pru didn't need) and swung out of the carpark into the shanty streets of lower Basingham. Pru cast him a glance but said nothing.

They sped through the narrow streets, cutting corners, and the pedal down to the boards on the straight, towards her place.

"You looking for a ticket?" she asked.

He grunted and eased off. "Sorry."

"Do you think Yates will do anything?" Pru asked.

"Depends."

"On what?"

"If he takes what we have told him seriously, he'll take some action, although as an official guest I don't know what. If he doesn't, he'll go back home having had a few pleasant days' holiday."

"But things aren't normal, are they?" Pru paused and then added "Do you think Sampson will turn up to the reception tonight? If not, there will be a very obvious empty chair."

They arrived at Pru's street and Hooper pulled over into the curb. Pru looked at him inquiringly. He nodded towards her house at the end of the street where a Rolls phantom was parked by her gate.

"Daddy," she said.

"I wonder what he wants?"

"I wonder why he's come in the Rolls."

"I bet he never does anything without a reason; it won't be just a social call."

"We had better find out," said Pru.

Hooper gently pushed the gear into first and the car began to move slowly down the street.

"Thanks for that," said Pru. "Both I and my car appreciate the careful handling."

Hooper looked at her and grinned. Pru smiled.

The limousine was blocking the gateway into Pru's garden but there was space behind it which Hooper pulled into effectively preventing the other car from moving.

The car's front doors opened simultaneously. From the driver's seat the tall massive figure of mute James unfurled onto the pavement. From the passenger seat the short squat shape of Zeke dropped his feet onto the road.

Pru opened her door, got out, and stood facing her father. Hooper stayed where he was.

"Good afternoon Prunella," he said, his cut glass English accent belying his east European appearance.

She didn't reply.

"Don't you want to know why I'm taking time out of my busy schedule to pay you a social call?"

"Social call?" she asked.

"Isn't your boyfriend going to join us? I'm sure he would have to approve of my proposal."

"He isn't my boyfriend and I don't need his approval for anything."

"No matter. What he thinks is immaterial to me."

Hooper opened his car door and, getting out, stood facing him. The four gazed at each other silently.

"Hmm. He is interested after all," Prune said.

"What is it?" Pru asked, a sharp impatience cutting the air.

"So harsh Prunella, and here I am offering you the most prestigious invitation the town has to offer."

"And what exactly is that?"

"I want you to accompany me to the reception for Chief Constable Yates tonight."

Pru gasped in surprise, and then widened into laughter. Hooper straightened up in interest and leaned forward.

"Father I never thought of you as stupid, but that is the craziest idea ever. I'm suspended from the force; I couldn't get through the door."

"Pru, no. That could be a good idea." Hooper butted in.

"It speaks," sneered Prune.

Pru spun to face Hooper, her face rising red with anger, but Hooper held up his hand and she subsided into silence.

"Well Mr. Hooper, do you tell her what to do?"

"Pru's my sergeant, I'm her boss."

"But you are suspended Mr. Hooper."

"We maintain the position."

"Very commendable DCI Hooper, very proper." Prune said sarcastically.

Hooper ignored the comment and asked, "What are you proposing Mr. Prune? Neither of us believes you are suggesting this out of heartfelt generosity."

"And you, Mr. Hooper, are most ungenerous. I have two seats for the reception, and I could take James here, but he's not such a good conversationalist as is my daughter." He laughed a wicked little laugh. "Are you James?" James looked down at him, hate brimming from his eyes.

"So, Mr. Hooper, why shouldn't I take my daughter to the reception? I grant you she couldn't go as Sergeant Prune, but no one will refuse her entry as my daughter."

"No." Hooper said.

"Can you be ready for seven, Prunella?"

Pru nodded her acceptance.

"We will call for you then. Unless you would rather come up to the house; you will have a much larger wardrobe to choose from there."

Pru shook her head.

"No? Then let us out Mr. Hooper, and we will be on our way. Oh, and Mr. Hooper just to show I have no animosity towards you, my invitation to come and ride with us on the estate still holds."

Hooper smiled. "As you know Mr. Prune, I don't ride."

"Ah yes. But very shortly, next week in fact, the Basingham Hunt will be setting out from the house. Why don't you come along and sample our stirrup cup? It's very impressive; all the guys and gels in their red and black. Maybe Pru would ride with us?" He looked at her questioningly.

Pru smiled and shrugged her shoulders.

Hooper moved the car and James expertly manoeuvred the limousine out of its confined position, and then drove off up the street. Pru and Hooper watched until they turned into the traffic. Pru went to her front door; she inserted the latch key and let herself in. Hooper followed her.

....

The taxi dropped Yates off at the canal at the south side of the town, after having given him a quick tour of the main area including the melee of streets that housed the light fingered, and worse. But no doubt he would become acquainted with them later, if he stayed that long.

"Nice caff, that sir" the driver had said as Yates paid him and asked him for his number for future use. Yates looked about him. The area was set with lawns and flower beds. Outside tables with multi-coloured brollys decking a paved patio in front of the café, but this morning they were empty, obviously the tourists hadn't arrived yet. Yates walked across and looked at the menu in the window.

The café was busy, but not full, with local workmen. He went in, looked around, and sat down at an empty table in the centre of the room. From here he thought he would be able to catch on to any local gossip which might be floating around. He picked up a local newspaper lying on the table; it was a few days old, and on the front was a picture of Ray Stacey and a headline blaring out the murder of a local businessman.

The waitress came over to take his order and he plumped for tea and a bacon sandwich. "Pot or a mug sir?" she asked.

Yates had noticed most of the men had pint mugs; the cups, he decided were reserved for the tourists.

"Mug, miss, and a bacon sandwich," he said, his face breaking into a welcoming smile.

The service was quick, and the waitress arrived back with a steaming pot of tea. "The sarnie will be a couple of minutes, sir."

Yates pointed to the paper. "Bad business, miss."

"Yes, Mr. Stacey used to come in from time to time," she replied quietly. "His place is a bit further up the canal."

"You knew him then?"

"Not really sir. He was a bit chatty when he came in."

Yates noticed an accent which he struggled to place. Latvian? "He came by himself, did he?"

The waitress paused and looked at him, suddenly realising she was being questioned. Yates leaned towards her confidentially, "I'm looking into what happened to him," he whispered.

She stood up straight and stepped back, doubt glazing her eyes. "I don't," she stopped. "Police?" she asked.

He nodded. She lifted her hand nervously to her mouth.

"Yes," he said.

"He was usually waiting for another man to come." She turned away and almost ran back to the counter.

Yates picked up his tea and began to turn the leaves of the paper. It had the usual articles of local events, people's successes and tragedies, and adverts for local businesses. He turned back to the front page and Stacey. A plate banged down on the table. His bacon butty with a miniature salad sat in front of him. A very large man stood over him, hostility written in his eyes and the clenched fists which rested on the table. "You upsetting my girl are you?"

Yates picked up his sandwich and took a bite, then raised his eyes and stared unblinkingly into the hostile face. "Did I? You must apologise for me."

"I think you should eat up and get out of here."

Yates took another bite and slowly cut a slice off the tomato. "Tasty sarnie," he said and followed sharply with "and who might you be?"

"I'm the owner of this place," snarled the man.

Yates said nothing but continued to stare at him. The man's gaze faulted, and Yates put down the sandwich. "Name?" he said, and brought out a notebook from his inside pocket, a move he knew always intimidated people.

The man stepped away, his aggressive stature melting into submission when he saw the notebook.

"You a policeman? I don't recognise you."

Yates ignored the question and was now standing dominantly above him said "I'm waiting."

"Sampson, Joseph Sampson."

"Sampson. That is interesting. You wouldn't be related to a certain police Assistant Chief Constable by any chance?"

"My brother."

"Indeed, and do you know where he might be, by any chance? I have been looking forward to meeting him."

Joseph Sampson looked down and away from Yates shaking his head. "I don't sir. He called earlier today, and then left. He didn't say where he was going."

Yates relaxed and put his notebook away. "Now Joseph, I think we understand each other." He handed him a card. "If he comes in, you tell him Chief Constable Yates would like a chat. That's my mobile number. Why don't you give me a quick call when he gets in touch?"

Yates picked up his binoculars and walked across the café to the door, pulled it open, and turned to Sampson who was standing watching him. He smiled one of his broad friendly smiles and said, "Nice sandwich Joseph. You should do well." and closed the door behind him.

Outside he muttered to himself, he's lying or I'm a Scotsman, and walked across the lawn towards the canal footpath. He didn't want to turn around but he could feel the eyes of Joseph Sampson watching him and thought I shall have to watch out. He looked at his watch; it was still four hours to the reception, plenty of time to walk back to the hotel and the delightful Miss Merson. He smiled at the thought.

He walked to the canal path and looked down into the clear water. A long narrow boat was heading down stream, a lady in a bikini, sunbathing on the flat top while her partner steered toward the oncoming lock.

"Great life," he called.

The lady lifted a tanned arm, and the man called, "Lazy days, mate," and they drifted on into the lowering sun.

Yates turned in the opposite direction and began his walk to Basingham. The canal path was walled at this point and the walking was easy. The sun warmed his back; he took off his jacket and folded it over his arm. On his right the clear water looked tempting enough to swim, and he laughed at the thought. Suddenly on the far bank a couple of children dived from the stone edge into the water making a pool of rings. The skipper of a passing long boat shouted at them to get out; it was dangerous to swim when there were so many boats passing up and down. The boys just waved and told him what to do. Kids, thought Yates, no sense of danger.

He walked on thinking of his contact with Joseph Sampson and what that might stir up. And then there was his speech for tonight. It was written and he would have a paper copy on the lectern, but he didn't need it. He knew it off by heart and would deliver it without a pause. He didn't think the event of the day had any place in it. And then there was the delectable Miss Merson.

Was she a Miss? He hadn't noticed any rings, but that meant nothing these days. He smiled inwardly, but she hadn't any place in tonight's proceedings either.

He suddenly realised the sun had left his back and he was beginning to feel chilled. Just ahead was the start of the woods, so he slipped his jacket back on, feeling sure it would be even cooler under the trees. The path swung to the left as he reached the beginning of the woods, and he climbed over a low stile to clear the barbed wire topped fence. He dropped into the high green bracken which was slightly trampled, and he knew someone had been over it recently and must be ahead of him. The path went both ways and he turned right along it, sure that this would lead him back to the canal. It wasn't far, but it was narrow, the trees were close together and, underfoot the ferns and snaking brambles clung to his feet and legs made a dense barrier, restricting his walking to small careful steps.

Yates broke through on to the canal path and turned left towards the town. The solid wall which had previously edged the path had disappeared, and the canal path now wound perilously along the edge of the water. He looked down at his shoes, hardly fit for reception tonight.

He began to walk along the muddy path, and in the distance he could see a large building. "Stacey's," he thought. He kept his eye on the path, the woodland encroaching tightly onto it making progress difficult. Up ahead he could see the path side had slithered into the canal and the water was leaking slowly into the wood. "God that looks like a jump, he thought."

Yates concentrated on the path. Should he try to run and then jump, or would a gentle jump be sufficient when he got to the leaking stream? As he psyched himself up and prepared for his jump, there was a rustle in the trees beside him and a large figure lurched into him. He struggled to keep his balance, but with arms flailing around his head he toppled headlong through the heavy bulrush foliage and into the water.

Yates' head surfaced and he glanced towards the bank, the figure had disappeared. He looked up and down the canal, no longboats in view. Never is anybody around when you want them, he thought. 'No problem.' He muttered, and executed a strong backstroke; he didn't move except to pull his head back under the water. He tried to thrash with his feet and that was when he found he was in serious trouble. His feet were firmly held by a tangle of underwater debris. He pulled again and felt a sharp tear down his ankle and winced as he thought he recognised the sharp prong of barbed wire. "Don't panic," he thought. "Float, that's it, float until somebody comes."

He forced himself into a quiet frame of mind, and listened intently. Yes, he thought so; he could hear the chug of a longboat coming up the stream. He shouted, but realised he couldn't be seen from the water, he was totally surrounded by reeds. He needed someone walking the towpath. What were the odds on that? He felt a twinge of panic fill his chest. He took a deep breath and let it out very slowly his panic subsided with it. "Could I submerge and release myself?" He sank but found he would have to bend double to get at his ankle. He couldn't hold his breath long enough. He surfaced again.

"You look as though you're in a fine mess," a voice called out.

Yates lifted up his head, the canal water lapping at his bottom lip. He gave a weak nod.

"Need a hand?"

He nodded again.

"Can you hang on a bit longer?"

He nodded again. The man raced off along the canal path. Two minutes later he was back and threw a life belt out to him. Yates grabbed it and pulled it over him. The man stood on the bank looking at him.

Yates looked closely at his rescuer. "Hooper?" he asked.

Hooper nodded. "I'll organise some help sir."

Hooper set off at a sprint along the path towards Basingham and the nearest phone, leaving Yates bobbing up and down in a life belt in the murky waters of Basingham canal.

Chapter 8

Christopher Wilkinson looked around the empty dining room; he was well satisfied. The tables were set with crisp white tablecloths and the hotel's best silver, even a small five candle candelabra sat in the centre of each table for when the dancing started. Dancing by candlelight - that would get Yatsy going. A pity he hadn't brought a partner with him; he could dance with his wife, or Sampson's.

Sampson, there's a thought. He hadn't seen him since their row in the office. The reality of the coming evening explained the smugness of his earlier satisfaction with the dining room.

Would Sampson turn up? Where was he now? He could ring Janice. Yes, that's what he'd do, he would ring Janice. He could do it from the hotel. She would know where he was. Why hadn't he thought of that before? Wilkinson hurried down the stairs and across the foyer to the reception desk.

"Good evening, Chief Constable. Is everything to your satisfaction upstairs?"

"Yes, Yes miss, I need to make an urgent phone call; have you anywhere I could be private?"

"Yes sir, that door, number five; it is a small sitting room and empty at the moment."

Wilkinson strode quickly across towards the door, thinking that's a pretty girl. He pushed it open and crossed the room to the phone. He sat on the arm of an easy chair and dialled Sampson's home number.

"Janice, is that you?"

"Yes, is that Chris?"

"Have you seen Paul? Do you know where he is?"

"No, and right now I don't care. He seems to have gone two sheets to the wind."

"I am worried about him Janice. If you know where he is you should tell me."

Janice said nothing.

"Look Janice, I want you to come to the reception tonight."

"What, without him?"

"He may just turn up. I'll send a car for you."

"Oh, very well."

Wilkinson put the phone down and left the room. He paused outside the door and looked over to the reception desk. He walked over. "Miss."

The dark haired girl turned towards him and smiled.

"Is Mr. Yates in?"

"He came in a few minutes ago sir and went straight up to his room. And a pretty mess he was in sir."

"Mess?"

"Yes sir. He went bird watching for the afternoon and fell in the canal."

"Fell in the canal?"

"Yes sir and he gave me a problem."

Wilkinson's eyes opened wide and he raised his eyebrows. "You? A problem?"

"Yes sir, he dropped the binoculars I had borrowed from the camera shop in the water. Even the divers couldn't find them."

"Divers?"

"Yes sir, he was trapped by the legs in some barbed wire, and almost drowned."

"Drowned?"

"Yes sir. It appears Mr. Hooper threw him a life belt and then phoned the fire brigade."

"Hooper?" Wilkinson sagged on to the reception desk. His earlier euphoria completely dissipated.

"Why don't you sit down sir and I'll bring you a cup of tea. You look as though you need one."

Wilkinson walked to an easy chair and sank into the soft cushions, his head fell back and he closed his eyes. A few moments later a hand was placed on his shoulder.

"There you are sir, hot and strong."

Wilkinson opened his eyes and the dark haired young lady was standing over a look of concern in her eyes.

"Are you alright sir?" she asked.

Wilkinson nodded. "Sit down, miss. What did you say your name was?"

"Merson, sir."

"Your first name; I can't keep calling you Miss Merson."

"Julia, sir, Julia Merson."

"Well, Julia Merson, and how do you know all this?"

"Are you questioning me as a policeman, sir?" She laughed and her voice tinkled across the room. Her laughter lifted Wilkinson's spirits and he began to chuckle. "Mr. Hooper came in to the desk to ask after Mr. Yates and I told him he was visiting the canal."

"That sounds like Hooper," he said.

A small silence fell between them, and Wilkinson thought that Hooper and Yates would, between them, be his downfall. And all for money he didn't need.

"I ought to get back to the desk sir. I will be off duty shortly and I want everything in order for my colleague."

Wilkinson placed a restraining hand on her arm. "One moment before you go, and this is a police command," he said, a pretence of sternness in his face. "I want you to come to our reception tonight."

"Your reception? But I don't have any connection to the police."

"No, but Chief Constable Yates doesn't have a partner to dance with tonight. So you, I think, are it."

....

Hooper was satisfied that Yates had suffered no serious harm and drove back to Pru's. The drive was uneventful and gave him time to muse over what to do with his evening. Given Pru had been commandeered by her father to go to the Yates reception; he would have to keep himself company.

I could always go to the pub, he thought. Not a good idea. He could go back to the hotel and hang about in the foyer, also not a good idea. He could go up to the bowls club and have another look around there.

He pulled into the front of the house. There wasn't a limo parked, and so Zeke hadn't arrived yet to poke his nose around his daughter's chosen place. He knew Zeke didn't approve but there was no chance of her going back to live with him at Prune House. He got out of the car and walked to the door giving their coded knock. After a couple of minutes the door opened and Pru stood there in her silk kimono style dressing gown.

"Not ready yet?" he asked, stepping inside.

"Too early, but I have only my dress to put on."

They walked through into the dining room and Hooper sat down at the long pine table, the table

Pru had been tied down on at the start of all this hassle. Pru continued through to the kitchen and poured water on to instant coffee. It was strong and he didn't complain.

Pru sat down opposite him, her elbows on the table propping up the steaming mug to her lips. "What will you do tonight?" she asked.

He slurped a tiny sip of the milkless liquid. "Been thinking about that."

"You could eavesdrop on the reception."

"Nah, I don't think I'll gain much from that. You could keep your ears open though. Don't stay with daddy, mix, you never know what someone might let slip."

There was a knock on the front door. Pru stood up and headed quickly for the stairs. "Answer that Herb," she said.

Hooper strolled through the front door and looked through the viewer. Sure enough, the squat dingo was standing there with his giant directly behind him. Hooper opened the door.

"You," said the dingo, "You're here every time I call."

"Just protecting your daughter for you."

Zeke pushed past him followed by his oversized lap-dog. "Where is she?"

"Putting on her glad-rags."

Hooper followed them into the dining room, sat down and picked up his coffee. He didn't offer them one.

"Take the weight off your feet Zeke," he said, pointing to the vacant chairs. "She won't be long."

The giant sat down, Zeke prowled around the room looking at his daughter's possessions. "She doesn't have much," he said.

"I told her; she's minimalist. She told me to mind my own business."

"You at a loose end tonight?"

Hooper spun round on his chair to look at the ugly little man appraising him. "Oh, I thought I might come and keep an eye on you. What are you going to do with Tarzan?"

"He can stay in the car. He's not very good at socializing, are you James?" James stood, and then walked around the table to face them both. His fists were clenched.

"I only asked, James, no offence."

James relaxed and perched on the edge of the table. Upstairs a door opened and then closed. There was the sound of footsteps on the stairs and the rustle of a gown. Pru appeared in the doorway. Her green, figure hugging dress just touched the floor. Her fiery red hair fell out over a mink coat falling to her waist.

"My dear," said Zeke, "you look absolutely stunning, just as my daughter should look."

James came sharply on to his feet, his eyes filled with lust for this young woman who he had first pushed around in a perambulator. Hooper smiled a slow smile. Pru looked towards him, and he winked and nodded approvingly. Her face widened into a shining smile

"'We had better be off," Zeke said, and taking his daughter's arm began to walk to the front door. Hooper headed quickly before them and opened it.

"Have a good time." he whispered as she passed.

Hooper went back into the dining room and sat down. Now, for tonight he thought. He had been interested to hear from Yates about his encounter with Sampson's brother. So he could go and visit Joseph Sampson and find out what was going on there, or, he could go home and check on his house; he hadn't been for a while. Home, he decided. That should be his next move. Yes, he would go now. He walked across Pru's polished parquet floored hall; he still didn't know how she kept it so bright and shining, and out of the door. The curtains twitched next door. He smiled to himself as he walked to the car. One of these days he'd give her a wave.

He turned in at the top of the street and the light was just beginning to fall into dusk. He banged down the brake. His house at the end was blazing like Christmas; every light was on, no curtains drawn. What the hell was going on? Sarah must be back. Or was someone else in? Who? Had Wilkinson sent some boys down to search? He started the stalled car and cruised slowly and quietly to his gate. There was Sarah's car. She was safe, she was back, it had been stupid to worry, he gave the door handle a sharp pull and pushed the door open wide with his foot and dropped his feet to the pavement, then stopped. Why hadn't she phoned first? Why was the house lit like Harrods? What was going on? Caution - that was the procedure here. Police caution. No going in with a battering ram.

He stood up and closed the car door quietly and walked across the lawn to the bay window. Keeping to one side he peeped into his sitting room. No one there from that angle. He lowered his head below windowsill level to get to the other side, and stepped into soft soil and a rose bush gripped his trousers. Damn, why the hell had he planted roses under his window. He struggled, the thorns digging into the calf of his legs. The light had faded; he couldn't see to unhook himself. He pulled viciously; he thought he heard his trouser tear but his leg was free.

This is ridiculous, he thought creeping around my own house, just go in and see what's happening. He reached the other side of the bay and looked into the room. Sarah was sitting on the sofa. She looked upset; her face was red and puffy; she looked as if she had been crying.

His training cried caution; his feelings cried to go to her. Keeping out of the light of the window, he walked round the garden and back to the front door. He inserted his key and pushed the door open. A man with his back to him spun round.

"You!" Hooper yelled.

His fist arced like a rocket from Hooper's knee and exploded on Paul Sampson's chin. He staggered backwards, his legs crumpled, and he fell to the floor, striking his head on the hall radiator as he went. Dazed, Sampson scrambled to his feet and headed for the door. Hooper looked at him for a second and then strode into the sitting room and looked at the shattered face of his wife. "You need a hospital," he said.

She shook her head. "Yes," he said, picking up the phone on the side table. Sarah put her finger on the rocker and cut off the call. "They'll ask questions," she said.

Hooper looked at her, her red swelling face was turning yellow, and tomorrow it would be black. "You're going to look a sight for a week or two."

She looked up at him again and began to weep, her shoulders gently shaking. He sat down at her side and put his arms around her. She leant into him, laying her head on his chest. His chin nestled into her lustrous blond hair. He sighed. "Did he do this to you?"

She nodded. "I am so sorry Herb," she said.

Hooper's eyes suddenly sharpened. He pulled away from her and turned her towards him. "Were you having an affair with him?" He asked, disbelief etching his face.

Sarah lowered her head, unable to look at his accusing eyes. She nodded. "I'm sorry. It was only meant to be a bit of…"

"Fun?" he screamed. He jumped up and stood in front of her, his fists banging his sides. "A bit of fun?"

"It got out of hand."

"You've been to bed with him?"

Sarah nodded again and looked down at her knees.

"You've been letting my boss seduce you," he said despairingly. He turned away from her.

"You're never here," she retaliated, her voice rising with indignation.

Hooper twisted around. "And does Janice know?" he shouted.

Sarah lifted her hand to her mouth. "I don't suppose so."

Hooper shook his head. "You don't know and you don't care. Now get to bed and don't get up until your face is normal again."

Hooper slumped into the easy chair and covered his face with his hands. He heard Sarah stand up and move across the room. When the door closed behind her, he uncovered his face and smashed his right fist into his left palm, and then he remembered the secret thoughts he'd had about Pru.

He listened to Sarah's footsteps on the stairs and then stood up and followed her. He went round the entire house switching off the lights. There was nothing else to do. The reception for Yates was starting about now. He'd intended to go and sit in the hotel foyer, but what was the point? Hooper stood on the landing of his house and looked around at the closed doors to the bedrooms, and the open doors to the rooms off the Hall. He was no longer thrilled by what he saw; tainted, every one, by the infidelity of the one person he had worshipped.

He went into the kitchen and put on the kettle and placed two mugs on the kitchen table. Strong and sweet, he thought. He went back upstairs and let himself into the marital bedroom. Sarah seemed to be asleep and he placed a mug on the low table beside the bed and sat down on the stool in front of the dressing table and sipped his own. Sarah seemed to sense his presence, she opened her eyes.

"There's some tea for you there," he said.

She glanced at the table and nodded, closing her eyes again.

"We need to talk."

She gave a slight nod and then suddenly stirred and sat up and reached for her tea. "How do I look?"

"I wouldn't look in the mirror for at least three weeks," he replied.

"Oh God!"

"Why did he beat you?"

"He was angry and took it out on me."

"The nutter."

"I think he is going deranged; his behaviour over the last few weeks has been erratic and getting more violent."

Hooper put his mug on the dressing table and walked around the room, thinking. "How long has this been going on?"

"About a year."

Hooper gazed at her and shook his head. "A year!" he exclaimed.

"Well, what you can do, I can do."

"What the hell does that mean?"

"It means Pru Prune."

He crashed down onto the dressing table stool. "You think I'm having an affair Pru?"

"You must be; you're never away from her. And the hours you've been keeping? And it's well known among police."

"Sarah, I am not having an affair with Pru."

Sarah turned her head away from him. "I'm starting to feel a little better; I think I'll get up."

....

Yates tumbled out of the taxi Hooper had called for him the moment they reached a house with a telephone. He walked up the hotel front steps and across the foyer to the desk for his key.

The mirror facing him as he entered the room told him a pretty story. Yates stood for a moment and then headed for the shower. A good wash down, a cup of tea, and an hour in bed would set him up nicely for tonight. His speech, well it would not be the nice, cosy, thank you talk he had planned. This police force needed some home truths that would set the local press on fire.

He threw his shirt and trousers on the floor, and the phone rang. "Yes?" he snapped loutishly, almost before the phone had reached his mouth.

The voice was low and smooth and sweet. "Hello Mr. Yates. I understand from Chief Constable

Wilkinson that I am to accompany you to the reception tonight?"

Charlie Yates was momentarily stricken with silence, and then his composure resurfaced.

"Oh, err, Miss Merson, I wasn't expecting…"

"Julia I think, Mr. Yates."

" Err, Oh, Yes. Charlie."

"Charlie or Charles Mr. Yates?"

Yates was feverishly struggling for words; he never struggled for words; get hold of yourself man. "Yes, well, I'm mostly called Charlie."

"I think I shall call you Charles."

"Oh."

"Do you mind?"

The turmoil in Yates' brain was gradually settling. "No, my Sunday name."

Her voice tinkled down the wire into his now cooling ears. "The one your mummy called you."

"I think you are teasing me Miss Merson."

"If we are going to have a light-hearted, pleasant evening we might as well start it that way."

Yates' heart lifted and he smiled into the phone. "I will see you in the foyer at seven Miss Merson, or rather, Julia."

"I'll be there Charles."

Yates put down the phone. He could have danced across the room to the shower. He wasn't that very formal Chief Constable; he was Charlie Yates going on a date with a beautiful young thing, and he couldn't wait.

The sharp ends of the water pierced the cuts and bruises on his body like a spear, and sanity began to reassert itself. He winced and began to soap the canal debris from his sore body. The sludge slowly dispersed into the shower tray and into the drain, with it went both anger and euphoria. He stepped out onto the bathroom tiles, dried, and walked to the wardrobe where the chief constable uniform was hung up and waiting to take possession of him.

The lift fell like a bird of prey, the doors opened and he stepped out. There she was, all in blue, midnight blue, like a bluebird ready to be captured. She was sitting with her legs crossed in an armchair, a small sherry on the table beside her and reading a magazine. It was the sort all hotels leave around for guests to pass their waiting time.

He approached her from an angle, just slightly behind her, so she wasn't aware of his presence until he was hovering over her. She suddenly looked up, and her face lit like a beam of light on a dark night. "Hello," she said, rising and holding out her hand. But for him the dark hair, cupping her sparkling face and shining eyes, the figure tracing blue dress said it all.

Chief Constable Yates said solemnly, "On the bottle already Miss Merson?"

"You will have to arrest me for DWYP Chief Constable."

"DWYP?" he asked.

"Drinking without your permission."

All Yates saw was the crinkles and dimples as a smile spread under a small snub nose. "Consider it done. Shall we find out what's going on?"

He laughed and held out his arm which she linked and said "Chief Constable, you will have people gossiping before the evening even begins."

They walked across the foyer and up the stairs to the rarely used ballroom, now commandeered as a reception room. The first person they met was Helen, Wilkinson's wife. She was standing with Janice Sampson just inside the door.

"Yates," he said. They introduced themselves.

"No husbands?" he said questioningly.

"No, but I see you two have met," said Helen.

Yates leaned over to her confidentially. "Yes, the brazen hussy rang me up while I was in the shower."

"Really," she said, and then pointed across the room, "Chris is over there organising something or another." She smiled at Julia and said, "Have a good evening Julia."

Yates dropped his hand to hers and gave it a squeeze of possession.

……..

Hooper followed his wife out of bed and grabbed her arm, spinning her towards him. "What is Sampson up to? Where have you been for the last two days?" he demanded.

"I can't tell you."

"Yes, you can."

"He'll kill me if I do."

"Who?"

"Paul Sampson, of course. He's paranoid about keeping his affairs and where we meet secret."

"Sarah, did Sampson murder Stacey?"

"'How should I know?"

"You're his mistress; who else would he tell if not you?"

"If you want to know what I think, I think he's going insane. He needs to be sectioned before he commits murder."

Sarah's voice rose to a jet engine screech as she pushed him violently away from her, and Hooper stumbled and fell backwards. He rolled over trying to catch her ankle as she fled out of the room. He heard the front door slam, a car stutter into life, and with screaming tyres, disappear into the distance.

Hooper rolled over and sat up. He gave the back of his head a rub thinking he might have a lump there in the morning. So, Sarah and Sampson had a secret bolt hole. Where could that be? It's doubtful that he would confide in Janice, but he could ask. That will have to wait; she will be buttoned up at the reception tonight like everyone of consequence in this case.

I might as well have that coffee now I've got the place to myself he muttered and pulled himself to his feet. The coffee was coal black, three heaped teaspoons in a mug; his ideal liquid for cogitating when he needed to solve a problem, except for beer and whisky, but there was no fun in drinking alone. That was only an option when Churchill's black dog was stalking him and licking the back of his neck. He thought to himself, that hadn't happened so much since he'd teamed up with Pru.

He sipped the hot coffee and decided there was no profit in just sitting there. He could either go down to Stacey's and see if anything was afoot there, go up to the club, but that should be dead as a dodo now, although no doubt Yates would want to look it over after today's incident, or he could go and sit in the hotel foyer and see who came to the reception. Sampson, would he try to slip in? There would be a seat on the top table for him.

That was it, the foyer, a corner out of the way and watching the Police's top talent arrive, that would be his most productive move. He gulped down his coffee and headed for the door. It was lucky it was not far to walk.

The foyer was heaving; two busloads of tourists had just arrived and were milling around the desk, signing in and collecting their keys. Cases and bags littered the floor and a solitary porter was trying to sort out who was going where and loading the lifts to avoid skirmishes on the stairs.

The confusion suited Hooper. He looked about him, and sure enough there was an unoccupied table tucked in beside the entrance door. He walked quickly across to it and sat down with his back to the wall. It afforded him a view of the entire foyer; he could see people as they entered and where they went. There was half an hour to go and the Uniforms began to arrive, but mostly it was the rank and file in civvies. Then he spotted Yates, top dressed as a Chief Constable should be, with a woman on his arm; dark haired and a deep blue dress, ravishing, the dog, where had he found her from?

Yates pushed through the crowd heading for the stairs and disappeared from view. Hooper was beginning to enjoy himself people watching. It was his favourite occupation. You could pick up on their foibles and eccentricities, watch how they behaved, invaluable information for an observant policeman, that is, if they weren't assaulting someone, or throwing something at you.

And then they were here, squat fat Zeke and his tall elegant daughter Pru. Hooper watched them unobserved. Pru was dressed in a long clinging gown of a subtle shade of green, somewhere between spring leaf green when the sun was catching them in a fluttering breeze, and the shadow green when the sun hid behind the flying puff-ball clouds.

But there was no fluttering in Pru's movement across the foyer, just a smooth elegance adjusted to pace her father. Hooper's eyes brightened and never left her until they too disappeared up the staircase to the reception. And then there he was, three metres behind them, James the muted giant. He followed Zeke and Pru to the staircase, and as they ascended, he turned around and crossed the foyer to the opposite wall and leaned against it. Hooper decided that he too had a watching brief, and after a quick glance around, their eyes met. They held each other's gaze for a long moment and then James looked away.

The foyer was alive with the movement of arriving policemen and their wives, all looking forward to an evening of eating, drinking and dancing. Hooper wondered if there were any left on the streets. He caught the eye of a circulating waiter, trying to drum up some trade before the shenanigans began, and ordered an orange juice. The waiter shrugged his shoulders in disgust. Hooper thought 'stuff you'. The crowd was thinning as people filtered upstairs to the reception for the start of their evening entertainment.

Hooper slurped his orange juice, thinking there wouldn't be much doing for the next couple of hours or more. He looked to check on giant James, 'now where the hell has he gone,' he muttered to himself as he realised James had disappeared.

Hooper, drink in hand, began to circulate the room, weaving between the throng of police constables. Making sure he didn't catch the eye of any of them, he worked his way around the foyer looking for any corners or alcoves where someone could observe unobtrusively. He wasn't there; not good news Hooper thought. You needed to know where a man like him was on an evening like this

....

Wilkinson was standing to the rear of the podium where the band was playing quiet music. The rush of people coming in was slowing down, but they were still rambling around working out their tables and places, even though they had all been given a table plan. There was a flurry of activity as the town's mayor and his wife arrived and Wilkinson hurried across to greet him, and then conduct him to the centre place on the top table. Yates and Julia followed him. That hotel receptionist had proved a good choice, Wilkinson thought. He caught his wife's eye and signalled her across. Helen and Janice Sampson moved away from the door toward the top table.

"I wonder where Paul is?" whispered Helen. "He ought to be here by now."

Janice shrugged but said nothing. They moved around the table and Helen sat down beside her husband, while Janice took her seat next to Sampson's empty chair. Yates sat beside Helen with Julia on his right. He could feel her nervousness and he squeezed her hand reassuringly.

Wilkinson remained standing and looking round the hall, he banged a gavel on the table. "Come on you lot, find your seats and sit down."

Wilkinson watched as the final few, scuffling their chairs, sat down and silence settled across the room. Wilkinson, already standing, called out. "Will all be upstanding for grace?"

The chairs scuffled once again as everyone stood up and he said grace. He then sat down and everyone followed him. Wilkinson turned to the Mayor and whispered in his ear and then stood up again and banged his gavel. "Ladies and gentlemen, I now invite Mr. Mayor to formally welcome our guest of honour the Chief Constable of Yorkshire, Mr. Charles Yates."

The mayor quickly introduced the Yorkshire Chief Constable, giving a short history of his career and achievements and the reason for his visit. He sat down and the hotel staff began to serve the meal.

Yates leaned close to Julia and whispered, "Enjoy your meal darling. "The fireworks begin when Wilkinson calls on me to speak."

"What do you mean?"

He winked at her and dug into his soup.

....

After scouring all the likely places James could be, Hooper went outside to the hotel carpark. A hundred metres away a pair of rear lights flicked on and Zeke's limousine began to edge out of its parking spot. Hooper raced across to his motor and was reversing out before James had the big car out of reverse gear. Limos were comfortable but slow.

Hooper followed the limousine out into the Basingham evening traffic. It was heavy and he dropped a few cars behind to make sure James didn't spot him. It soon became obvious that James was heading back instead of waiting at the hotel.

Hooper thought 'why'. He pulled out of the heavy traffic and into the back streets and put his foot down, zipping along empty office lined roads, deserted as their inhabitants made the slow journey home, and he gradually overtook James. He parked out of sight and waited for the big limo to arrive and drive through the electronically controlled gates. He was certain that no one would be watching, Zeke was out and James wasn't back at his post. He ran through the trees which bordered the formal gardens, and saw the car take a turn, not to the garages but to the stables.

Keeping low he reached the corner of the house. James got out of the car and walked to the stables; there was a low neighing as he entered. Hooper could hear James's low soothing noises as he quieted them down.

Hooper crept to the stable entrance. It was a long building and all the stalls were full. James was walking slowly down the length, nuzzling each horse as he reached it. He walked on to the end; the horses became restless as they sensed the presence of Hooper. He turned around suspicious that something was amiss but he couldn't see Hooper in the low light.

Hooper, stooping low to the ground, watched. He couldn't see very well but James lifted one of the saddles down from its hook. He laid it on the floor in front of him and fiddled it this way and that, but Hooper couldn't see what he was doing. And then seemingly satisfied he hung the saddle back on its hook. Hooper decided it was time to leave and ran back across the gardens into the woods and back over the wall.

He had only just reached his car when the limo emerged from the gates and set off back to town. Hooper let him get a start and then followed. He kept a good hundred metres behind but was not surprised when James turned into the hotel car park and parked in the place he'd left an hour before. Hooper reversed into the space he'd left earlier, on this night there was not going to be any casual parkers in the car park, too many bobbies around.

Hooper reversed into his space and sat low in his seat to see what James would do next. The limo door opened and James got out. A lighter flared and he lit a cigarette; he closed the door and stood smoking and looking around. He began walking and Hooper thought he was heading for the hotel entrance but he didn't. He came straight towards him. Hooper watched him all the way across until he was standing looking down at him. James just stood and looked at him, and then he motioned for Hooper to roll down his window. He turned his hand in an anti-clockwise direction until the window was fully down. He nodded and grunted, he reached into his pocket and took out the lighter, clicked the button until it flared into a four-inch flame. Still holding Hooper's eyes he drew a hand across his throat and then threw the lighter into Hooper's lap. As Hooper panicked, he burst out laughing and walked away.

…………..

The clatter of pots being collected and the buzz of conversation rolled around the room. Waitresses bustled around, hurrying to clear the tables so the speeches could begin. Wilkinson stood up and banged his gavel to still the chatter. The room dropped silent.

"Good evening again," he said. "Before we commence the dancing, I would like our honoured guest, Chief Constable Yates to say a few words."

He looked down the row of guests to where Yates sat. A slight smile puckered Yates lips, and gave Julia's hand a small squeeze. He acknowledged Wilkinson with a nod and stood up.

"Thank you, Chief Constable, for this magnificent reception. After all, I'm only here to do a job." He stopped. Not a smile broke his lips as he looked out over the faces of the collected policemen. "And what an unpleasant job it is."

He raised his arm and slowly jabbed a finger at his audience and worked round the room he said. "Which of you is a crooked policeman? Which of you am I after?"

The room stirred uneasily; constables began to look at each other. Wilkinson jumped to his feet and sat down again as Yates gave him a warning glance.

"This afternoon I was attacked and assaulted while taking a walk along the canal. Which one of you knew I was there? Which one of you organised that attack? There is no doubt in my mind that someone in this room will be going to prison." Yates stood tall facing the silent crowded room, just nodding his head at them.

"It doesn't matter to me if the whole of the Basingham police force is against me. I have the authority to command your compliance and assistance, and if I don't get it, to bring in assistance from outside."

The silence was as dead as a cemetery at midnight. Not a chair scraped, not a cough sullied the silence. He held them mesmerised by his hypnotic stare. Suddenly he relaxed, his whole framework seemed to drop, a broad smile beamed out across the hall.

"Now, ladies and gentlemen, let's get on with the evening. Miss Merson and I will lead the dancing." He glanced down at Julia and held out his hand. She looked up at him shyly and took hold of it, and he led her on to the floor.

....

Hooper snatched up the burning lighter and flung it out of the car window as he watched James walk back to the limo. He slammed the door and walked across to the hotel and entered the foyer. Hooper followed him. Once inside, the noise startled him. He could hear the band playing, but there were people coming down the stairs from the reception hall chattering animatedly. James was not leaning up the wall, so where was he? Hooper walked over to the staircase and stood there for a moment trying to hear what people were saying as they passed him.

James, he concluded, must have gone upstairs, so he decided to go and see what was happening. The door into the reception room was open and he went inside and stood where he could see all across the room. There were a number of couples dancing, but there was a queue of people waiting to collect their coats. Something had happened. He spotted Pru standing to one side with her father and James. Charlie Yates was on the dance floor swinging round that lovely receptionist as though he hadn't a care in the world. Wilkinson and his wife were on the dance floor and Janice Sampson was being whirled around by a young single constable who'd had the nerve to ask his boss's wife to dance. She looked to be enjoying the attention because she was laughing at what the young man was saying. There was no sign of Sampson.

Hooper wondered if he dared to ask Pru to dance, but he wasn't supposed to be here; he wasn't invited, he was the bad apple, suspended. He chuckled to himself; he wasn't going to be the bad apple for long. Now that Yates was here, they would be able to clear up that racket that was going on at Stacey's.

He moved further into the room and sat at an empty table, feeling sure no one would notice him for a while at least.

"Well, look what the cat's brought in," said a voice on his shoulder.

Hooper looked up. "Well, Well. Trench, I might have known you'd be skulking around somewhere."

"How did you get a ticket?"

"I haven't. I'm gate crashing, and so is that dumb yob with Zeke Prune."

"Ah, James, the dumb hard man cum bodyguard."

"What's everyone packing up for Trench?" asked Hooper.

"You weren't here for that then?"

"For what?"

"Yates threatened to arrest everyone in the room."

Hooper started laughing. "You're joking."

"I'm not, and they'd just had dinner. Shook everybody rigid he did."

"I must go across and congratulate him. Did he include Wilkinson?"

Trench nodded.

Hooper stood up and nodded to Trench, walked across the room to where Yates and Julia were exiting the dance floor.

"Recovered then?" he asked.

Yates turned around. "I didn't expect to see you here."

"Always poking my nose in somewhere."

Yates turned back to Julia. "If it wasn't for this man, I wouldn't be here tonight."

"And do you rescue damsels in distress too Mr. Hooper?"

She nodded across the room. Hooper followed her gaze. Pru seemed to be crying, and was having an argument with both her father and James.

"I think I'll go and…"

"I'll come with you," said Yates.

"Why don't we all go?" said Julia. "You can introduce us."

The three of them traced a line through scattered tables, turned over chairs and half sloshed policemen. Some arguments had started between constables and their wives. Wives fearing for their husbands' careers were grilling them, banging the tables with their fists. Others were having quiet rational discussions. The trio weren't listening. A problem for another day.

They reached the other side of the room unnoticed. Hooper stood directly in front of Prune, Yates positioned himself at James's shoulder and slightly behind. Julia slipped round to the weeping Pru's side and slipped arm through hers. Pru looked around into the smiling comforting eyes of the girl standing beside her and gripped Julia's hand. Confidence like life blood surged from her toes, injecting a sudden firmness into her limped bones. Her shoulders firmed, her face set into aggressiveness. "No father I will not....."

"Prune," Hooper almost snarled.

Prune's head snapped round at the new voice.

"Hooper," he spat.

James stepped back at Prune's anger and collided with the solid body of Yates, and looked him in the eyes. His face spread wide with astonishment and fear, like an expanding comic balloon.

"Yes," said Yates, grabbing his arm. "I thought it was you. East End, London. When I was a constable, you were up for murder and escaped."

James gave his arm a vicious tug pulling it out of Yates's grip, and his right fist swept up in a sharp powerful arc spinning Yates jaw like a top. Yates staggered and fell to the ground, while James spun on his heel and fled for the entrance.

Zeke Prune, his ally and bodyguard gone, his daughter, bolstered by this strange girl, into total defiance, stepped away from Hooper. "Another day, another time, Mr. Hooper."

Prune began to walk after his servant. Then he stopped, and turned, his face a gruesome smile, his voice smooth as velvet he said, "My offer still stands. Come to the hall on hunt day. It will be the best day of your life."

They watched him walk away through the hubbub of a shattered evening. The deserted tables, upturned chairs, and upturned police lives. Hooper offered Yates his hand and pulled him to his feet. "Now you know how it is on the street." Hooper muttered. "Aren't you glad you climbed the ladder and left it down below?'"

"Oh, I don't know; a bit of excitement now and then does you good," rubbing his chin.

"Herb knows all about that," Pru said. "He's never out of trouble; it follows him like his shadow."

"What about you Julia, do you like trouble?" Yates asked.

"Oh, I get my fair share. I don't envy whoever is on duty down stairs tonight, having to clear up after this fiasco."

She nodded towards the door, where, at that moment a black tied, black evening suited figure appeared in the doorway, paused, and marched across to where a stricken-faced Wilkinson looked about him.

"Who's going to pay?" Julia said, "That's what's on his mind. Not his insurance if he can help it."

They laughed. "Not our problem," chuckled Hooper.

"You speak for yourself," Yates replied.

They dropped into silence looking at each other.

"Shouldn't we go outside and see what my father and James are doing?" asked Pru, her voice lifting her to her old self.

"Of course," said Yates, suddenly remembering this was a policewoman, personally embroiled in something very nasty, which could end her career. He led the way across the room, down the stairs and out into the ill lit car park. They stopped on the steps and looked around. There was no sign of Zeke Prune, James, or the limousine.

"Gone," said Hooper.

"I think we had better call it a night and go home," said Yates.

"You are home," Julia said, her voice tinkling into the night and lightening the moment. "At least for the next couple of nights."

"Miss Julia Merson, my host, and solver of all my problems, I think I had better take you home."

She linked his arm and they walked towards the cars.

Hooper looked at Pru. "Home James," he said.

She thumped his shoulder playfully and they walked down the steps and over to the car.

"You drive," he said, yawning. "A good night, Pru?" he asked.

"It is now," she replied.

Chapter 9

Sampson sat in his darkened car and watched them go. He'd thought about brazening it out and attending the reception but thoughts of Hooper and Yates had put him off. Hooper would definitely be after him after the incident with Sarah and he wasn't sure if Yates would recognise him from the canal incident. In any case, his jaw hurt. As he sat, he saw Wilkinson and Helen leave accompanying Janice, his wife.

"Can I trust her to help me?" he thought. "I wonder if they'll have a threesome." In his head the wild visions of sedate Wilkinson struggling in bed with two women sent shoals of invidious sexual images swimming and diving through the flooded caverns of his mind. His head began to whirl as the grey curtain of his insanity descended upon him. There in the car he began to shout, laugh, banging his fists on the doors, roof, wheel, and then scream, his lungs bursting.

Hooper and Pru reached the car; they separated for Pru to open the driver's door and Hooper to edge his way to the passenger side. He stopped and held up his hand, motioning her to stop. "What's that?" Hooper said.

Pru leaned her back against the car and listened intently, gazing into the ill lit car park where James had walked away leaving Hooper with a flaring cigarette lighter burning in his lap.

"Sounds a bit like someone screaming," said Pru.

Hooper walked around the car and stood beside her, the darkness covering their closeness. His old awareness of her presence made his body tense and his bones seemed to stiffen. He pushed himself to his feet and away from her. "Let's find out," he said.

They slowly walked back the way they had come, taking almost the same line James had taken before them. The majority of the cars had gone and the remaining ones were empty, but they worked their way along, examining each one. The noise, though weak, was getting louder. Hooper stopped and listened; his ears cocked like a radio detector trying to find the direction from which the sound was coming. Suddenly, Pru was beside him, she pulled on his arm; he froze, and she pointed to where a car, parked in a bay obscured by overhanging shrubs, seemed to be shaking as though rocked by an invisible hand. They walked towards it, six feet apart. The car seemed full of activity as though someone inside it was fighting. Pru had moved out away from Hooper and they approached it from different angles, Hooper from the side and Pru from the front, the team was in action again. Hooper was about six feet away when the flailing activity inside stopped, and the car engine screamed into life. On spinning wheels, it shot forward. Pru hurled herself to one side as it bore down upon her. It swerved erratically around her and sped for the exit, disappearing into the night and the city.

"Now who do you suppose that was?" Hooper said as Pru walked towards him.

She shrugged her shoulders, releasing the band that held her long hair in a ponytail and let it fall around her. "I don't know but I think it was Sampson."

"Sampson?"

"There was a seat for him in the hall, but he never shewed."

They stood looking at each other.

"No use trying to follow him."

Pru shook her head. "Besides, evening gowns are not the ideal dress for chasing villains."

Hooper looked her up and down, and thought, even in the dark with the red hair hanging loose about her shoulders, that she looked stunning.

"Let's get you home," he said, and turned back to the car. He took the wheel, and she slumped down into the passenger seat.

"You back to normal then?" she asked.

He laughed across at her and let in the gear. They arrived at her front door some ten minutes later and she said, "Coming in then?"

"If the spare bed is still made up?"

"It is. You made it when you got up this morning."

"OK, OK, I can still roll into it as it is." And he followed her to the front door.

....

He walked back into the other room of the old dungeon. A glimmer of light penetrated the blackness through the iron barred slit which served as a window. He could see Jimmy spread face down on the earth floor and kicked him viscously in the side. The boy cried. "Let me go!"

Mrs. Gardner said, "Leave the child alone."

He turned toward her. She was splayed on the wall, her wrists and ankles shackled by the old iron rings which imprisoned the early inhabitants

"Mrs. Gardner, I really think you should look at your own predicament."

"What do you mean? You will have to let us go sometime."

"Why Mrs. Gardner? I could simply lock this place up and leave you."

She dropped her head with a small whimper, "No."

He walked close up to her and gently lifted her head and gazed at her face. He leaned forward to kiss her. She twisted away. He tightened his grip and pushed her head back hard against the damp wall and pressed his body up against her. She tried to lift her knee up in self-defence but screamed as the shackle tore into her ankle.

He laughed. "You resist me?"

He began to unfasten the buttons down the front of her dress until it fell open exposing bra covered breasts.

"Mrs. Gardner!" he said, "A bra that opens at the front. How very convenient."

He doubled his fist and putting all his weight behind it struck her directly on her nipple. She cried out and sagged on her restraints. "I am going to leave you now to anticipate the pleasures we shall enjoy together shortly."

Sarah was desperate. She needed to get away from her husband before he forced her to tell him about the castle. But where would Paul be now? If she could get to there she could hide; no one would know where she was. But if Paul was there; Oh God, if Paul was there.

Still, she thought, she had nowhere else to go. She slashed at the accelerator, and with drive gravel decimating the flower beds and lawn, the car rocketed through the gates. The car careered through the streets. Horns blasted and head lights flashed her like lighthouses in a panic. But she didn't stop. All she could think of was hiding. Hide from Herb, hide from Paul. She had thought he was her salvation; Paul, was her sanctuary; Paul was her soul mate.

Sarah's panic began to quieten; her foot eased off the pedal and the car eased down to thirty and then twenty. The police station car park, she thought, no one will think twice about Herb's car being parked in there. Sarah turned in at the gates and pulled into an empty space as far away from the front door as possible. She looked about but there was nobody to be seen. Exiting the car as quietly as possible, she walked towards the exit under the lee of the high hedges that bordered the car park perimeter. Once outside she relaxed, anonymity, that's what she craved. She went into a twenty-four-hour store and bought some provisions and bottled water.

The door into the castle was locked, which told her Sampson wasn't there. At least she was safe for now; they never locked the door from the inside unless they were both there.

She let herself in and closed the door behind her. It was dark, and quiet, except for a small whimpering which seemed to be coming from the far end of the cellar. She paused, slipped her hood on and then very cautiously headed downstairs... Light flooded the cellar as she pushed down the light switch. Jimmy lay where he had been lying since he arrived here. He was very still; she hoped he was asleep. She glanced over at the wall. There were chains on the wall, hanging empty. Sarah stiffened and listened. Through the silence she could hear a simper, no louder than the mewing of a kitten. She knew distress when she heard it. Sarah walked slowly down the passage to the end room and slowly pushed open the door.

"Is someone there?" a small voice whispered in the darkness.

Sarah's feet seemed weighted to the ground, as though roots were burrowing into long dead soil, and she could no longer move.

"Is someone there?"

The voice stirred her, and she moved towards the wall and the light switch. The lights, low and atmospheric, filtered through the room to the horror before her.

Mrs. Gardner was splayed out on the bed, her clothes in a neat pile on the chair beside her, her hands and feet tied firmly to the bedhead and foot rails. Her face was a bloody smear of a face. Her cheeks had been slashed from her eyes to her mouth and then battered over with the bowling bowl which had been placed neatly beside her head on the pillow.

Sarah knew this was the end for her. She looked at the battered figure and knew she had to ring for assistance. On the wall above the bed head, was written, with my compliments, James.

Sarah gasped and staggered back. How did anyone have access to this place except her and Paul; it was their secret. And who was James? She thought she knew only one James, the dumb man who was always with the father of Herb's partner Pru, Zeke Prune.

With the thought, dread and fear spread through her. She had to get away, leave Basingham, disappear, and say nothing to anyone. Just go. But where? It would have to be either the loneliest place on earth, or the busiest. There was only one place, London.

She turned round and hurried along the passage into the prison chamber. She released one of Jimmy's hands and placed a bottle of water where he could reach it.

At the top of the stairs, she looked back into the chamber where she had had so much fun and pleasure. A chamber of fun, a chamber of horrors. Sarah stepped out into the night and closed the door behind her. One more job and it was over. Once outside the castle, Sarah didn't wait. She opened the booth door and walked quickly towards the railway station. At that time of night, the station was deserted, but there was a light on in the ticket office. She knocked on the window and a weary eyed clerk slid open the window. "Yes?" he said.

Sarah knew then she would be remembered and paused, the clerk looked up and said. "How can I help you madam?"

"Can I get to Oxford and what time is there a train?" she muttered.

"Five in the morning, with no changes."

"That's alright." She delved in her purse for cash. When she had paid she realised there was very little money left and she would have to go to the bank to draw some. I'm leaving a trail she thought, so much for disappearing. How much money was there in the account? Four thousand pounds. She would have to clear the account. Herb would be angry. But she wouldn't be seeing him again. How long would it take to get all that money? How much could she draw out at one go? Five hundred a day? Sarah's erratic planning raced through her tired brain. She sat down on the hard waiting room seat. It was a long wait ahead.

Sarah's head dropped to her chin to the top of her open shirt. Her hand gripped her bag where the precious Debit cards lay. Her access to freedom.

"Asleep?" a voice asked.

She jerked her head up. Through half open eyes she vaguely saw the figure of a man. He was standing just in front of her, looking down at her, only about an arm's length. Too close she thought, but she didn't mind. He had dark hair, just turning grey, she couldn't see his eyes in the dim light, but his smile lit up his face.

"Nodding," she said.

"You must have been nodding for rather a long time, the next train is due. That is if you're going to Oxford?"

"Yes, I am."

"So am I."

They looked at each other for a few moments, Sarah sitting, him standing.

"Why don't you sit down?"

'Not worth it; the train will be here in a few minutes. That's why I woke you."

"Thanks." She struggled to push herself up from the hard seat.

"Need a hand?" he said, offering his hand.

Sarah laughed looking up into his face, and took it. His grip was warm and firm and gave her a gentle pull up onto her feet.

"Alan," he said.

"Sarah," she answered.

"The train is coming in now; have you any luggage?"

"Travelling light."

He smiled at her and held the door open for her. They walked out of the waiting room and onto the platform. As the train pulled to a halt he opened a carriage door. "Shall we share a carriage?" he asked. Sarah nodded.

He held open the door and they stepped in, Sarah first. She walked to the far side of the carriage; Alan followed her and sat opposite her. Their knees were almost touching.

"Old carriages," he said. "I thought these had been dispensed with."

The guard walked down the length of the train slamming the doors shut, and the train began to move slowly out of the station.

Sarah thought, there; that's my old life gone and my new life begins today. A smile spread over her face, her eyes brightened and she looked directly at the man in front of her. She stretched her legs out and their knees touched.

The journey took just over half an hour, and as the train pulled into the station they prepared to leave.

"The next time you are in Oxford, Sarah, you should come and visit me."

"Alan, nothing would give me greater pleasure."

Sarah watched him walk towards the exit as she dropped a small roll of notes in her bag. "That was better than Paul Sampson, and it fixes my income problems," she muttered to herself and then checked which platform the London train would leave from.

....

Pru couldn't sleep. The events of the evening played over and over in her mind. I'll make some coffee, she decided. She headed for the kitchen. As she crossed the landing she heard sounds from Hooper's room.

"Can't you sleep either?" inquired Pru.

"Nope. Are you making coffee?" asked Hooper hopefully.

"Yes, alright," said Pru.

She walked into the kitchen and put on the kettle. Pru sat down at the kitchen table and looked around her. A photo of Hooper and Sarah at some country location sat on a Welsh dresser. There was no sign of any children, and she thought, childless then. I wonder whose choice.

The kettle began to make impatient boiling noises, and she made the coffee strong and black. Smiling to herself and thinking, this will wake him up.

Hooper was lying on the bed with his eyes closed when she entered the room, a mug in each hand. With a smile still twitching the corners of her mouth she went over and placed them on the bedside table. Turning to where he lay she reached out to give him a shake. He caught her hand, she was surprised by how firm and warm it felt. The hand pulled her, and without resistance she fell over the bed to the space beyond him, and she lay beside him. He pulled her closer. Pru kissed him, thinking what am I doing. His hands began to explore her virgin body, and their union was passionate and long, and the coffee went cold.

Chapter 10

Sunlight was streaming through the windows when Pru awoke. She stretched a feline stretch; she yawned and looked into the sunshine, a sleepy happy smile creeping over her face as she remembered the events of a few hours ago.

"What a wonderful day," she said to herself, but mainly to the sunshine.

"Yes, and the coffee's cold," said a voice beside her.

She turned over quickly and thumped the prone body beside her in the ribs with her fist. "Herb Hooper, you unspeakable wretch, you can go and make some fresh."

Hooper pulled her towards him and found her lips with his and they united in languorous harmony until they lay exhausted in tousled linen, their limbs entwined, unwilling to untie the knot that they had tied. Pru's face lay at the side of Hooper's cheek. She gently nibbled his ear and whispered, "Herb, shall we have some coffee now?"

"Philistine," he said, pushing her away and jumping out of bed. "Madam, you shall have coffee in bed for the rest of your life."

"Miss, if you please."

Hooper pulled his tongue out at her, and with a juvenile whoop disappeared through the bedroom door pulling on his dressing gown.

Pru lay there not moving, supremely relaxed. She felt happy; she had never felt this way before. She knew her partnership with Herb had changed. It couldn't quite go back to DCI and sergeant. The thought cast a shadow on the sunlit morning. Suddenly a bright, laughter filled voice shouted from downstairs.

"Rise and shine sergeant, your coffee is ready and we have work to do."

Pru rolled over and jumped out of bed. She slipped on the sweater and slacks of the night before and found a pair of his oversized slippers and headed for the door. She was going downstairs dressed even if he wasn't. He was already sitting at the table when she entered the kitchen. He grinned sheepishly and pointed to the mug of steaming coffee.

"I thought you said I was getting this in bed?" she said with a laugh tinkling though her voice.

"Weekends only; we have work to do."

"Work?"

"Yes, I think we should give Charlie Yates a ring."

"Do you think he'll be up?"

"Of course, he'll be up. He's a Chief Constable, very duty oriented."

"And what about the delectable Miss Merton? He seemed very immersed in her charms."

"Charlie, bowled over?"

"He's human you know."

Hooper looked at her, disbelief spreading across his face. He shook his head. "He's only just met her; she was only his companion for the night."

"It happens."

They gazed at each other, separated by the table. He reached across and she took his hand.

"I think I've been in love with you since the day we met. I just wouldn't, and couldn't, admit it."

"The day Wilkinson introduced us, I thought, I wonder if he's married."

Hooper pursed his lips and lifted his eyebrows questioningly.

"And you were, and still are."

"Sarah, she's just another problem. God knows where she is now."

Pru picked up the mugs and walked over to the sink. "You had better ring Mr. Yates, Herb. We have to get started sometime."

………….

Zeke Prune was sitting at his executive size desk looking at the paper in front of him. James was at the other side watching him.

"Not a good night last night. My daughter is infatuated with that idiot Hooper. I won't have her slumming with an oaf like him. He is married, so there is no future in that."

Zeke walked over to the window smashing his fist into the palm of his hand. He placed his hands heavily on the glass and drummed with his finger nails, the sound ringing round the room like agitated cymbals. He turned away from the window and James began talking to him in sign language.

"No, James," he said quietly, his voice hissing through his teeth like a dentist's water jet. "You will see to Mr. Hooper at the hunt. He has been invited and it would be very agreeable to see him trampled under some horse's hooves."

Zeke looked up, noting the sceptical look on James' face. "But James, I know how resourceful you are.'"

"Yes, I do all your dirty work," he said in sign language.

Zeke Prune walked back across the room and sat down opposite his subordinate. "James, I plucked you out of that East End cesspit just when the law was about to snatch you and place you behind bars stronger than a drain grate. I gave you a new name. Your fellow wallowers in that cesspit are lifers in various prisons. While you, James, are living a life of luxury. I have paid you well. You are now a wealthy man. So, James, keep your end of the bargain, and right now that means, get rid of Hooper."

James stirred uneasily in his seat and dropped his eyes to the floor. He hated this lecture on his past whenever Prune wanted to make him feel grateful and obligated to him. It also reminded him that Prune probably set up that police raid which had caught them all. It also reminded him that his younger brother was with him that night, and had been hauled in with the rest. His brother was so innocent; he'd never committed any crime, but was doing life.

James mulled over these thoughts as he looked back at Prune, and his hatred welling up until he could hardly hold back from strangling him with his bare hands. And one day I will do it, he thought.

Prune resumed his seat and looked again at the list of riders and guests he had invited to the hunt. The first week in April, he thought, that will be the last hunt of the year. I wonder if I could arrange a fete for the local church to start as the hunt returns. That would mean the place will be heaving with people when we get back.

"James, I want you to take a message to the vicar suggesting that we have a church fete after the hunt, all in aid of the church funds of course." Prune smiled at him. "A church fete, James, will ensure this place is awash with people. You won't be able to move. James, you might even like to spend a couple of Sunday mornings listening to the vicar promising you salvation - if you confess your sins of course."

Prune began to laugh. He rose from his chair and said, "Come along James; let's go to the stables. I want to decide which horse I will ride."

They finished their drinks and standing up, walked towards the door when the doorbell rang. They looked at each other questioningly.

"Who can this be?" said Zeke, knowing unexpected visitors were very rare. James shrugged shoulders and put his hand in his pocket covering the small pistol which lay there. He moved to the door ahead of Prune and opened it. James held up his hand, signalling the person to wait, and opened the door a little further. Prune moved forward to the door where Joe could see him.

"Ah, Mr. Prune, the boat arrived a day early, I thought I'd bring your private package."

Prune reached past James and took the small, paper wrapped package from him and slipped it in his pocket.

"That was thoughtful of you Joe, but you shouldn't have bothered. You know the system; James would have collected it in the morning."

Joe shuffled his feet uneasily. I don't like these two, he thought. "Well sir, I thought it might be the safest."

"Why, what has happened?"

"I'd heard a new police chief had been brought in to look into the problem at the canal, and if he came down tomorrow it would be better if there was nothing for him to find."

"And the current set of people?"

"I've moved them on sir; well, they'll be gone in the early hours."

"Good job Joe. I can't invite you in; we are busy at the moment."

"That's OK sir; I'll go back to base."

The two of them stood at the open door and watched him walk down the drive.

"I wonder if there was more than meets the eye in that little visit," said Zeke.

Together they followed him down the drive for a short distance, and then cut away towards the stables.

"Let's go and look at those beautiful horses. I'm really looking forward to this hunt day."

James walked beside Prune across the cobbled forecourt to the stable block, his mind ticking over the things he had in store for Zeke Prune on that fateful day.

The horses sniggered and shuffled about in their stables as they entered. There were six highly temperamental animals, all fidgeting and looking round to see who was there. Zeke and James walked down the length of the stable, stroking their hind quarters and talking to each animal, calming them. Zeke was in front and reached White Ice first.

"Now my white beauty," he said, "how is my champion today?"

The grey turned his head, nodding as if he understood every word.

"Pity he can't talk. I can't ask him if he'd like to come to the hunt." Zeke replied.

James slowly ran his hands over him, White Ice shivered with pleasure.

"I don't think you would enjoy that very much," Zeke mused, "would you boy?"

The horse shivered again and seemed to shake his head.

"I know you don't like jumping hedges and real streams."

Zeke stroked White Ice's ears and whispered to him, "You'll be ok boy, won't you?"

Zeke came out of the stall and said, "Come on James, White Ice it is. The white horse will win the day."

"You are cruel as ever, even to the horses; you know he hates those locations," thought James.

"Horses are there for my pleasure James, and they will do my bidding," said Zeke as if he had heard James's unspoken thoughts.

Zeke gave White Ice a hard slap on the rump and, pushing past James, he strode towards the door. James patted White Ice and followed him.

....

Yates' eyes flashed open and he was immediately awake. No slowly coming to and the rubbing of eyes to push consciousness into his brain. When his eyes opened, the world was bright and shining.

He lay on his back and looked at the ceiling and smiled. It was white and plain like the background to a black and white photograph, and on it appeared a picture of Julia Merton.

Without realising it, a smile broadened his features and he began to chuckle. How long has it been since he last woke up thinking of a woman. And what a wonderful woman she was! He reached across to the bedside table for the telephone, and then the clock caught his eye, five thirty; hardly the time to wake a young lady from her slumbers. He put the phone back on the cradle and it burst into life. Who on earth at this time in the morning; he let it ring and just looked at it and hoped there wasn't any further trouble.

"Yates" he snapped at it.

"Good morning Chief Constable," a female voice said with a laugh. "Have I woken you up?"

Yates relaxed back onto the white linen sheets. "No Miss Merton you have not, but what are you feeling so bright and breezy about at his time in the morning, and where are you right now?"

"I am lying in bed thinking what a wonderful night I had last night, that I ought to thank you for that, and that I ought to get up because I'm on the early shift, and the Metropole management doesn't look kindly on late starters, and I wanted to hear your voice and see if it was sleepy."

"I suggest, Miss Head Receptionist, that you get your skates on and bring your chief guest an early morning cup of tea."

"Head receptionists don't bring guests cups of tea. And I won't be there for another hour." Julia replied.

"And I will be about my business by then. But as you are starting work so early, you could join me for dinner tonight."

"You will have the staff gossiping, and I'm not sure the manager would approve."

There was a pause. Yates didn't speak; he just pictured the woman at the other end of the phone line. "We…"

Julia interrupted, "You could come here and I could cook."

"Or we could send out for a pizza."

"I'd rather cook. I'll cook you a pizza if you're that keen."

"I'm more into roast beef."

"I'll make you scrambled eggs on brown toast."

"I'm sure we can compromise. Shall we say eight? Always allowing for police work, it always seems to get in the way of social engagements."

"I have noticed. Yes, eight will do fine. See you then."

The phone clicked off and Yates put down the phone and headed for the shower. Halfway across the room, the phone sprang into life again and brought Yates to a dead stop. That thing has a life of its own, he thought. He walked back to the bedside table and picked up the handset. "Yes," he said.

"Hooper here," said the voice at the other end.

Yates sagged onto the edge of the bed. "Another who can't sleep," he said, "What's the matter with everyone this morning?"

Hooper looked over at Pru who was standing at the sink drying the mugs and glasses she had just washed. Very domesticated, he thought. "We're all still recovering from your welcome party," he said. "I was wondering what you wanted to do now and if you wanted my help."

Yates walked to the window and eased the curtain open, where a sliver of morning light from the breaking dawn indicated a fine day to come.

"I was just going to invite you to breakfast, but I don't think that is such a good idea. We need to meet somewhere out of the way a little."

"Yes, why don't you forsake the uniform this morning? I'll give you Pru's address, and you can take a taxi there."

"Good idea. No one will think twice about a guest leaving a hotel." Yates replied.

"You haven't looked round Stacey's garage on the canal side yet, or the bowling green where he was killed. Where do you want to start?"

"I think we'll leave that until later in the day. As the investigating officer I think I should call in at the station first and assert my authority there. It won't hurt to let them know who's the boss now. The fun is over Hooper, we have to get down to business."

"Yes sir," Hooper said quietly, recognising the steel and determination in Yate's voice. "Then what's next? Do you want me involved?"

"Discreetly Hooper; I don't think we should be seen together for the moment."

"I don't think either the bowls club or Stacey's garage will be very busy. The bowls club is taped off, although I don't know if there's a constable on duty, but I believe the garage is still working."

"Right Hooper, the bowling club at ten. What time is it now?"

"Just after six thirty sir," Hooper replied. Pru was now leaning on him with her hands over his shoulder tickling him under the chin. She turned her wrist so that he could see her watch. He gave her a dig in the ribs with his elbow. She pouted and playfully bit his ear.

"That gives us plenty of time."

"Yes sir. Will you be in uniform sir?"

Yates thought for a moment. "Yes Hooper, at the station on this first day, I think so. I can dress in civics when the rank and file have had a look at me."

"Right sir."

"The bowling club at ten then."

"Yes sir."

Yates put the phone down on the cradle and thought I wonder if that man will be an asset or a liability. There was a knock at the door. "Yes," he bellowed.

"Your early morning tea sir," a young girl's voice said.

He slipped back into bed. "Come in," he called.

The door opened and a nervous young girl of about sixteen appeared holding a tray. "I've brought you a croissant and butter too sir, compliments of Miss Merton sir."

Yates' irritation disappeared.

....

Hooper and Pru were the first to arrive at the club. They pulled into an already crowded car park, full of staff cars from the nearby school. Hooper pulled on the handbrake and they sat in silence, fully aware of where they were, and what had happened there.

"I need to get my car back from Sarah. I don't like driving yours."

Hooper glanced across at Pru; the colour had drained from her cheeks. He placed his hand on hers and gave it a gentle squeeze.

"Head up Pru; it won't be so bad," he said.

"I'm thinking of that bowl and that tennis ball."

"They're evidence now, all bagged up in the station."

Pru gave him a green smile. "What a police sergeant I make."

"You are OK, the best sergeant I ever had."

He leaned over to her and kissed her on the cheek.

A car turned into the carpark and Hooper could see the peaked cap of a police chief constable. "He's here," he said, and, opening the door, slid out onto the rutted soil surface, the potholes full of water from the recent rain.

Yates' stopped in front of him, his polished shoes sinking into an inch of mud. "Good morning, Hooper; not much use polishing your shoes this morning."

He nodded at Pru as she emerged from the car.

"You look a little green this morning. Have a good night last night?"

"Not exactly sir."

He looked back at Hooper. "Where are we then?"

Hooper nodded at the lane and they began the long walk to the bowling green entrance.

"Is this the only way out?" Yates asked.

"Yes sir,' Hooper replied, 'unless he opted for the field, but that is nearly a mile of open country."

"I can't see him doing that, can you?"

"No sir, and we know he was seen by young Jimmy and Mrs. Gardner and they are both missing."

"Abducted, do you think?"

"That's my take on it sir, but what Chief Constable Wilkinson and Mr. Sampson think about it I'm not quite sure."

The constable on the gate into the green saluted and opened it. They stood just inside and looked to where an area of the green was covered with a tarpaulin and taped off with police tape.

"At least the crime scene is secure," Yates said.

"The clubhouse has also been ransacked sir, but that was done later."

"Connected do you think?"

"I believe so, given that we found the diamond, we assume it is connected to the murder but we have no evidence to support that."

Yates looked across the green towards the clubhouse. "Can we still get access?"

"If the code hasn't been changed, we should be able to."

"Let's try," said Yates.

They walked over to the clubhouse, Pru following them but saying nothing. She knew full well that her social position was the cause of Yates being here at all. She sighed inwardly and thought I'm a sergeant and they are DCI and Chief Constable.

The three of them stopped at the door. Yates held up his hand and Hooper and Pru stopped in their tracks. Yates walked to the end of the building and then rounded the side. He came back a few minutes later holding a piece of paper. He held it out to Hooper.

"Do you think this is of any significance, Detective Chief Inspector?"

Hooper looked at it thoughtfully. "Well sir, it's an information sheet for the old castle in town. As a matter of fact it is just opposite the station in Churchfields."

"'I can see what it is, Detective Chief Inspector, but is it of any use to us, does it tell us anything? You are the local here, does it tell you anything?"

Hooper stood looking at the crumpled sheet of paper and then handed it to Pru. "Well sir, when we were here last it was dark, and we were chasing the lady who caused all the damage inside. She could have been the one to drop it," Pru said.

Hooper nodded, "That's right; we don't keep advertising info inside the club for local attractions because we don't get that many visitors."

"Do you think it is worth a visit?"

"It has been closed to the public for many years so how old this advert is I don't know."

"Sir,'" Pru said.

Yates looked directly at her for the first time. "Yes sergeant?"

"Well sir, it may belong to my father."

"Your father?" Yates gasped.

Hooper turned towards her with a look of hopelessness on his face.

"My father, you see sir, is a large landowner in this area. He owns property all over the county and, knowing him, he probably owns that too."

Yates and Hooper looked at each other and Yates motioned him to try the door. Hooper typed in the code, the door opened and he gave a thumbs up. Yates stepped gingerly over the threshold into a narrow hall, where notice boards covered with club lists of information and events lined the walls on both sides. On his left was another door; he opened it; another passage led to the bowling hall. On his right was a serving hatch, on his left a door stood open. He paused for a moment to look into it, and it was obviously a changing room. Ladies' coats and cardigans were hanging on hooks where their owners had left them.

Adjacent to the hatch was a further door; it too was standing open. He approached it cautiously placing each foot softly in front of the other. He peered round the edge of the door frame, and jerked suddenly to his full height. Motioning the others to follow he went into the club kitchen. The kettle was still steaming.

"Christ," Hooper shouted, 'someone is here.'

He spun round on his heel and dashed into the bowling hall. The figure of a man appeared in a doorway at the other end of the hall. He saw Hooper and the mug he was holding crashed to the floor. He raced across to the quick release doors and out onto the path.

"Stop, Police!" shouted Hooper, but the man kept going.

Hooper crashed through another, nearer door, but the figure was already gone. He came back into the hall and Yates, with Pru trailing him, came from the kitchen. "I think that was Sampson," he said.

Pru began to pick up the overturned chairs and they sat down. "I'll make some coffee," she said. "There's no point in wasting a boiling kettle," and went back into the kitchen.

Hooper looked around the hall. No one had been in since the club secretary had ransacked it.

"'How sure are you that it was Sampson?" Yates asked.

"Pretty sure that it was Sampson. No wonder he'd disappeared; hiding under our noses."

Yates smiled at Hooper. "Very clever of him, hiding where no one would think of looking, and a police guard to boot. I had better call the station and let them know we have seen him."

"I wonder how he got in; the site is enclosed with chain link fencing."

"We'll have a look round before we leave."

Pru appeared with the coffee. "I found some biscuits too," she said.

Yates picked up a custard cream. "Very civilized, sergeant," he said.

Hooper picked up a mug. "There's not much more to see here sir. Where would you like to go next, Stacey's garage or the castle?"

"The castle is probably locked sir. I could, perhaps, get a key from home." Pru said.

"Very well sergeant. You go and get the castle key if you can, and Detective Chief Inspector Hooper and I will meet you there in an hour and a half. Is that a plan, Hooper?"

Hooper nodded his agreement. "Shall we inspect the perimeter fence sir?"

When they got to the back of the clubhouse it was obvious how Sampson was entering. In his haste to leave he had left the chain link fencing bent open.

"He must have had wire cutters for that," Hooper said.

"Yes, he must," Yates muttered. "Let's get off to Stacey's Garage now and see what we can find there."

"Right sir, that's down on the canal."

....

Hooper drove quickly through the town and down the long country lane to the canal dock. The lane was deserted. There was no sign of life.

"Not much happening here, Hooper," Yates said.

"No sir but we are a bit late. I imagine all the people are shipped out to their respective farms early."

Hooper slowed to a stop at the entrance to the yard. There was no sign of life or any vehicles. He drove into the yard and stopped. Nothing happened. Hooper and Yates sat in the car looking around and waiting. After a few moments Hooper said, "Those are new sir."

He pointed towards the office. At each side of the door was a small wooden building. They were not large enough to be called a shed but too large for an average size dog. "They look like dog kennels."

"A bit big for kennels don't you think sir?" replied Hooper.

"Let's take a look, shall we?"

Hooper set the hand brake, Yates opened his car door, and Hooper followed him. They were fifty yards from the office when, as though on que, two very large Bull Mastiff dogs exited the buildings beside the office door. Hooper and Yates stopped walking. The dogs didn't. They walked to the full length of their chains, and then stopped. They didn't bark. They bared their teeth and growled a low growl.

"Some guard dogs." Hooper said.

"Are they legal? They're not muzzled."

At that moment the garage roller shutter began to open and a man appeared. He snapped his fingers and said, "Kennel." The dogs, cowed by his command, slunk into their kennels. He kept walking towards them.

"Buster's replacement." Hooper said. "Dogs instead of a gun."

"Both illegal in a public place," Yates muttered.

The man smiled a broad smile. "Good morning gentlemen; and what can I do for the police this morning?" He paused. "I think I've seen one of you before?" he nodded toward Hooper. "Thought you were a tourist."

"Your name for a start," snapped Yates ignoring the remarks about Hooper.

"Joe, sir."

"Joe what?"

"Just Joe sir, that will do."

"Well, Just Joe, I have been brought into the area to investigate the murder of Mr. Stacey and I want to take a look around. He was your boss I believe."

"Before my time sir; I never met him."

"We have come to look round the place to see if we can find anything to help us."

"Strictly private property sir. No entrance to anyone. Instructions from the boss, sir."

"And who might that be?"

"Mr. Prune, sir."

"Mr. Prune; he seems to own everything around here."

Hooper began to move forwards towards the garage. "Right Joe, then I'll go and take a look…"

"Not without a warrant sir." He moved to block Hooper's path.

"Jason," he called out; a dog appeared from one of the kennels.

Hooper stopped.

"You can let us have a casual look around now, or we can come back with a truck load of armed police," Yates said. "'We could just shoot your dangerous dogs."

"Not my dogs sir. Ask Mr. Prune sir. His orders; no one is to enter."

Hooper moved to his right, away from the canal; the movement caused a rattle of chains and the other dog came out of his kennel. "Sensitive, aren't they?" he said.

"Well trained guard dogs sir." Joe replied.

Hooper stood still and looked across the forecourt at the caravans partially hidden in the woods. "Anyone still living in them Joe?" he said.

"Not permanently. They're not in my jurisdiction."

Yates walked to his left; the dog tracked him and began growling.

"Sit Jason," snapped Joe. The dog subsided to his haunches.

"Just what are your responsibilities here?" Yates asked.

"I don't see that as any of your business."

Yates stood silently gazing at the man for a few seconds. "I would like to remind you this is a murder inquiry. Everything is my business. I advise you to cooperate with me."

"I'm just another guard dog, sir."

"'But one that can speak."

"I don't think the dogs would have much to say if they could sir. Mr. Prune wouldn't approve."

Hooper walked back to Joe. "You're a bit of a smart alec aren't you?"

A smile drifted across Joe's face. He shrugged his shoulders.

"Well, tell me this. Has anyone else been here this morning?"

"No sir. I haven't seen a soul since the waggons left."

"And what did the waggons contain?" Yates asked.

Joe paused, and then smiled again. "Just the goods which came in on the boats."

Yates' face hardened, "And that was?"

"Ask Mr. Prune sir."

"Ask Mr. Prune," Yates mused, "Joe I think we are going round in circles."

"Are we sir?"

Yates turned to Hooper. "I think we should go and get that search warrant, DCI Hooper."

Hooper nodded and went back to the car. They sat for a few moments and watched. The dogs went back into their kennels and the man walked back to his glass fronted office and picked up the phone.

"We didn't get very far there," Hooper said.

"Oh, I don't know. We rattled his cage."

Hooper nodded towards the office. "He's probably reporting to Prune right now."

....

Hooper turned the car around and headed for the exit. The morning traffic was gathering momentum but the vehicles were nose to tail and they made slow progress.

"The castle sir, that seems to be the other place of interest in this case."

"And the castle is opposite the police station you say?"

"Yes sir. I believe it is structurally unstable and dangerous, and that's why the public aren't allowed near it. What I didn't know was that Prune owned it."

"'Does that man own this town?"

"There is that smell about. I think he believes he owns the police too."

Yates tapped his foot in the well of the car. "Hooper, you and I are going to have to drown his ambitions and bring King Prune down to the bottom of the fishing pool."

Hooper chuckled and pressed his foot on the accelerator as a gap opened in the traffic. The traffic was heavy through the town; at first they made good progress and then slowed to a stop. Half an hour later they pulled into the station car park, and pulled in at the side of Pru's car.

"She's beaten us to it," Yates said.

"A fast girl is our Pru," Hooper grinned. "I can't see any activity around the castle. I wonder if she's inside the station."

Hooper jumped out of the car and headed for the station entrance. He bungled open the door and barged in. Trench was at the desk.

"Is Pru about?" Hooper asked.

"I've not seen her."

"Her car is in the carpark."

"Well, she's not been in here."

Hooper paused, still looking at Trench.

"You want something else?" he said sharply; "I'm busy."

"You wouldn't have a key to the castle by any chance, would you?"

"And why would I have a key to the castle?"

Hooper shrugged and turned to leave.

"You're not thinking of going there, are you?"

Hooper stopped with his hand on the door. "Yes."

"You know it's not safe."

"Then you'll know where to send the search party if I don't reappear."

Trench dropped his eyes to his desk in dismissal.

Hooper left the station and went down the steps to where Yates was waiting.

"She hasn't been in there this morning, sir."

Yates nodded. "Let's have a look at this castle of yours, Detective Chief Inspector." They began to walk towards the castle. "It doesn't look much. Why is it kept?"

"The whole of Churchfields is listed sir, something to do with King John."

"And now it belongs to Prune, a big come down."

The castle was set in the middle of Churchfields and surrounded by ancient oak trees. They walked around outside, and Yates read the board about its historical significance.

"The sergeant doesn't seem to be here. Shall we take a look at the gate?"

Hooper was no longer smiling; his face was breached with worry and his eyes were sombre and lightless. He knew she should have arrived. She should be here. First his wife, disappearing without a trace, and now Pru.

"You look worried, Detective Chief Inspector," said Yates.

"Too many people are disappearing; the sergeant should be here by now," he replied.

He led the way to the front of the castle and they walked up to the gate and looked at it closely. It was fastened with a heavy chain and a padlock. Yates took hold of it and rattled it. "I don't think this is the original, Detective Chief Inspector. It looks fairly new to me."

"Circa this year, sir, would be my guess."

Yates stepped a few paces back from the gate to take an overall view of the ancient building. "Let's wander around the place and see what we can see," Yates said.

They set off through the trees surrounding the castle. The bottom of the walls had shrubs and brushwood growing out of the foundations to about a metre high, and Hooper wondered if they were obscuring anything. He pulled some of the shrubs away from the walls and crawled underneath. He found a small window covered with mediaeval iron bars. He tried to look through into the room beyond, but years of dirt obscured his view. "Hey sir," he called, "look here."

Yates looked over Hooper's shoulder at the window.

"An ancient window, probably into a dungeon," he said.

Hooper looked up at him. "Except, sir, like the gate, these bars ain't so old. Somebody's been mucking about with this place."

Hooper crawled out from under the shrub and stood up. "Shall we see if there are any others, sir?"

They walked slowly around the building poking behind the vegetation, but it was the only window they could find.

"Did you look through that window, Hooper?" asked Yates.

"Yes, but the glass was too dirty to see anything."

After half an hour their investigation was complete and they were back at the gates.

"I wonder where your sergeant has got to?" Yates asked.

Hooper rattled the gates again. "That has been on my mind for some time sir; she ought to have been here by now."

They stood around and paced backwards and forwards through the trees. Yates looked over to the police station across at the other side of Churchfields.

"Will there be any chain cutters in the station?" Yates asked.

"I doubt it, sir."

"Well, we can't just stand around here like a pair of scarecrows waiting for a lost bird."

"We could go to her father's place and see if she is still there," said Hooper.

Yates nodded his agreement and they walked briskly over to the police station car park. Hooper opened the driver's door and Yates slipped into the passenger side. "Is it far?" asked Yates.

"Twenty minutes," Hooper replied. "That's why she should be here."

Hooper let in the gear and reversed out and into the busy town traffic. A silence fell between them and

Hooper struggled for something to say. "Did you enjoy your reception, sir?" he asked.

Yates turned his head to Hooper, a broad smile across his face. "Eventful, wouldn't you say, Detective Chief Inspector?"

"Yes sir, I think we could call it that."

"This investigation I'm supposed to be conducting seems to be taking longer than I expected. I thought I would be back in North Yorkshire in a couple or three days."

"Who was it who coined the phrase sir, events, dear boy, events?" Hooper smiled.

"Well, we have certainly had plenty of those, and I've met some good people besides bad."

"Are you thinking of staying long, sir?"

"I will have to stay until this is all over and this crooked top management has got it just deserts. And then, Detective Chief Inspector, I have some leave due and I think I will take a little holiday."

"Anywhere in mind sir?"

"Somewhere warm and anonymous."

"Anyone in mind to go with sir?"

"Detective Chief Inspector Hooper, I think you are phishing," he laughed.

Hooper smiled and said, "I think we are here sir."

Hooper brought the car to a halt outside the large gates which led into the Prune estates. He got out of the car and pressed the signal button on the electronic gate.

"Yes?" a voice said.

"Police," said Hooper. "Let us in please."

The gates slowly opened, they drove in and up the long drive to the front door.

"A big house," said Yates.

"This is how the rich live," Hooper replied.

"And you say this is where your sergeant lives?"

"Used to; she moved out and bought herself a small house at the bottom end of town."

"She still has some influential friends; it was her friends in North Yorkshire that brought me down here."

"So I understand, sir."

"If she has so much money, why is she in the police?"

"I asked the same question sir."

"And?"

"The reply I got was she wanted a career."

"Hmm, it takes all sorts to make a world."

Yates led the way to the large oak door, Hooper standing unobtrusively behind him giving Yates the commanding position. The door opened as he was about to press the bell. The tall figure of James filled the doorway.

"Police," said Yates. "I want to see Mr. Prune."

James shook his head.

"It's alright James, let them in; after all if we have the honour of Chief Constable Yates calling on us it must be important."

James opened the door wider to give them access. Prune was standing in a doorway across the hall, his short broad stature filling half of the doorway, and silhouetted by the light from the large window behind him. "What can I do for you Mr. Yates?"

"Is your daughter here?"

"I haven't seen her since last night's reception."

"She said you had a key to Basingham Castle and she came to ask you for it," Yates said.

"Yes, we have a key as it is one of my properties. Why would she want it?"

"She was going to show us around the place."

"There isn't very much to see, but I'm sure James will have the key; under lock and key," he smiled at his own joke.

"James, go and get the key for these nice policemen."

James closed the door and left them standing looking at each other. "You seem concerned Mr. Yates?"

"Your daughter, a police sergeant, remember, was supposed to meet us at the castle to let us look around it."

"Police sergeant indeed," Prune scoffed. "She always was a silly girl."

"Not so silly," Hooper intervened, "She's a good officer."

James came back into the hall and they all turned to face him. James shook his head and shewed his empty hands.

"Mr. Prune, your daughter's car is in the police station car park, your key to the castle is missing, and she didn't meet us as arranged earlier this morning. I think we have a problem, don't you?"

"She was always a law unto herself," Prune said.

Yates turned to Hooper. "I think we had better get back to the station and organise a search, Detective Chief Inspector."

Hooper's mind was already racing over the possibilities. Could she have gone back home? But why would she have left her car in the carpark? Could she be in the station somewhere? But the desk sergeant would have seen her. That left only one option: she must be in the castle itself.

"Yes sir, but I think she must be in the castle. I don't know how, with that padlock fastening it, but that seems the most likely place."

Yates nodded his agreement. "I think we should break in," he said.

Hooper began a three point turn when an e-type Jaguar with James at the wheel raced around the corner of the house and down the long drive to the gates. Hooper crashed through his gears and floored the accelerator, but as the gates came into view they were already closing and the Jaguar had disappeared.

"Damn," said Yates. "Now what?"

"Back to the house and roust Prune out wherever he is hiding."

Prune was standing on his front doorstep with a broad smile on his face as they arrived back at the house. "Ah, Chief Constable, Detective Chief Inspector, the trouble with a long drive and electronic gates is it does imprison you when your car isn't equipped to automatically open them."

Yates climbed out of the car and walked slowly up the steps to the front door. He stood in front of the smiling man and said.

"Mr. Prune, I think you are deliberately obstructing the police in the execution of their duty and if you don't open those gates immediately, I will arrest you."

Prune stepped back into his house, a nervous chuckle rattled in his throat. "And how will you get off the premises, Mr. Yates?"

"Oh, that is quite simple Mr. Prune. I will have your gates torn down."

"I don't think there is any need for such wilful damage." He stepped back into the hall and pressed a button. "There. I think you will find the gates are open now."

Yates followed him into the hall and sat on the edge of a large oak refectory table.

"Was there something else Chief Constable?" asked Prune.

"There is always something else in a police investigation."

Hooper appeared in the doorway. "Don't you care about what's happened to your daughter?"

"She is perfectly capable of looking after herself. Always has been."

Yates leaned forward looking down at the smaller man. "And the other thing is, why was your man in such a hurry, and where is he going? Such a lot of questions Mr. Prune; when are you going to start answering them?"

Prune moved to his front door and opened it wide. "I don't remember inviting you in, and the front gates are open so I would be very much obliged if you would leave."

Yates stood up and, with Hooper following him, walked to the door; then he turned and looked at the short broad shouldered man in front of him. "Make no mistake Mr. Prune; you will answer them, sooner or later."

Yates walked out onto the stone steps and winced as the door slammed behind him. "Well, what now Detective Chief Inspector Hooper, what now?"

They walked slowly down Prune's front steps, side by side to Hooper's car.

"I think this is all tied up with this castle sir. We have too many people missing and it is locked up like a prison, not some off-limits tourist attraction."

They opened the car doors and thumped down inside. Hooper turned the key and fired the engine.

"Right Hooper, go over the list of missing people once again."

Hooper closed his car door and removed his foot from the accelerator. "Well sir, first there's our murdered man Ray Stacey; the second to go missing was the boy Jimmy, and then Mrs. Gardner. They all have a direct connection to the bowling club. Then there is Sampson, a senior police officer.

I'm not sure he's being held captive because he's kept appearing from time to time and then disappearing again. He seems to be very slick at finding places to hide. And then there's my wife Sarah and my sergeant Prunella Prune who both seem to have done a disappearing act. I think Pru's disappearance may have something to do with her father."

Yates tapped his foot on the car floor. "Pretty mess, Detective Chief Inspector."

Hooper didn't reply, he sat and waited for his next instruction. When none were forthcoming, he said, "We mustn't forget the canal and Stacey's garage sir. We have to keep our eye on that too."

Yates glanced up at Hooper. "I think possibly all the locations are still linked in some way. We are now fairly certain that the immigrants were brought in on the long boats, but I suspect the diamonds you told me about were as well."

He suddenly sat up sharply in his seat. "Come on Detective Chief Inspector, if there's only you and I who are still straight, we had better get a move on. Let's do the rounds again starting with the canal."

Hooper depressed the clutch, revved the engine, pushed the gear lever into first and drove away from the house, but he was thinking I wonder if we are leaving Pru behind.

....

Zeke Prune watched them go from an upstairs window, a smile breaking across his face. He walked across the hall and unlocked another door. The stairs behind it were steep and lit by electric lights. He ascended them carefully; he didn't think Prunella would attack him, but you could never tell. She was sitting in an armchair when he got to the top of the staircase.

"You can't keep me here forever, father," she said.

"I thought you liked your old nursery, Prunella."

"Not when it's a prison. How long are you going to keep me here?" she said.

"How long would you like to stay with your old father? It would be like coming home for a holiday."

"In a room without a window and no doubt that perv James serving me meals, that sounds like fun."

Pru stood up and walked over to the bed and picked up a doll. She lifted it up for him to see. "You want me to play with Becky again, is that it?"

"Don't be silly. Now that your friends have gone on a wild goose chase to find you, come downstairs and we can talk about this properly."

"And what about your pet puppy; is he in on this?"

"I don't want James to hear what I have to say."

"Ah, secrets, secrets."

Pru walked across the room toward her father and followed him down the stairs. "No James around?" she asked.

"No, I sent him off to the canal hoping to get your friends to follow him and they did. That means we have the house to ourselves for a short while."

"Well father, what is this great secret you want to share with me?"

Prune looked at his daughter. Could he trust her? She might be flesh and blood but she was still the police. "I have to disappear."

Pru looked at him, her mouth cracking into a smile and then into laughter. "Father, you disappear? You are the most recognisable human being on this planet."

"The world is a big place," he replied.

"It is also well policed," Pru said," even in South America. You may be able to go where you can't be extradited, but not where you can't be found."

"I wasn't thinking of South America; it is too obvious."

Pru looked at her father. What a strange man, she thought. Was he really guilty of all the atrocities he was accused of, people trafficking, murder? He is a rich man; why would he do all those things? Prune sat down.

"Come, sit down Pru and let's have a chat before James comes back. Before anything else happens I have set my heart on having a hunt, but you know that, and I want you to organise it."

"Me, why me? Everyone knows I have left home. Why would I suddenly come back to do that?"

"You are still family. You know the hunt people, you have ridden with them. They are more likely to accept a proposal from you than me."

Pru walked over to the window and gazed across the family acres. "It's been a long time since there was a fox hunt here, and they are a pest, but resistance to hunting is growing, and hunting with hounds arouses the worst type of opposition. There are likely to be hundreds of protesters here."

"More the merrier," Prune chuckled, "more the merrier."

Pru turned on him quickly. "You want trouble," she said.

Prune shrugged his shoulders. "Why would I want trouble?"

"I don't know, but I think you have some ulterior motive. You always have."

Prune didn't move; he just stood there looking at his daughter and she looked at him.

"Are you going to do it for me?'" he said.

"I suppose so; the hunt will organise the event once I've suggested it to them. You, no doubt, will organise the stirrup cup."

"The wine cellar is full. You will make sure your Mr. Hooper and Mr. Yates are invited won't you? And of course, Mr. Yates's new lady friend, Julia Merton isn't it?"

Pru crossed the room and looked down at her father, "Why Julia Merton father, what has she done to rile you?"

Prune smiled and said, "Nothing dear daughter; I just want everyone to be happy on the day."

....

James sped past the two policemen. He had a grin on his face but he didn't think they noticed. He was well pleased that he was out through the gates and the fuzz was locked in. He was sure that ugly little rat Prune wouldn't let them out, and he could get down to the canal without hindrance.

At least he wouldn't open the gates immediately; he must think that another shipment of his little blue riches had arrived and he would want those in his pocket. But then, thought James, so do I. My tiny share has made me rich, but not rich enough, not yet. And I still have to settle my score with him. Shall I cut out his tongue before I kill him, or could I devise a nice slow death for him? What could that be? Very slow strangulation perhaps, or the ladies choice, poison. The bastard has to suffer for what he did to me.

He pulled into the canal car park and parked by the office door. There was a light on in the office and Joe was sitting reading, but there was no sign of a canal boat. Must have been and gone he thought. As James pulled to a stop he noticed Joe pick up the rifle and put it under the desk within easy reach. Cautious, thought James, so he lifted his hand in greeting, thinking and I'll kill that swine too before this charade is over. James got out of the car and walked around the car to the office door and walked in. Joe stood up and held out his hand.

"Snazzy car you have there," he said.

James handed Joe an envelope.

"Don't know why he's sent me this. I know you are going to come and collect the packages when they arrive."

James stood up sharply. What the hell was Zeke up to? Trying to get him out of the way? He stretched for the door and out and into the car, the whole movement a seamless flow, leaving Joe with the words he was about to say unuttered.

The e-type's wheels spun viciously on the loose McAdam and then dug in and gripped the surface. The front wheels and bonnet lifted and the Jag shot forward as though rockets were shooting from the exhaust. James brought the car under control and then floored the accelerator pedal and the car surged forwards. He knew in future he couldn't be very far from Zeke, the bug that posed as a man, the man whose fingers dug into everything; every enterprise, every business, even the local plumber paid him off by servicing his rentals for free. James was determined that the empire was not going to slip through his fingers when he finally pulled the rug from Zeke's feet and he got rid of him. His daughter was another matter; her fate would be another pleasure he looked forward to. He pressed a button and the mansion gates slid open, the car wheels spat out gravel and the car streaked up the drive.

He noticed the car standing a little beyond the door but ignored it. He ran up the steps and hurriedly pushed his key in the lock. Suddenly he felt a knee in his back and an arm around his neck pulling and bending him backward. He stretched for the knife lashed to his calf but a hand whipped his arm up to his shoulders; he screamed as the shoulder dislocated. He slumped to the ground and two men stepped over him and into the house. He watched them cross the hall, silently and cautiously approach the staircase.

He staggered painfully to his feet and followed the two men up the broad staircase. They reached the landing and stopped. James leaned against the wall watching them. They nodded towards the doors. James raised two fingers and pointed to the door. They looked at him and he nodded.

At that moment the door opened and Zeke came out holding Pru around the neck.

"Ah, Mr. Hooper, and Mr. Yates too. Is this the baggage you are looking for?" he said, throwing her on the floor.

"Take her!" he snarled, "as long as she comes back to do what she's promised."

Hooper bent down and helped Pru to her feet. "You Ok?" he asked.

She nodded and leaned against him.

"Get out, the lot of you!" Zeke yelled at them.

"You!" he shouted pointing at James, "Get in here!"

James edged around the trio and followed Zeke into the room.

……..

Chapter 11

Hooper, his arm round Pru's waist, followed by Yates, tumbled down the stairs and out into the gardens slamming the large oak door behind them. They quickly crossed to the car, Yates taking the wheel and Hooper and Pru sliding into the back seats.

"What was all that about?" Hooper asked.

"What was that about?" answered Pru.

"Your father said you had to go back and do what you'd agreed."

"He is absolutely insane about wanting a hunt to begin at the house and wants me to arrange it."

"Why you?"

"Because he knows no-one will accept if the invite comes from him."

"Why won't they, it's a great estate to chase over?"

"Because the Master of hounds has no time for him, like most people around here. Whereas, if I ask them, they will all come."

"In that case why was he treating you so roughly?"

"Because I had just refused."

"Why had you done that?"

"Because I disagree with the way he runs the estate. You know that's why I left home in the first place."

"Oh, yes," Hooper muttered.

"Now you've settled that, where am I driving to?" said Yates from the front of the car.

"My place," Pru said. "I need to brush up somewhat."

"I'll drop you two off and then I'll head for my hotel." Yates replied.

"Ah, Ah. Is the delectable Miss Merton on the desk tonight?" joked Hooper.

Pru dug him in the ribs with her elbow.

"I wouldn't know," he said innocently.

Hooper looked across to Pru and they began to laugh. "You know sir, I believe any Chief Constable would know exactly what he was doing and, no doubt he would plan his strategy. That's how he became Chief Constable."

"You're a cynic Hooper."

Yates pulled the car into the front of Pru's house and Hooper and Pru got out and limped towards her front door, fumbling for her keys.

"I'll ring you Hooper,' said Yates. "We have to make a plan to clear this mess up. I will have to be thinking of moving back north soon."

Hooper nodded, "Yes sir."

Hooper followed Pru into the house. The kitchen was cold and the phone was beeping a message. The cat was sitting on the table and began a loud purr as Pru entered.

"Oh, you're back," said Pru.

Hooper sat down at the table, and the cat jumped down brushing around Pru's ankles, seeking attention. Hooper drummed the table with his fingers impatiently. "The phone Pru; there's a message."

"It's probably father. It can wait until we've had coffee and showered. I'm sick of my father for one day."

After coffee she headed upstairs to the shower. "Wash up!" she shouted.

Hooper nodded, cleared the pots into the kitchen, and ran water into the sink. On the table was a copy of 'Hare and Hounds' magazine. He picked it up, turned off the water, and began to read.

A few minutes later Pru appeared in the doorway.

"Not done yet?"

He held up the magazine. "What's with this then?"

"If I'm going to organise a fox hunt, I thought I had better get up to date with what is going on now that it's banned," she replied.

"How can you have a hunt if it's banned?"

"You have a drag hunt."

"What's that?"

"You are an ignoramus for a police Detective Chief Inspector."

"I'm a towny by nature."

"Rubbish."

"Well, I'm not sufficiently genned up to know just what goes on."

Pru said nothing and rinsed the coffee mugs in the sink; then she threw a tea towel at him, which he caught deftly. "What do you want me to do with this?" he asked innocently.

He stood up and looked at her, standing with her hips resting on the edge of the sink, her shoulders leaning backwards and her legs forward, feet slightly apart. Her eyes shone an invitation and he dropped the towel and walked across to her; she opened her arms and he fell into her embrace.

....

Zeke was just pouring himself a drink when his mobile phone rang. He glanced at the number and frowned. This could be good news. "Yes," he said quietly. "I was not expecting to hear from you."

Zeke's frown deepened. "Thank you," he said, ending the call. He slipped the phone back into his pocket.

He spun round quickly as he heard the outside door open and close. He relaxed when he realised it was only James. He waved him away; this was not news to share with the hired help. On the other hand, James might be of some help.

"James, I want us on maximum security alert, alright? Doors locked 24/7, check under the cars before you drive them. Ok?"

James looked puzzled but nodded. Zeke gestured for him to continue his business.

The hunt had gathered. The morning of the first of April was fresh, an early morning frost had cleared, but a slight mist threaded through the trees leaving visibility impaired. Zeke looked across the front steps of his mansion at the milling horses, snorting and stamping, anxious to be off, waiting for James to bring his mount, White Ice. He knew, of all the horses in his stable, White Ice, was the best. He was fast, he was fearless, but he didn't like jumping. Nevertheless, today he would outride the field.

James walked White Ice to the bottom of the front steps where Zeke was waiting to mount. He turned to face the stallion and moved close to nuzzle the horse and whisper in his ear. White Ice nodded his head as though taking instructions from his master.

Zeke came down the steps and pushed James away. "Leave the horse alone and fetch me a mounting block," he said, taking hold of the reins.

James moved away and walked back toward the stables, his eyes glittering with hate. "I'll have you," he thought to himself.

"Good morning Mr. Prune. It's a fine day for a hunt." Zeke looked up to find the hunt master looking down at him from a magnificent mare of about fifteen hands.

"Yes, we should have some good riding today,' he replied. "James has just gone to get me a mounting block; White Ice is a little difficult to mount at sixteen hands."

"I would have thought you would have preferred a smaller mount."

"There are smaller horses in the stable but none with the fire of this beauty."

The hunt master smiled and nodded. "Have a good ride Mr. Prune and thanks for loaning us your estate."

"My pleasure," he said to his retreating back.

Zeke looked across towards the stable to where James was just locking the door. He walked briskly back and placed the block in position. Zeke walked up the few steps which allowed him to easily put his foot in the stirrup and mount. He looked down at James and nodded his thanks.

"Hooper is a very inexperienced rider. That low jump you have arranged should attract him and the water beyond it should cause him to take a nasty fall."

Zeke smiled and nodded again. "I knew I could rely on you James. Always reliable."

James nodded in return and moved away from the crowded forecourt and on to the house steps. He smiled to himself and thought, "You are in for a far greater shock than Hooper, and hopefully finito."

The hunt master gradually formed the horses into a loose formation and they began to head out, away from the house and past the stables towards the open fields and parkland.

Hooper dropped in at the back of the packed horses, feeling safe away from the huge beasts. He pulled over to one side where he could see Zeke Prune up at the front just behind the hunt master. The size of White Ice stood out among the rest of the horses, its colour and size making it distinctive. He could also see Pru positioned immediately behind her father sitting tall astride her mount.

She even looks elegant on a horse he thought to himself, smiling indulgently. Suddenly, he realised the horses were picking up pace and he touched the horse's side and she started to trot.

Out in front, the drag was laying a scent and the hounds began baying as they recognised the familiar smell of a fox. The chase was on.

Hooper began to hang on to the horse's reins as the speed increased. Panic surged through his body; he gripped with his knees, knowing it was a long fall to the ground. He couldn't afford a fall; he needed to keep Zeke in sight. He must know what the man was up to.

They raced across the open fields towards a patch of woodland. The track narrowed to an open gate; the hounds raced through it, but the horse riders strung out knowing they couldn't get through together. From the gate a fence and hedge stretched across the field blocking the riders' way but some decided to jump the fence.

Hooper watched Zeke as he approached the hedge, it was obvious he intended to jump and not take the gate. Hooper could see that Zeke was increasing speed, his great white horse driving to the highest part of the hedge. Hooper watched as the huge animal rose into the air to clear the hedge. But as it reached its pinnacle Zeke twisted in the saddle and fell towards the ground. The hounds and horses raced on.

Hooper pulled on his reins and his horse slowly reduced speed to a trot. At the fence he stopped and dismounted. He ran across the few yards to where he thought Zeke had fallen, but he couldn't see him. Looking over the fence he saw a broad shallow stream which would also have had to be cleared in the jump. He still couldn't see him.

Hooper ran to the gate and round to the other side of the hedge; there was still no sign of Zeke or White Ice. Hooper jumped over the stream and walked slowly down the length of the hedge to where it ended and a low fence began. He noted that new barbed wire had been placed about six inches above the top rail. That, he thought, would have been invisible to a galloping horse and rider. I wonder if it was meant for me; that's where I would have aimed for if I hadn't stopped. Hooper looked around. It was obvious that the majority of the riders had filtered through the gate, but where they had jumped the hedge there were deep hoof marks where the heavy horses had landed. To one side where he estimated Zeke had jumped the hedge there were marks in the mud and what looked like knee. Zeke must have landed in the stream. He smiled to himself at the thought of Zeke crawling out on all fours.

Hooper examined the prints, thinking it's a pity I can't take casts of those, and then stepped into the stream to look at a bright object resting on the bottom. He bent down and pulled it out of the mud. A metal ring, attached to a length of leather, sat in his hands. He remembered being shown how to saddle his horse. This looks like a part of a harness he muttered to himself turning it over. He looked at the ring and thought that looks normal. He turned it over and then looked at the other end. This has been cut almost all the way through but not quite. Designed to snap under pressure; dirty work afoot. He rolled the strap up and put it in his pocket. No evidence bags so that will have to do.

Hooper walked back and through the gate to his horse which was standing patiently waiting for him. He looked up at the saddle and then at the stirrup and shook his head. He couldn't mount the beast again without assistance; he would have to walk back. He took hold of the reins and gave a little tug. "Come on sweetheart," he muttered. The horse gave a little snort as though she was replying. "You're pissed off too, are you?" he said.

The horse turned and began to follow him. An hour later they walked through the gates of Zeke's manor house and up the long drive to the front door. He could hear a commotion of some kind, but as he had not been to an event like this before he didn't know what to expect. The drive was lined with trees and shrubs and they restricted his view, but as he came round the last bend he could see Pru leaning disconsolately against the door frame at the top of the steps. The steps were crowded with people and Yates was trying to get some sort of order among them.

Pru suddenly caught sight of him and ran down the steps towards him. "Daddy hasn't come back," she said.

Hooper took her hand. "I saw him fall at that big hedge in front of the stream."

"What, by the gate?"

"Yes."

"Didn't he go through the gate?"

"No. He went to jump the highest part of the hedge and I definitely saw him fall. I was right at the back of the bunch; I could see him clearly. Everyone else kept riding, most went through the gate."

"But daddy didn't?"

'No, it looked as though he was anxious to get to the head of the field and jumped the hedge instead. I saw him fall. When I reached the hedge, I dismounted and looked around but there was no sign of him."

"And then you couldn't remount and you had to walk back," a little laugh tinkling through her voice

She took his arm and they began to walk towards the crowd. "What's going off?" he asked.

"Chief Constable Yates has assumed his rank and is trying to get the riders organised for questioning."

"I'd better go and help," he said.

Yates waved a welcome as they reached the milling group and signalled him over.

"I'll go and help," he said. "Catch you when we're finished."

"No, I'll come too. I might as well resume my sergeantly duties."

They moved into the middle of the mass. Hooper went over to Yates, and Pru went across to the Master of the Hounds and pulled on his sleeve. "Can't you quieten this lot down?' she shouted. "Yates and Detective Chief Inspector Hooper need to ask them questions."

The hunt leader began to wave his whip in the air and shouted, "Come on now, quieten down."

The hunt members gradually turned towards him and the garbled talk stopped.

"You all know," he said "that our host Mr. Prune has not returned from the chase, but his horse has. Fortunately, we have two policemen riding with us and they want to ask us a few questions so please form a line and let us get this over and we can all go home."

"What do we know? We were galloping like mad," called a voice.

Yates held up his hand for attention. "I'm sorry," he said, "you won't be able to go home just yet. When we have finished with the questions, I would like the hunt master to arrange a search of the area. He could be lying in a ditch injured."

A general murmur broke out, some nodding and some groaning. "That could take hours," someone shouted.

"Yes, it could," replied Yates, "but you are the best people to do it, and on your horses, you'll do it quicker than people from the village doing it on foot."

Hooper turned his back to the crowd and faced Yates, "I think he's done a runner. Let's go inside for a minute."

Yates looked at Hooper questioningly and led the way into the mansion followed by Pru. "What's all this, then Herb?" he asked.

Hooper pulled the leather strap out of his pocket and gave it to him. Yates examined the piece of strapping and looked up at him. "So?"

"I found it in the stream where he fell. I bet the harness on White Ice is loose."

"It is a piece of harness," said Pru, "there is no doubt about that. Someone has messed with his saddle."

Yates examined the strapping again. "And it has been partially cut through."

"Attempted murder?" asked Hooper.

"I think so," Yates replied, "Just when I was thinking I might go home."

Hooper's face broadened into a wide smile. "No chance of that yet sir." He briefly related to Yates how he had seen James messing with one of the saddles.

"Stabbed in the back by his own man. He'll not like that," observed Yates. "Anyway, let's start questioning this mob; someone must have seen something."

"Not many people would have the opportunity to do this. Dad's very hot on security; that is why we employ James."

"Unless it was James," observed Hooper.

"There is one other thing," said Pru.

Yates and Hooper stopped in their move to the door and faced her. "Yes?" asked Yates.

"Has anyone seen James?"

They stood motionless, and then looked at each other. "Now, there's a thing," said Hooper.

"Could he be in the house?" asked Yates.

"Did he go on the hunt at all? I didn't see him," Pru said.

"But you were at the front, Pru." Hooper said.

"And I was in the middle of the bunch," mused Yates.

"I was at the back and none of us saw him, so he wasn't there."

The three of them looked at each other silently, the significance of his absence becoming apparent. "He's done a bunk," Yates muttered, "and that means two people are unaccounted for."

"He won't have gone empty handed," said Pru.

"Which car has he taken and where would he go?" added Hooper.

"I bet he has a pocket full of diamonds," Pru said. Where would he go to get rid of those? London? Birmingham?"

"Well, as he comes from the East End my guess would be London," Yates said.

"Not too many enemies there?" asked Hooper.

"He's been with my father a long time; would people have forgotten him?"

"Unlikely. Those people don't forget," Yates said.

The crowd in front of them was getting restless; some of them still mounted, some standing around holding their horses by their heads. "Are you three going to stop chatting and tell us what to do?" a voice shouted.

Yates turned towards them, held up his hands, and the talking fell silent. "We may need to get hold of you again, so we will take down your names and addresses and then you can go."

"Pru," said Yates, "you go through the house very carefully and make sure both your father and James are not here while we get on with this job."

Pru glanced across at Hooper who smiled and nodded. Pru spun on her heel and dashed through the open door and into the hall. She skidded on the highly polished parquet but reached the huge staircase without falling.

"Steady girl," shouted Hooper, "we don't want to lose you too."

She kicked off her riding boots and ran nimbly up the wide oak staircase to the first landing. She paused. Next floor she thought and skipped along the landing to the next staircase. At the top she paused; six rooms up here she muttered to herself, which first? Pru looked around for the best place to start, and noticed the door to the attic at the far end and a separate, much smaller staircase, not a continuation of the major stairs. The door was closed, but not quite shut. She stood and stared at it. Should she tackle it on her own, or should she call Herb? If she called Herb and he was up there she would warn him. Pru moved silently in her stockinged feet towards the attic staircase door. She reached out and placed her fingertips on the door edge. Would it creak if she moved it? She debated with herself, should she, or shouldn't she?

She increased the pressure on the edge of the door, paused, and breathed in slowly, a deep lung filling breath, as though the tension of her body would prevent it from screaming that telltale squeak. Pru eased it towards her. Silence. She let her breath flow out. The door opened and she moved to the bottom of the attic stairs and listened. Pru could hear the sound of someone moving about very carefully. The stairs were uncarpeted; would they creak if she mounted them? At that moment, she heard a squeak like chalk on a blackboard, and then a loud bang. Disregarding the noise, she rushed up the stairs.

A tumbled chair lay beneath an open skylight window; she quickly picked it up and stood on it. She couldn't quite see outside, she needed to be higher. There was a small table over by the bed. She dragged it across and placed the chair upon it. She looked at the rickety arrangement and then climbed on the table, and then on to the chair. It wobbled beneath her. She put her head through the open window and looked out across the blue slate roof. The slates were cracked. Someone had clambered over them.

She ought to call Herb. There was no time. Pru placed her hands on the skylight frame and heaved herself up past the supporting stay and through the narrow opening and out onto slate roof. The roof was vast; she hadn't realised how big a roof was. Which way had he gone? She could see the telltale scratch marks leading her, but could she follow them? She struggled to her feet. The roof was fairly shallow but her feet still slipped as she tried to walk.

Pru decided she would have to run, and then above her she saw the ridge and the round ridge tiles. Catching hold of the skylight, she pulled herself up the shallow pitch to the top of the window. From here she tried another step. Her stockinged feet slipped as she reached for the ridge, she stopped, then crouched down. If she lay down would she be able to reach the ridge tiles?

Pru lay down with her toes against the top of the skylight window and stretched upwards just as she would on a diving board. She could just get her hands over the ridge tile. She gave a push with her toes and pulled with her arms and scrambled up the slates and over the ridge. She sat there, her legs straggling the ridge for a moment, and then heaved herself up onto her feet and began to run across the rooftop.

She reached the far gable where she had seen James disappear and sat down. The slope down to the gutter wasn't too steep, and with her hands and heels acting as brakes she slowly slid down the slates. When she reached the bottom she dropped her heels into the gutter and stopped.

She could hear noises and leaned forward to look down to the ground. Below her she could see the fall-pipe reaching the ground four stories below her and James sliding down the last six feet to the earth and freedom.

"Herb!" She shouted at the top of her voice but she knew it was hopeless; they would never hear her at the front of the building.

"Hello," a voice said from behind her. "What are you doing down there?"

Pru turned round and saw Herb's head peeping over the edge of the skylight.

"Chasing James," she said, "but he's gone."

'Well, just hang on there for a minute and I'll find some rope or something to get you out of there."

....

The crowd and their horses had gone, Hooper, Pru, none the worse for her scramble across the roof, and Yates were standing on the steps outside of the front door.

"We may as well go inside and sit down," said Pru. "I'm exhausted."

Hooper looked up at the sky. The sunshine of the early morning was slowly being covered with rolling dark clouds and a light drizzle was floating in on the edge of a cold breeze. "The weather is changing," he said.

Pru opened the front door and walked to the lounge followed by the other two. "Sit down," she said. "I'll put some coffee on."

Hooper and Yates slumped into deep armchairs.

"Where do we go from here?" asked Hooper.

Yates pursed his lips. "The devious devil has hopped it for now, but he can't have gone far yet."

"I suppose the point is where will he try to go," said Pru as she came back with a pot of coffee.

"Oh, daddy's best silver, is it?" Hooper said with a smile stretching over his face.

"Nothing but the best for the Prunes," Pru quipped.

Yates smiled at their banter and said, "It's OK for you two but that won't find James."

Pru poured the coffee and looked up at Yates. "Black, two sugars please," he said. "As he comes from the East End of London it's quite possible that is where he will run to, but he could be in as much danger there as here. He wasn't loved in the East End."

"If he can't go there, where is another likely place?" said Hooper. "Where else has he been or has connections? We don't want him disappearing into the ether too."

Pru picked up her cup, sipped her coffee and looked at them. "He may have a pocket full of diamonds, but they won't buy him his next cup of coffee. He'll need cash," she said.

"Where can he sell them?" Hooper said.

"Let's look at this from a different angle," Yates said. "What does he need on the run?' Money and a roof over his head."

They dropped into silence, and then Hooper stood up and walked over to the window. "He'll have access to money," he said.

"How do you make that out?" Yates asked.

"If Pru's dad was making a lot of money, you can be sure he was paying his bodyguard well, even if he was dressed up as a butler, or a personal servant. My choice is he was a bodyguard."

"He isn't short of money," said Pru.

"That still leaves two options for us to pursue: transport and a place, or places, to get his head down, and of course hide," said Yates.

Pru gasped, "Good heavens! I won't be a moment," and rushed for the door, out into the hall and outside. She dashed round the house to the stables where some of the hunters were sitting astride their horses chatting.

"Have you seen James?" she asked.

"Yes, he seemed in a hurry and took one of the horses from the stable. He left with Jane and Alan McPherson."

"Right, thanks," said Pru.

Pru turned round and made her way back to the house and the lounge where she had left Hooper and Yates. They looked up at her as she entered.

"Well?" asked Hooper.

"Scotland," she said, "that is where he'll be headed."

"Why?" said Yates.

"Because he took a horse and went off with the McPhersons who just happen to be great friends of my father and have a place in Scotland."

"Do you think your father could be there too?" asked Hooper.

"He could be, or in Ireland; they have a place there as well."

"Do you know where these houses are?" said Yates.

"Scotland? In the highlands, on a loch somewhere; maybe Loch Lochy? No idea. I think he has somewhere in Ireland as well. We used to have a house at Mizen Head."

Yates pursed his lips in thought. "I can get the Scottish police on to it easily enough. The Irish will be more problematic, I don't know anyone there."

Yates gulped down his coffee and jumped up. "Where is the phone?" he asked.

"You can dial from that extension," Pru said, nodding towards a table by the window.

Charlie Yates smiled his thanks and walked over to the table, thinking which of his contacts in Scotland would be the best person to contact. He decided to hedge his bets and ring both the Chief Constable in Edinburgh and the one in Glasgow; that way he would have both sides of the country covered.

....

James heaved himself up and out of the skylight window and on to the blue slates of the roof. He could hear Pru shouting downstairs to alert Hooper and Yates to his whereabouts. The slates were quite dry and he laughed to himself when he found that his shoe soles gripped the surface and he could move over the roof with ease. He stood up and looked around assessing just where he was. He decided he was at the rear of the house. The garages and stables must be just below him somewhere, but how to reach them? A rainwater fall pipe, where would they be? At the corners of the building? He walked gingerly over the slates towards the edge of the building; occasionally he heard one crack under his weight. He could see that the gable end of the house protruded up above the roof and knew that would give him something to hold on to.

He heard a noise behind him and glanced back and saw Pru trying to climb out through the skylight behind him. He did not dare hurry; the position was too precarious. What did she think she could do by following him? He stayed calm. He reached the gable wall. It was capped by long flat flagstones and the last one was horizontal, enabling him to sit down and look over the edge.

He looked down to the ground four stories below him. He could see the downpipe stretching like an iron lifeline to freedom. He looked behind him. Pru was now walking in her stockinged feet astride the ridge towards him. What did she think she was going to do, arrest him? Not much chance of that. He made his decision.

James turned over onto his stomach and gradually inched his way over the edge of the roof. He held onto the edges of the parapet wall and felt for the downpipe with his toes. He knew what he was feeling for, the bobbins that held the pipe from the surface of the wall. He pushed himself a little further over and tried to push his toes behind the pipe. His shoes were too big, they wouldn't go; it was six feet to the next set of bobbins. He looked up, Pru was almost to the end of the ridge. What did she think she was going to do, pull him back onto the roof with his hair?

He kicked off his shoes and heard them fall to the ground. He eased his body over the edge and reached down and grasped the top of the downpipe. Slowly, he lowered his body until he was fully stretched out and clinging with hands and toes to the pipe. He began to climb downwards, his fingers and toes lacerated between the rusting metal and the ageing stone.

Two lengths of pipe to every story; skin torn with every move. Blood began to run down his hands, and he had no doubt that blood was dripping from his feet to the earth beneath. He looked up and saw

Pru gazing down at him. Surely she wasn't going to follow him. Suddenly he could hear Hooper shouting and she looked away from him and moved away from the parapet edge.

James paused and looked towards the ground. Not far now he mused and then into a car and away. He dropped the last six feet, lightly on his toes. The garages and stables over to the left, he dashed in that direction, and then suddenly he heard the neighing of a horse. He stopped and listened; he could hear someone talking. He hoped it wasn't Yates; Hooper wouldn't have had time to get there. He continued towards the stables at a casual walk until he could see four people on their horses. They were obviously discussing the disastrous hunt and as they heard him they turned to face him.

"Hello James," called Mrs. MacPherson. "Looks like Zeke has disappeared. We are heading off home; would you like to come with us?"

James nodded.

"There's a horse still saddled in the stable. Why don't you mount that and we'll return her in a day or so."

James walked quickly into the stable, and emerged a few moments later mounted, but not feeling very comfortable.

"Right James, are you ready?" asked Mrs. MacPherson.

James nodded again. He knew that Yates and Hooper wouldn't be far behind, but he also knew they wouldn't be able to follow.

....

Hooper ran across the front of the building and around the corner and down the side towards the rear, where he knew the stables were. Yates and Pru trailed in his wake like pet dogs. He was sure it was Scottish voices he could hear but as he rounded the edge of the house wall, he could see the backs of three riders as they moved away, through a yard gate, into the fields and away from the house.

Yates appeared at his shoulder. "They've gone," he said. "What shall we do now?"

"You can make those phone calls," replied Hooper.

Yates spun on his heel and ran back to the house knowing he should get his colleagues in Scotland alerted to the situation as soon as possible. He knew he now had to assume that these Scottish people were part of the racket. If they were, it put the whole game on a different level; the canal and the long boats were not necessarily the only point of entry into the country. The trade, he thought, was spreading through Scotland; that was a step he had to try and prevent. Well, it would be a start to warn his opposite numbers of this threat, but he was sure they already had the problem from other sources.

The phone was picked up immediately and the light Scottish lilt of the telephonist twinkled down the line, "Hello, Edinburgh police, can I help you?"

"Yes," replied Yates, "Chief Constable MacGovern please?"

The broad tones of MacGovern bellowed into Yates's ear. "Now Charlie, what can I do for you?"

"Hi Mac, You can help me catch a couple nasty pieces of work who are heading your way."

"That will be a pleasure, Charlie. Tell me more."

"Right Mac. First guy comes from the London East End gangs. That's where I met him when I worked for the Met."

"Are you sure it's the same man? It's been a long time since you were in the Met."

"Yes it is, but there's no doubt about it; he recognised me as soon as he saw me."

"Aye right."

"He was only a kid then, early teens, but nasty then. Slick with a knife. He was suspected of a couple of murders, mainly gangland, but nothing was proved."

"Mmm," MacGovern muttered.

"He's turned up here posing as a butler for a wealthy landowner called Prune. Have you ever heard of him? He seems to be involved in scams all over the country."

"Och no, laddie," MacGovern replied.

"OK, Mac, but both these characters are lethal. If you come across them they'll be posing as innocent citizens, so watch out."

"Right laddie. I'll have warnings put out, and I'll keep you informed whatever happens. Do you know what they're involved in Charlie?"

"People smuggling, Mac. That's for sure. We know they bring them into an inland port at Basingham on canal long boats, and then ship them out around the country. They may be using them as slave labour. I don't know if he'll reach as far as you."

"On the other hand, if he's that organised he may be shipping them up the Clyde."

"That's not too far-fetched Mac. Perhaps you'd better get a few eyes and ears out there and see what's brewing."

Yates put down the phone and looked at Hooper. "At least that's alerted Mac; he'll not hang around."

Hooper nodded his agreement and strolled over to the window. The grounds seemed empty now. Most of the hunt folk had left; only a few were still standing around gossiping. Hooper turned as Pru came into the room, her red hair tangled and limp.

"You look as though you've been dragged through a hedge," he quipped.

Pru stopped dead, placed her hands on her hips and shook her head. Her long hair flicked about and dropped into some semblance of tidiness. She delved in a pocket and brought out a hair band, slickly slipping it on and creating a ponytail. "So would you if you'd been scrambling across roofs," she said.

Yates covered his smile with his hand. "Anyone want a drink? Now we've shovelled that little problem onto Mac, we can manage a break"

"Hooper can have tea," Pru said, "We can't have him laid out on the carpet with anything stronger. I'll have Scotland's best."

"Whisky?" Hooper exclaimed. "You? Whisky?"

"I'll put the kettle on," said Yates, 'I don't want you two tiddly."

He walked out of the room chuckling to himself.

Pru sat down and looked over to Hooper. "Seriously Herb, what are we going to do? We still have a number of people missing even if daddy and James have hopped it to Scotland."

Hooper's smile faded into a frown and he looked at her. "Charlie will be going home soon, and we urgently need to find young Jimmy and Mrs. Gardner."

"You are still the boss, Herb. You will have to decide our course of action. The station is out of action and we won't get any help from there."

Hooper nodded his head. "And we are officially still suspended."

Yates came back into the room with three steaming mugs of tea; he placed the tray on the coffee table.

"You're right, Herb. I do need to get home, and I suppose I could do something about getting your suspension lifted, with your chief officers under a cloud."

Hooper picked up his coffee and walked over to the window. The day was deteriorating. Black clouds were settling on the hills as dark as the thoughts trickling into his head. Pru could see his reflection in the window and she knew a depression was descending on him.

"Herb," she called.

He turned from the window, his face dull, expressionless. The Bell, he thought, down by the church, now that's the place, sod tea and coffee. He turned from the window to face them. "I think I'll head home; perhaps there's a message from Sarah."

Pru's head shot up. She wasn't deceived. He wasn't thinking of Sarah. She walked across the deep pile carpet of her father's sitting room and hooked her arm through his. "Herb," she said, "The Bell is not a good idea."

He looked down at her, a slow sly smile creeping over his face. "I wasn't thinking of going to the Bell," he said.

"Shall I run you home Herb? If Sarah does happen to be there I'd like to meet her," Yates butted in.

"You need to go and pack for your journey home Charlie. You've done enough here. I suspect you have a lot to do up in Yorkshire, Charlie, especially as a certain young lady will be following you there."

Yates rose from his chair, still holding his cup of coffee. "Would you like another of these?" he said, holding up his cup. "We're still on duty."

Pru pulled on Hooper's arm. "I think we should head for my place; the cat needs feeding, and then Herb can decide what we are going to do next."

Hooper resisted the pressure on his arm but Pru smiled at him and said, "You drive, Herb; you know my dear little cat will be starving."

He grinned a weak smile. The thoughts of the Bell and its warmth and alcoholic smell receded as he realised the chance of a drink were diminishing by the second. "OK'" he said.

They made their way across the room. As they passed Yates, he gave him a wink and said, "Don't forget that fair maid."

Yates grinned and gave him a thumbs up.

Chapter 12

Hooper sat down at Pru's kitchen table. "More cups and kettles," he called. "No bottles and glasses lying around?"

The rattle in the kitchen stopped. "Don't keep them."

"I bet there is one tucked away for a late-night snifter."

There was no reply, just the sound of a boiling kettle. Pru came into the kitchen and placed two mugs on the table. "We haven't come to talk about tea and booze."

"So, what have we come to talk about sergeant? Feeding the cat?"

"Well, how about finding young Jimmy, Mrs. Gardner, and even our boss Sampson?"

"Not my wife Sarah then?"

"She ran away from you Herb. She'll come back if, and when, she feels like it."

The kettle clicked off and Pru walked back into the scullery. Hooper tittled the cats' ears while he listened to the water gurgling into the teapot. The teapot banged on to the table beside him. Pru took the other chair in silence. Hooper picked it up and filled the two mugs. "Strong," he said.

"I need it," she said.

"Well," said Hooper," a bottle of…"

They looked at each other and broke out into laughter. "OK Pru, you win. We ought to get our thinking caps on about Jimmy and Mrs. Gardner."

They sat quietly together sipping their tea, musing over the events of the past few days.

"Herb."

"Yes?"

"Do you think we ought to get those blue stones we found checked to see if they are diamonds?"

Herb nodded.

Pru retrieved the stones from their hiding place. Hooper put down his mug and held his hand out and Pru dropped them into his palm. He rolled the glassy beads around with his finger and then picked one up and held it up to the light. The bead glinted in the bright light. It isn't solid blue, he thought; it's clearer with a strong blue cast to it. "Pru, if you were buying a ring, would you buy it with this stone set in it?"

She took one of the stones from him and examined it. "It's quite large, and if it were a diamond with that blue cast it would cost a fortune."

She held it up to the light again. "But it looks like one. It's not blue enough to be a sapphire. Do you remember Princess Diana's engagement ring? That was a blue sapphire set in diamonds."

Hooper grunted his agreement. "Where could we get it checked?"

"It would need a proper jeweller, not your average high street jewellery shop."

"Let's do that," Hooper grunted again. "Your dad brought these in on the canal boats didn't he?" he asked

Pru nodded. "Yes, there were lots of them and then they disappeared."

"I wonder if they are fake. I bet your dad was going to sell them as real-coloured diamonds and make a fortune."

Pru sighed and dropped her head on to her chest. "He's a real villain, isn't he?" she said sadly.

Hooper continued to roll the stone around the palm of his hand. "Do you know how jewellers go about identifying a stone?"

Pru leaned forward and looked over Hooper's shoulder at the blue stone flashing light as it moved about. "I think you would need a London jeweller, a really top class one."

"Do you know of one? Some of your classy friends must buy their jewellery somewhere."

Pru sat back down in her chair and then leaned forward placing her elbows on the table and her chin on her hands.

"I think you could start with Cartier's; they are as upmarket as you can get, or you could go to Hatton Garden; on the other hand, there is Goldsmiths. You need someone who employs a lapidary."

"What's a lapidary?"

"That's a chap who cuts stones," she said. "He can take a rough stone and cut it and facet it so that it gleams when you look at it in a shop window or when you try it on your finger. I'll get in touch with Annabel and see if she can pass it to someone to have a look. She's got lots of boyfriends who owe her favours."

Hooper hummed to himself, still rolling the stone in the palm of his hand. He placed the stone on the table but that didn't make the stone look any better. Pru said, "Just a minute Herb," and went back into the kitchen. A few moments later she came back with a notebook of white paper. She tore out a page and placed it on the table. "Put it on there," she said.

Hooper placed the stone on the table.

"There," said Pru, "look how much brighter it looks."

Hooper rolled the stone around on the paper. "I suppose so." He looked up at Pru. "But," he said, "Who would your father try to sell these to, knowing they're fakes?"

"My guess would be back street jewellers, or men and women who try to flog them in their local pub."

"Well, we know how gullible people are."

"Just remember Herb, when that stone is set in a ring or a necklace you won't be able to see any difference between them."

"Hm, fake blue diamonds at knockdown prices; shall I buy you one Pru?"

"Don't be cheeky. I'm a genuine girl only."

Hooper laughed. "Expensive to the end. You'd better ask daddy." Hooper continued to roll the stone around in the palm of his hand while Pru looked in silence.

"What are you thinking about Herb?" she asked.

He glanced up at her and smiled, shaking his head. "Once we get an answer from your friend we will have to start thinking like policemen again."

"Yes. Basingham does seem a bit short of those at the moment. Do you have any plans now that Mr. Yates has gone?"

Hooper looked up at her again and shook his head. "Have you any ideas?"

"Herb, you're the boss; you're the Detective Chief Inspector. You should be setting up an investigation, not me'"

Hooper shrugged his shoulders. "I've run out of steam I suppose."

Pru stood up and walked behind him. Taking hold of his shoulders she began to shake him until his head began to roll about. Hooper began to laugh and struggled to free himself. "Well, have you an idea where to start?"

"Don't you think we ought to try and find Jimmy?" Pru said.

Hooper pushed his chair away from the table and stood up, a sudden surge of enthusiasm surging through him. "Come on then, let's get on with it."

Pru threw Hooper's coat at him and grabbed her own before he could change his mind.

"What's our first move?" she said.

Hooper leaned forward his hands on the table, thinking. After a moment, he said, "There is also the question of Sampson. Where is he?" He sat down again.

Pru pulled out her chair and sat down. "They both have to be somewhere," she said.

"Obviously."

Pru drummed her fingers on the table.

"Don't do that; it spoils my train of thought."

Pru nudged him with her elbow and smiled a wide smile. "What about Mrs. Sampson?"

"What about her?"

"Do you think she will know where her husband is?" she said.

Hooper looked at her. "She'll never tell us."

"No, but we know where she lives and we could keep an eye on her."

"Pru, you'll make Detective Chief Inspector yet."

"Shall we go and call on her?"

Hooper shook his head. "That's a bit heavy handed; you will go and call on her."

Pru ran her hands through her long red hair. "Me?" she said. "Without you?"

"Yes, the feminine touch, Pru."

"But what shall I say to her?"

"You could ask if she's been out to lunch with Mrs. Wilkinson lately; that would break the ice."

"Wouldn't she think that is strange?"

"You could say that you aren't very busy these days and thought you would like someone to go to lunch with."

"That's a bit weak, Herb."

"In that case, go in full blast and say you're looking for her husband, and does she know where he is?"

"That will put her on the defensive."

Hooper stood up and mooched about the room, came back to the table, picked up his empty coffee cup and put it back down again. He looked across the table. "Pru, you have to make a choice: a friend in need, or an investigating cop, one or the other."

Pru walked through the hall and lifted her coat off the hook, slowly buttoned it up and started to walk to the door. "Are you coming? What are you going to do?"

"I think I might sniff around the canal and see what is going off there."

"OK," she said, "I know where she lives, I think I'll go and park outside for a while and see if she comes out. What do you think about that?"

"That might be better than calling on her," he said. "Give me a ring if anything significant happens."

They went out into the yard to their cars. "Let's meet back here in about four hours," Hooper said.

Hooper arrived at the canal and stopped in the road leading down to the canal dock. He could see the yard quite clearly through the trees which boarded Stacey's parking area. There didn't seem to be anyone about, although he couldn't be sure if Joe had come back and was lurking in the office with his rifle. He edged nearer to the yard. Creeping from tree to tree keeping the office in view, he didn't want to be caught out by Joe's vigilance again.

Across to the right where the woodland had sheltered the caravans, he could see the area seemed deserted. There were still a couple of vans but not the number which had been there previously. He couldn't see any people. The place was empty. Hooper left the shelter of the trees and stepped into the open yard. There was no shout telling him to hold it right there. Buster's, now Joe's office, door didn't open. He paused, looking over to the office; you could never tell with Joe, he might wait until he had you primed like Cock Robin, but it wouldn't be a bow and arrow which had you in his sights.

Hooper slowly began to walk towards the caravans keeping close to the woods and walking the perimeter of the yard. If there was anyone in the vans he didn't want to be seen. Cautiously, he edged closer to the vans. No one appeared in the windows. His position in the trees gave cover from any watchful eyes. He stopped and looked around. There was no movement by the office and no sign of anyone by the vans. Hooper stepped out from his shelter and walked towards the vans. He looked through the window of the first van, it looked unoccupied. He tried the door handle, it opened. He went inside. There were mugs neatly arranged on the sink draining board, they were dry, so was the draining board. He went through to the next room. A bedroom, bed neatly made. Down one side were two bunk beds, again neatly made up. He opened a drawer; children's clothes lay folded ready for use. He ran his fingers over the dressing tabletop, his finger ploughed through a layer of dust.

Hooper mused to himself, "Who ever lived here was expecting to come back but they haven't been here for some time."

He left the van and walked to the other one. He walked around it. It was dirty like the first one. It was obvious no-one had washed either van for some time. He tried the door, unlocked; he went in. The van was neat and tidy but dust lay over the furniture like frost. He opened the drawers one by one. They were all tidy. In the bottom drawer were some men's shirts; he lifted them up. In the bottom was a wallet. He opened it, inside was a number of foreign notes, but he didn't recognise the currency. Nobody has been living here lately he thought to himself again, although they did expect to come back. He placed the wallet back where he had found it and closed the door. There was no key so he couldn't lock it.

He stood outside looking round. 'The place is deserted, he thought. I might as well have a look in the office and the garage. He walked across to the garage. The huge roller doors were locked but a side door gave him access.

Once inside, the area staggered him; it looked like a football pitch. One truck was parked in one corner but it looked like a dinky toy in the massive building. Hooper strode over to it and climbed up into the tractor. There was a coat lying on the passenger seat. He picked it up and searched the pockets, but there was nothing to identify its owner. He climbed down and went round to the trailer. Again, a few items of clothing littered the floor, obviously left there by the poor souls who'd been carted round the country as slave labour. "Zeke," thought Hooper, "nasty bastard, deserves all he gets."

Hooper walked back across the garage to the office door and let himself in. He hadn't expected to find anything but decided to search through the cupboards and drawers. They were empty except for a small key in the top drawer of the desk. Hooper picked it up and then realised there was one cupboard he hadn't looked in. It was a tall cupboard and it was locked. He tried the key and the door opened.

Hooper stepped back in amazement. Inside stood three rifles, two hand guns, and on the shelves boxes of ammunition. "Oh my God," he muttered. "Buster's armoury. Something will have to be done about that."

His phone began vibrating in his pocket. He pulled it out, Pru. "Hi Pru. Did you get anything?"

"Herb, I didn't have to wait very long. I followed her into town and she's come to Conners Kettle Wine Bar."

"So?" he said.

"Guess who she's met here."

"Come on Pru, get on with it."

' "Mrs. Wilkinson."

Hooper let out a low whistle. "Can you get a table and watch them?"

"I could go across and say hello."

"What would that achieve? No, sit and wait; if they see you see how they react."

"OK, then what?"

"If they don't see you, follow Mrs. Sampson when they leave. Don't sit by the door Pru."

"OK," she said.

"This place is deserted. I'm wondering what to do next. I've found some guns. Must be Buster's. I'll have to let the station know somehow."

"I'd better find a table, Herb or they'll see me hanging around the door."

"Keep me in the loop, Pru."

"Will do."

Hooper closed the phone and put it in his pocket. He left Buster's office and walked out into the yard and paused. "No need for secrecy now," he muttered to himself. "I'd better have a look at the canal while I'm here."

He walked over to the wharf. The stone construction edged the whole length of Stacy's car park and mooring bollards were set every hundred yards along its length. He looked across the water, now covered in leaves and broken twigs from the surrounding woodlands. The canal here, he realised, opened into a huge basin which enabled the long boats to turn around and head back the way they had come. This was the end of a branch of the canal. Stacey had chosen his site well, or was it Zeke Prune?

Hooper thought, I wonder what this was for originally. What did narrow boats bring to Basingham when this was built? Coal?

His musings were interrupted by the sound of an engine. A low regular chug, not a car he thought; besides it is coming from the canal, not the road. Hooper chased over to the far end of the wharf, jumped over the fence and into the woods. Here he had an uninterrupted view of whatever was approaching the basin. Slowly the prow of a large narrow boat came into view. He was shocked, the boat was covered in balloons, an accordion was playing and the happy sound of people singing floated over the air. Somebody was having a concert.

He stepped further back into the wood, a few extra trees at this point wouldn't hurt, he thought. The low music went on. The boat came slowly into the basin, it almost seemed, cautiously. Hooper dropped to one knee. Suddenly, a head appeared at the rear end of the boat. The person surveyed the car park for a few moments, then looked back into the cabin. The music stopped. Inquisitive faces appeared in the windows and then disappeared as though instructed. The head reappeared and again cautiously inspected the large empty area in front him. The man raised himself higher, and then began to climb the ladder onto the roof. Hooper realised he was carrying a rifle.

He called out to someone inside and the boat slowed and came to a stop. The man shouted again, it seemed to Hooper he was trying to attract someone's attention. He walked along the roof and climbed down a ladder into the bow. Hooper could see the boat clearly now and he was sure it must be six feet from the wharf side. The man would have to jump or get his partner to manoeuver the boat closer to the dock. He shouted again and the engine started, moving the long boat into dock side. He put down his rifle and picked up a coil of rope and threw it towards a bollard, and then jumped on to the dock. The boat edged in toward the wharf and the man began to curl the rope around the stanchion.

Hooper was now lying flat in the trees and he knew he couldn't be seen, especially in the fading light.

"Stop!" he shouted. "Police!"

The man dropped the rope and spun around. He raised his hands in surrender and then called out to his partner. Another man appeared in the stern of the boat with a rifle and began shooting wildly into the trees. Hooper lay still. He realised he was in a fix now; he should have kept quiet. The bullets continued to fly into the trees above him, luckily at waist high. Christ, he thought this is rural England, not New York; this is not supposed to happen.

He flattened his head to the woodland floor, damp grass and old leaves sticking to his cheeks and digging into his ears. Time to get out, he thought. How? He pressed his hands down and pushed, he moved a couple of inches. He tried again. Again a couple of inches. Could he turn around? He'd be better off going forward; he'd be able to see where he was going.

He splayed his legs, and then bent sidewards from his waist. The bullets continued to clip the tree branches above him. He pulled himself to his right, in front of him a couple of metres away was a large oak tree, the trunk was wide, it would afford him better cover. He inched toward it. He was facing away from the canal now. He had to get out of the line of fire.

The frequency of the shooting had decreased but seemed to have become more targeted. Hooper reached the tree. He sat with his back against the trunk and his legs out in front of him. How to stand up without drawing attention to himself? The shooting was still focused on the same spot; they thought they had him pinned down.

He bent his legs and pressed his hands on the trunk, gradually working his way into a standing position. The bullets stopped, but he couldn't see what was happening. Jesus, if Pru could see me now. Think. He heard footsteps slowly crossing the car park. They're coming to take a look, he thought. Time to get out. Where is the car from here? Could he move without inviting another shot? Then he realised they couldn't leave the people in the boat. They couldn't risk them unloading unescorted.

He relaxed and looked carefully through the trees. He could see his car on the roadside about a hundred metres away. Could he risk moving away from the shelter of the oak tree into the scrappy trunks of the silver birch which made up most of the wood? He had no choice; he couldn't stay where he was. He dare not run, that would make too much noise. Hooper looked at the floor around him, grass littered with old dry tree branches. He bent low and took his first step, trusting his weight on it. No noise. Holding his breath he stepped out of the shelter of his life saving oak. No bullets.

Tree by tree he slowly tracked to the path which led to the road, knowing when he reached it, he would be exposed if the boat men were still searching for him. Bending low, he stealthily crept along the footpath until he reached his car and breathed a sigh of relief. Still keeping low, hiding behind the car, he unlocked the door and slipped in. The car engine was quiet enough but would starting bring the men chasing through the woods to find him?

He engaged reverse gear and drove quietly away from the woods, his body relaxing the further he moved. His mouth was dry; he licked his lips but they felt parched. He watched the road through his mirror. It suddenly seemed to fill with vision of a pint glass of beer. The pub. Pru wouldn't like it but the urge surged through his body. There was safety in numbers. He'd sent Pru off to the Kettle. Yes, that was the answer, the pub. He must have a drink.

....

Pru looked around the tearoom. From the centre of the high ceiling hung a huge old fashioned copper kettle. Conner, she thought, must have had that specially made; it was too big for any fire range she'd ever seen. The two women were sitting directly underneath it, deep in conversation. She needed a table where they were unlikely to notice her but where she could keep an eye on them. The tearoom was large and it was busy, but she spotted a table with two chairs over by the far wall and walked over to it. She hadn't been noticed; they were far too busy. She signalled a waiter and ordered a Latte. Now, what to do while she kept them in view.

She opened her bag and picked out her phone. Snazzy, she smiled to herself. Text Herb and let him know she was in position. He'd be pleased. After that she could keep the phone to her ear and pretend to be talking while she watched Mrs. Sampson and Mrs. Wilkinson.

How long could she spend drinking a cup of coffee? The decision was made for her. After fifteen minutes Mrs. Sampson stood up and picked up her handbag and her shopping bag. Pru thought it looked heavy. She knew Mrs. Sampson hadn't been shopping, so what could she have in the bag?

The two women said goodbye and Mrs. Sampson began to walk to the exit. Pru waited until she was halfway across the room and stood up to follow her. She didn't want to lose sight of her in the busy street outside. What she didn't notice was that Mrs. Wilkinson had seen her, and quickly removed a phone from her handbag.

Pru reached the glass door and saw Mrs. Sampson turn right. She pushed through the doors and caught sight of her twenty metres ahead. She suddenly stopped and delved in her bag and brought out her phone. Pru moved to the side and looked in the shop window as Mrs. Sampson turned around. Pru was sure she must have been seen and turned away from the shop and continued to walk. As she caught up with Mrs. Sampson, she feigned surprise and said, "Oh, hello, Janice. Janice, I was sorry to hear your husband is missing. Have you heard from him?"

Mrs. Sampson turned sharply towards her. "What business is that of yours? You and Hooper are suspended," she snapped. "My husband is your boss and what he does is no business of yours."

Pru stepped back in surprise at the hostility. "I thought you were concerned about him, Janice, I thought you wanted to help him."

"You get back to your estates and feed your chickens."

She turned smartly away and strode over to her car.

"You're not getting away that easily," Pru said silently to herself and quickly ran to her car. Pru eased her car out of her parking place to where she could see Mrs. Sampson and the car park exit. Cars were busily moving in and out regularly; she thought she might have missed her as she moved off. No. there she was. Pru let in the clutch and moved forward, letting a number of other cars out in front of her but keeping Mrs. Sampson's car in view.

Pru wasn't skilled at tailing someone. Mrs. Sampson was keeping to the speed limit and to the left hand side: she was a cautious driver. Other cars came speeding past all hurrying to their destination, others, trying to make progress in the outer lanes, cut across her, breaking into the line of traffic forcing her further behind. Pru pulled out into the middle lane and accelerated. She could just see the roof of Mrs. Simpson's blue car some two hundred metres ahead, when another car exactly the same colour cut across the lanes and settled two cars behind.

"Sod it," she muttered to herself. "That's going to make life difficult. I wonder where she's going."

The traffic was slowing; there was a traffic light ahead. It was just turning red. Mrs. Simpson's left indicator came on.

"Ah," thought Pru, "She's going to the police station." And then she thought, "Why is she going there? Her husband won't be there."

As the traffic began to move Pru nosed her way back into the nearside lane. Horns blared, drivers shook their fists. She ignored them; she had to make the turning. If she could get into the back streets and out of this melee, she would get to the station quickly - hopefully, before Mrs. Sampson. Her destination was an educated guess, but where else could she be going? Pru depressed the pedal and the car surged forward. She knew it was a thirty-mile limit, but she had to get there fast. The roads were busy with both vehicles and pedestrians going about their business. It was ten minutes from here to the station and Mrs. Sampson was in front of her. She cut corners, horns blasted the air; she tried to beat people to pedestrian crossings. She didn't have a blue light that would have given her priority.

Then, there was the station. She zoomed into the carpark and jumped out of the car. No Mrs. Sampson's car. Pru looked around her. "Where the hell has she gone?"

Pru walked across towards the station doors and began to climb the few steps. She paused; she didn't know what sort of reception she would get in there. She stopped and stared across the tarmac yard. Beyond the boundary wall she could see the old patch of woodland and the ancient castle which King John had once used as a weekend retreat. The castle was all locked up now with iron gates and padlocks to prevent kids going into the dungeons to play. Her musings stopped. On the far side of the castle, through the trees she could see something blue, was that Mrs. Sampson's car?

Pru ran down the steps and across the car park. She wasn't sure how far it was to the castle but it was a good run. Five minutes she thought. The walls of the castle were hidden from her, only the top of the tower was visible. There was no sign of Mrs. Sampson. Pru lengthened her stride. She was sure Mrs. Sampson was going to the castle. But why?

At the edge of the wood, she stopped. She looked around her; this wasn't a busy area of town but there were people about. No-one was taking any notice of her. There were no police; only a solitary man walking up the steps to the station door. Now she was here, what should she do? What would Herb do? Herb would go in dragging her with him. But Herb wasn't with her. I am Sergeant Prune, she said to herself to bolster her confidence. I have every right, and a duty, to investigate if I think there is a misdemeanour taking place.

Pru took a deep breath and stepped into the wood. There was a police station at her back; she was ok. It was quite safe. She pushed her way through the bracken and nettles which smothered the floor, brambles plucked at her legs, digging holes which began to bleed. Damn, she thought, I'm not dressed for this. Over to her left it looked grassier. She gritted her teeth and pushed her way through and out of the ferns. Here the trees were more open and she could t walk more easily. She increased her speed; the castle wasn't far from here. Then she realised she could also be seen and stopped again. It wasn't a good idea to approach the castle head on. She would need to plan her approach so she couldn't be seen.

The castle was an ancient building in the town, and was, after having been repaired and made safe by the local council, had been handed over to the ancient monuments' organisation. They, in their wisdom, only opened it to the public four times a year. Pru knew it should be closed and locked at this time of year. However, she was certain that Mrs. Sampson was heading for it.

From where she stood Pru could only see the back of the building which was a blank wall. Turning round and looking behind her, Pru saw that the police station was beginning to be obscured by the trees, and no-one else seemed to be coming through the wood. There wasn't anyone in front of her. She walked quickly over to the wall of the castle. I'm safe here for a moment, she thought. I can't be seen. Pru edged her way to the nearest corner and looked round. There was no-one in sight. She turned the corner and paused. The wall seemed to extend for twenty metres or so and then stopped. What happened then, she mused. I wish

Herb was here. The wall must drop back, she thought. I wonder if that is where the entrance is.

Pru put her back to the wall and slowly worked her way along, stopping every couple of steps to listen. She couldn't hear anything. Twenty metres seemed like miles. She stepped forward, gently placing each foot down as quietly as she could. Reaching the end of the wall, she thought, now what's round this corner?

She was certain that Mrs. Sampson had approached the castle from the opposite direction to herself, but she hadn't seen or heard anything of her. So where could she be? She ventured a peep round the corner of the wall. Ah, the iron gate sealing off the entrance into the castle. Pru, keeping her back tight to the wall, sidled around the corner and stopped. The gate was two arms lengths away. Her breathing heightened.

She drew in a deep breath to stem her panting and the aching bones which were reluctant to move another step. "It's only a couple of metres," she muttered to herself and forced her rigid foot to creep toward the gate. "Another six inches," she thought.

"Come on girl," she urged herself, terror seeping through her veins. Quietly, slowly, step by step, she closed the gap. She reached the gate. Again, she stopped. What should she do now?

Listen. She tried to tune her ears for any sounds coming from beyond the gate. Nothing. Pru moved in front of the gate to look through it. She could see a door had been opened inwards but it didn't appear to be a room.

'Then she saw the staircase which dropped into darkness. Should she go in, she wondered. Pru shuddered; she needed Herb here for that. She looked at the gate. It was fastened with a chain and a padlock. The chain was loose she realised, and the padlock was open. And, the keys had been left in the lock. Stealing further forward she reached the edge of the gate. Her hands were shaking as she removed the keys. The gate needed a little push for it to go into its housing. Would it make a noise? Gently she eased it forward. It clinked quietly into place.

The tension in her breast slackened and her breathing eased as she laced the chain through the iron loop, slipped the padlock through the iron links of the chain and turned the key. Whoever was in the castle cellar wasn't going anywhere soon she thought. Pru turned about and fled.

Hooper, as arranged with Pru, headed back to her house. The house looked dark. He sat in his car and pondered, Pru's car wasn't there. Should he let himself in or take a walk around the back first?

Cautious reconnaissance was the order of the day. He opened the car door and got out, closing the door but not slamming it shut. The next-door curtains didn't flutter; there were no watchers.

The drive was gravel with a grass edge; he walked on the grass. There were no doors or windows on the side of the house. Reaching the end of the wall, he paused and carefully looked across the back of the house. Pru's car was parked untidily, half in half out of the garage. In a hurry, he thought. The kitchen window had the curtains drawn but the light was on. Should he knock on the door, or let himself in? Front door or back? He knocked on the front: he thought she probably would have the chain on. He walked back down the side of the house and gently tapped on the door. There was no response. Then he remembered three rings of the bell. It sounded very loud. The next-door window curtain moved slightly; the old girl missed nothing.

There were footsteps beyond the door and the rattle of a chain being fixed. The door cracked open, enough for an eye to peep through. Hooper heard a great sigh of relief and the door was thrown open and Pru fell into his arms.

"Pru, you hadn't got the chain on," he whispered, running his hands through her long red hair, and conscious of her hourglass body pressed hard against him.

"I thought you might let yourself in."

"It still isn't safe," he said, nibbling her ear.

"I'm so glad you're here," Pru replied. "So glad." She gasped, "I was so scared."

"Tell me," he said, a broad smile breaking across his face.

Pru pouted. "It wasn't funny," she said.

"I can't believe you were scared, you who can dive off the top diving board."

"That's different."

"OK. What happened?" he asked.

"Well," she paused, "I followed Mrs. Sampson from town as far as the police station, but then I lost her."

"You lost her. How?"

"I don't know; she just disappeared from sight."

"We'll have to up your following skills."

"No need. I'm leaving, Herb."

"Leaving what?"

"The police."

"Why?"

"The estate. Now daddy's gone, someone will have to look after it. There's only me."

"Hm,'" he said, "You'd better tell me what happened."

"Yes. Right. When I got to the station I thought I could see her car at the far side of the woods, beyond the castle. So, I decided to walk through the woods in that direction."

"Hm, very scary."

"Don't be nasty," she said.

"Go on."

"I couldn't see anything but I could hear the occasional rustle which I assumed was Mrs. S. walking through the long grass."

"Mm, very perceptive."

"Beast," she cried, "I was terrified. I didn't know if she had anybody with her."

"OK, what happened then?"

"I got to the castle."

"And?"

"The iron gate down into the castle was unlocked."

"It's never unlocked," Hooper said.

"Well it was. The chain was hanging loose and the padlock was open."

"What did you do?"

"I put the chain back and relocked the padlock and put the key in my pocket."

Hooper gasped and began to laugh. "You mean that whoever is in the castle is locked in there?"

"Mm, yes," she said cockily.

"You clever darling."

"So, Mr. Police Detective Chief Inspector, what are you, or we, going to do now?"

"We could starve them out. Just leave them there until they're banging on the gate screaming to be let out."

"That doesn't seem fair."

"Fair! Pru they're a bunch of thieves and murderers in there."

"Yes, but what if Mrs. Gardener and young Jimmy are down there?"

"Yes, well, that's a possibility."

"Mrs. Gardner and Jimmy have been missing for quite a while."

"Mm, I know."

"You don't seem worried."

"I am but there's a problem, isn't there?"

"What problem?" Pru said as she walked into the kitchen and water rattled the bottom of an empty kettle. "Coffee?" she called.

"Need you ask, Pru? We're not officially the police any longer, are we? And we ought to have backup when we go to that place."

Pru came back to the kitchen door and studied the back of Hooper's head. Leaning against the door frame she took a deep breath, knowing her next words were going to upset him. She had mentioned it before but he didn't believe her.

"Yes we need that, and if we're not police I'm not going to rejoin." Pru said quietly.

Hooper spun round on his chair to face her. "What! Why?' You keep saying that. What about me? What will I do without you?"

Pru shrugged her shoulders. "You'll get another sergeant, and somebody will have to look after daddy's estate. There's only me. I'll have to give this place up and move back to Prune House."

"I thought you hated that place?"

"Nevertheless, I don't have any other options."

Hooper turned away from her and put his elbows on the table, dropping his head into the palm of his hands, despair flooding his eyes and face. "Well, I suppose we ought to give some thought to the castle." Herb said thoughtfully.

Pru turned back into the kitchen at the tiny rumble of a boiling kettle. A moment later, she walked back into the dining room carrying two mugs of steaming coffee and sat down beside him placing the mugs on the table.

"You mean it, don't you?' he asked.

Pru nodded her head. "No choice."

They sat in silence, the coffee cooling until it no longer had steam rising from it. Hooper gazed at it with unseeing eyes, his mind spinning her words around his head. He was going to lose her.

"We can still see each other." Pru said.

"Yes," he replied, his voice low and expressionless. "I suppose."

"Come on Herb, perk up, it's not that bad, and we have things to do."

"Yes, the castle," he said looking up at her. "What to do about the castle?"

Herb looked at the girl sitting at his side; he knew he wanted her at his side forever, but that was impossible. The social gulf between them was as long as the barrier reef; it stretched on into infinity: her wealth and friends, the huge estates and land, compared to the terrace house with an outside privy, a bricked yard and the front door opening onto the street. He might have achieved Detective Chief Inspector but that didn't raise the class. She'd be slumming being with him. He was a drunk who couldn't keep out of the Bell.

He turned away from her and gazed at his coffee cup. The coffee was cold, no steam. "You're right, Pru. We ought to take a look at the castle," he said standing up and pushing the chair away.

Pru sat up straight and smiled. "Great," she replied enthusiastically. "I won't be so scared with you around."

"You, scared! You've never been scared in your life."

"Don't kid yourself."

"My car," he said, "and we'll call at the station and see if we can rustle up some reserves. A couple of constables wouldn't come amiss."

Chapter 13

There were no constables available at the police station; they had missed the shift change by half an hour. Hooper came out onto the steps where Pru was waiting for him. He shrugged his shoulders. "We're on our own," he said. "You've got the key?"

Pru nodded. They stood for a moment at the top of the steps and looked across the woodland to where a castle turret peaked above the trees. "Come on," he said, "no point in standing here."

They walked down the steps and through the car park, the road snaked away back to town.

"Someday they'll improve the access to this place and cut down half those trees."

Pru glanced at him. "They're protected aren't they?"

"Could be. Let's take the footpath; it wanders a bit but there's no rush."

They walked side by side along the narrow path, their arms touching, each conscious of the other, neither willing to break the silence. They came to a fork in the path. "This way," Hooper said going to the left. "That loops back to town."

Pru followed him, a little behind him now. She made no comment and they slumped into silence. The trees in the wood began to get denser the further they went towards the castle. Hooper began to look around him. "If we let anybody out of this place they'll get away easily," he said.

"Assuming they need to get away," replied Pru.

Hooper chuckled. "Mrs. Sampson won't appreciate being locked in. She'll be itching to get away."

Pru touched Hooper on the shoulder; he stopped and turned round. "Herb, I wonder who is in that place? We know where daddy is, and we have an idea where James is, but where are the others? They couldn't all have holed up here could they?"

Hooper's shoulders dropped. "If they are, we've got a problem. Wilkinson is still the Chief Constable I suppose."

The castle loomed up through the trees. It was off the main path through the wood, but a smaller path led towards it. Hooper and Pru veered off along it. Grass, weeds, and fern, were beginning to encroach upon it since the Basingham council had deemed it unsafe. As they neared the old building they could see the path led directly to the iron gates.

Pru nudged Hooper and pointed over to where Mrs. Sampson's car was still parked.

Hooper smiled. "Well she hasn't managed to leave," he muttered. Pru smiled back, a nervous smile, which spread slowly over her face. She had been here and wasn't relishing a further visit.

"No," she replied quietly.

They slowed their pace and Hooper took the lead. About twenty-five metres from the castle he stopped; they were now in full view of the castle and if anyone could look out they would be seen. Pru came up to his side and they gazed at the building in silence. "What now?" she asked.

"You got the key?"

Pru nodded and delved in her bag. She handed it to Hooper and they began to walk towards the gate. At the gate Hooper peered through the bars but he couldn't see anything. He rattled the chain and padlock but it was firmly locked. He inserted the key; it turned easily. He slowly and quietly unwound the chain and placed it and the padlock on the ground. There was no door after the gate, just the old stone door frame with the remains of the original iron hinge set in lead and the blackness of the dungeon before him. Hooper stood looking into darkness; he could feel Pru grasping his sleeve. He listened intently. He could hear the murmur of voices, but they seemed a long way away.

....

Zeke Prune knew this was his chance. The horse was pounding towards the hedge. The hedge was low, broken by the hooves of the hunt riders who had gone before him, an easy jump.

The horse started to rise over the hedge and at that moment Zeke pulled back on the reins, the horse faltered mid-air confused by his rider's signal. At that moment Zeke flung himself from the saddle. He landed in several inches of water but expertly broke his fall and lay still. Twenty-five metres away another rider cleared the hedge and raced on.

"Damn, I thought I was the last; I wonder if he saw me," Zeke thought. He began to crawl along the ditch, the water slopping around his knees and elbows. Images of his flight from the east many years ago flashed through his mind. A hundred metres away from the hunt's crossing point he stopped and rolled into a sitting position, the fast-flowing stream lapping around his legs and buttocks. He sat there straining to hear galloping hooves but there was none. He stood up and looked around. His horse had fled on, following the pack and the howling dogs. He trudged on further down the stream to a break in the hedge which was filled in with wooden fencing. He climbed over and began the hike back to the house. It would be empty until the hunt returned and he would be home in three quarters of an hour.

Zeke arrived at the house, his clothes beginning to dry on him from the light breeze that had sprung up. He walked into the barn and dug out his case of clothes from behind the bales of hay. He changed into the dry garments and stuffed his damp ones into the case; he would have to get rid of those later.

He looked around the barn and across the yard to the mansion he was accustomed to living in. The ease and luxury of unbridled wealth, however it was gained. A quick thought shot across his brain; the legitimate and illegitimate ways he'd used to get that wealth, but that was over. His contact had made it very clear that his Russian boss was extremely angry about the missing diamonds and the fact that one of the fakes he had made had turned up at a jeweller's in London. How the hell had that happened! His contact had made it clear that the Russians had realised he was trying to pull a fast one. He needed a new identity, a new country, a new start and damn quick. He would have to realise his assets at a later date. A pity about Pru. A pity about James, but there was always some criminal or another who he could bend to his will.

Zeke walked quickly to the back of the house to the footpath which led to Basingham and his first steps to freedom. He'd dressed in a blue open necked shirt, jeans, walking boots, and carried a rucksack on his back. The typical walker, he thought, but he'd rather go by car or horse than shanks pony. But needs must come first, and this was the start of his new life.

The footpath ended five miles later at the end of a long row of terrace houses. They were all in need of repair, except for the odd one here and there which had been bought by the occupant and had been repaired and painted to make it liveable.

Zeke paused at the entrance to the street and looked up its long length. About a hundred houses he thought, I wonder if it is one of the streets I own, a money earner; do nothing to them and collect the rent every week, no arrears allowed. A no-brainer, a cash cow.

He walked up the street and at the top joined a busy road. Shops, betting shops, pubs and the odd boarding house lined the street. He had never been there before, but likewise no one would know him. He walked along looking for number fifty-four, Mrs. Price, that's what she said her name was. A large cardboard sign in the window announced she had vacancies and a dozen stone steps climbed to the front door. The sign pleased him; there wouldn't be too many people at the breakfast table. He looked at his watch. It was three o' clock, just about right for a hiker finishing his walk. He walked on; he'd have to get rid of the suitcase first; a hiker would hardly be carrying a case as well as a rucksack on his back.

In front of him a small sign on a lamppost pointed to the railway station. He took the turning. There would be waste bins there, and possibly a cafe where he could get a cup of railway tea. He knew he had to slip into his new persona, Zeke Prune was dead and Joshua Binns had started his public life. As he walked, he slipped off his gold Rolex and put it in his pocket. Would Joshua Binns be the owner of a Rolex watch? He was loath to dump that in a public waste bin. He would have to get himself another, less conspicuous brand. What sort of watch did ordinary people buy? He didn't like being ordinary; he liked having a Rolex and staying at the Ritz, not a mean boarding house.

He, Joshua, no, Josh arrived at the station and headed for the cafe. There was a money machine in the corner; he might as well try out his new debit card. He typed in a hundred pounds and Joshua Binns's account dispensed the money. He smiled as he took it; at least that arrangement was working.

Now what was he going to do with the case with the hunting gear in it? He walked to the counter and ordered tea and a ham salad sandwich, "Are there any waste bins around dear?" he asked.

"You might find one at the back of the station, but I don't think they like the public using them. How do you like your tea?"

"Black, love, no milk or sugar."

"Sit down and I'll bring your sandwich across."

He sat at a table in the corner where he could look out of the window. The view wasn't like the view from Prune House. He sighed and took a sip of his tea. The waitress arrived with his sandwich and handed him a Daily Mail.

"Thank you," he said, thinking he could spend some time reading it and then find those waste bins as the light dropped. Then he would have to book in at Mrs. Price's boarding house. He scowled at the thought but needs must. He sat in the cafe and drank several cups of tea and as the light faded the streetlamps outside began to switch on. The stream of customers had dropped to a trickle, and the lady behind the counter began to cash up.

"Haven't you got a home to go to dearie?" she called. "Elsie will be in shortly for the night shift.

There are a few trains to come through yet, and when the London train gets in there'll be a fair crush in here." She headed for the door as a small dark-haired lady walked in. "Hi Elsie," she said. "He's drinking tea by the bucket." Elsie looked across at him and smiled. Josh smiled back and nodded. It was time to go. He was getting too recognizable. Elsie thought he's an ugly sod; even our Joanie wouldn't want him in bed for an hour.

Josh stood up and slung his backpack over one shoulder and picked up his case. He waved to Elsie and moved to the door. Elsie watched him until he'd walked past the window towards the station. She made a cup of coffee and sat down where Josh had been sitting, and she had a clear view of what was happening on the street. She was ready for the crush of the London train arriving.

Josh turned left out of the door and passed the cafe window; he knew she was watching him, nosey bitch. The lights around the station had come on and ignoring the entrance to the platform he headed for a side gate. It was unlocked. He lifted the latch and gently opened the gate, hoping the staff would be having a cup of tea before the next train arrived and the crush began. The yard was empty. Over in one corner, sure enough, were the large waste bins. He crossed to them.

Opening the case, he looked at the riding clothes, expensive gear to be dumped. A good job he'd been wearing black and not red, that would have been a dead giveaway. He quickly put one piece of clothing in each bin and his case in another; hopefully no one would connect them. He left the yard unseen and walked back towards the cafe. He had a quick glance at the window. There, sure enough the nosy bitch was sitting looking out. He didn't falter but he knew she would watch him all the way up the street.

Elsie stood up as the now familiar, short stubby figure walked past the window. His gait was not of a man used to walking. Her son worked at a local riding stables and this fella walked a bit like him, as though he would rather be on a horse than his feet. There was something different about him though. Elsie couldn't place it. She watched him all the way up the street, and then she knew he wasn't carrying his case. Now, I wonder why that would be, she muttered to herself.

Josh Binns turned on to the high street and headed towards Mrs. Price's establishment. He could feel the piercing eyes of that cow in the cafe were no longer on his back and he wondered how much she would remember him. He would try not to make an impression on Mrs. Price.

He climbed the steps to the front door and pressed the bell. The door was opened by a tall, slim, pretty woman with blonde hair tied back in a pony tail. At five feet eight she smiled down on him.

"Mr. Binns?" she asked.

Josh smiled and held out his hand. "Mrs. Price," he said.

"Have you had a good day's walk?" she asked.

"Long enough," he said, "about fifteen miles."

"You'll be wanting something to eat. Dinner won't be long. Come, I'll show you to your room and you can get freshened up."

He followed her inside. It was a typical Victorian house. The front door led into a large hall from which the staircase ascended to the bedrooms. Mrs. Price opened the first door she came to.

"I have four rooms on this floor and this is the largest Mr. Binns. Is this alright for you?"

"Thank you, Mrs. Price, it is excellent."

She handed him the keys. "Come down in an hour or so and I'll have a meal ready."

"About tomorrow, Mrs. Price."

"Yes"

"I have some work to do. Do you mind if I stay in my room all day?"

"Well I usually come in and flick round with a duster, but I suppose it won't matter for once." she replied, making her way to the door.

Zeke Prune alias Josh Binns had found his bolt hole. He looked around the room. Pink flowered wallpaper adorned the walls, a pink bed spread covered the bed, pink curtains hung at the windows, a pink flowered carpet lay on the floor.

He dumped his rucksack on the bed and walked across the room and drew the curtains. He turned around and looked around the room. "I'll bet she calls this the pink room," he muttered to himself. "I wonder if the next one is blue."

The room was quite large with a comfortable looking armchair close to the window, a wardrobe and a chest of drawers, although he wouldn't need those. He sat down. Now he thought I have to plan my next move. I have no doubt someone will be looking for me if it's only that Hooper and Yates. And I'll bet they put out a general alert and that means Scotland too.

He delved in his rucksack and found a pad and a pen; lucky, he thought. Trust Pru to have such things when she goes walking. I wouldn't go out of the house unless it was in a car or on a horse. One thing is for sure I can't take a train direct to Edinburgh; they're sure to be waiting for me there. What about heading for Wales? Where could he take a bus to from Basingham? He couldn't go back to the railway station that was certain. Now there was an idea. He would take local buses, and use places like this to stay, or small pubs. He took his watch out of his pocket, and an hour had passed. He would have to buy a less conspicuous watch, a solid gold Rolex was hardly a thing to flash around.

He stood up and stretched; he'd better have a quick shower. The pink room was already growing on him. He felt sure Mrs. Price wouldn't mind if he stayed a day or two extra. The shower was hot and that pleased him. It also had a seat, very thoughtful. He sat down and let the water spray over him. He turned the heat to the hottest he could bear; he relaxed and let the water spray over him, soothing his aching bones. He sat in the shower mulling over his problems; they didn't seem so great here in the shower.

Tomorrow would be a different matter. Reality would kick in and he would have to get his thinking cap on. For a start it probably wouldn't be a good idea to stay here; he should move on and not let Mrs. Price get to know him. The less she saw of him, the less she would remember if asked. After all he wasn't that far from home, and there were people in Basingham who knew him. He turned off the shower and slid back the door, picked up Mrs. Price's luxury towel, and thought, dinner awaited. He couldn't remember the last time he felt so hungry.

Over the soup he turned over his problem; a gradual progression to Scotland where his new loch side cottage waited for him. No need to rush though. Perhaps he'd head for Historic Hastings first, and then perhaps a month on a houseboat on the Norfolk

Broads. He could head north using the canals. Perhaps he could call in at Stratford upon Avon and take in a show. The first thing to do would be get some information: a book on boarding houses, if there was one, an atlas, or map of the UK, a book on caravan parks where he could hire a van for a night or a week, bus routes, that would be useful. Yes, that should keep him on the move and not be too noticeable. A day here, a week there. Tomorrow he would sketch out a plan. He needed to stay off the internet until he could get a new untraceable mobile phone.

....

Hooper paused in the castle doorway and looked down into the dark abyss before him. He turned around and looked at Pru. She lifted her head questioningly. "Go home," he said. "I don't want you down here."

"No Herb, where you go I go."

"Don't argue Pru. Go home. I'll follow you shortly."

She shrugged her shoulders.

"Give me the key," he said.

Pru dug into her bag and handed it over. "Why?" she said.

"Because I don't want you to get hurt."

"There might be someone down there who needs my assistance."

"'I'll ring you if there is."

"Why don't I just wait here?"

"Please Pru, do as I ask and go home."

Pru stood for a moment looking at him, a scowl crossing her face. "Alright," she said, and turned on her heels and marched down the footpath to her car.

Hooper watched her for a moment. Why had he done that? They had done everything together since she had become his sergeant. She was the bravest woman he knew, the bravest person he knew. Who else would dive from a sixty-foot diving board?

He dismissed the thought and turned back to the task in hand. She was at the end of the telephone anyway. Should he call her back? No, he needed silence right now. Shouting wasn't an option.

He pulled the iron gate shut behind himself, laced the chain through it and locked the padlock., No one was going to do a runner. Beyond the stone door frame was blackness. He moved just inside and stopped, even in this intense darkness he knew his eyes would acclimatise and some sight would be possible. The light from outside filtered into the vast ancient hall. He looked down at his feet, now just discernible. He looked around; surely lights would have been installed, the public was allowed from time to time. But, right now he didn't want a lot of light.

Gradually, his eyes adjusted. He gulped. He was standing in a huge hall, at the top of a great stone staircase which fell below him. There was no banister rail. Did the ancient owners of the place expect their visitors to fall to their deaths before dinner? Above him a floor had been replaced excluding the natural light. Hooper slowly began to descend the staircase, putting each foot down carefully and quietly. He reached the bottom and again stopped. He looked about. The darkness was not quite absolute. Some way away he thought he could see a glimmer of light on the floor. He stood still, listening for any sounds. Silence, and then a shuffling sound.

"Anyone there?" he whispered.

"Yes, Yes," a female voice called. "Over here, Oh thank God!"

Hooper bounded over the stone flagged floor in the direction of the voice. Why hadn't he brought a torch? Ten steps and his impetus ceased. There, in the low light of the ancient cellar, a woman hung to the wall. Her arms and legs splayed out like a cross and manacled to iron hoops. A metal ring encircled her neck, attached to the wall with a long loose chain. A reflection of Stacey on the bowling green thought Hooper. Her hair, long, stringy and unkempt, hung about her, straggling her face and shoulders. Whoever did this is a madman, Hooper muttered.

"Over there," she gasped, "Jimmy; is he alright?"

Hooper turned from her, and there on the floor was the missing boy; the boy at the bowling green who he'd given half a crown to go home. He too was splayed out and manacled. His wrists and ankles padlocked to iron rings on the floor. Mercifully he was sleeping.

He crossed the room back to the woman. "You must be Mrs. Gardner," he said.

She nodded. "How long have you been here?"

Mrs. Gardner shook her head. "I've lost track of time."

"Is there anyone else here?"

"Yes, they're in the room by the stairs."

"Does this place have any lights?"

"Yes, he turns them on when he brings us some food."

"Do you know him?"

Mrs. Gardner shook her head. "He's big, taller than you. Can you get us out?"

"I'm going to get the police and ambulance. Can you hold on a bit longer?"

She nodded and dropped her chin to her chest as though it was too heavy for her neck to carry.

Hooper walked to the staircase and climbed to the top. The mediaeval scene below churned his stomach. It was unbelievable. He slumped to the ground and fiddled in his pockets until he found his phone. What was the emergency number? He couldn't remember. Pru was listed in names. How did you find names on this blasted device? Then he remembered, Pru had put an icon, or something, for him to list phone numbers. He pressed on the button and the screen lit, bright and colourful.

He looked at it through blurred, wet eyes, unable to remember what she said he had to do. Then he saw it, a bright red patch, the colour of her hair, with Pru written in the middle. She'd said just touch it and she would answer.

"Herb."

"Pru, get the police and an ambulance here quick."

He dropped the phone and Pru could hear his retching. Hooper turned on to his side as his stomach boiled and heaved, but it was empty and nothing more was emitted.

Hooper sat there on the grass, his back to the castle wall. "Where is the nearest pub" was running through his head. No, a pint would taste of vomit.

Perhaps a scalding hot shower would drive the stench and the scene from his mind.

Hooper heard a rustle of grass and opened his eyes. Pru was running towards him, her red hair streaming out behind her. The most beautiful sight he had ever seen he thought. She stopped in front of him, the iron gate separating them.

"Oh Herb," she muttered, the wet tear-stained face and the yellow bile of his vomiting clinging to his clothes. "Give me the key," she said.

He lifted his head, such banal words he thought with the terrible pictures racing through his head like a movie film.

"Herb, the key," she repeated.

"The key? Oh yes."

He fiddled in his pockets until he found it. Pru reached through the iron bars to take it. Hooper held up his hand. "Don't go down there Pru; wait 'til they come."

In the distance the wailing sound of a siren cut through the air. To Hooper it sounded like a reprieve.

…………..

Hooper and Pru sat side by side, their backs against the castle wall. Pru gently held the limp hand of Herbert Hooper, normally so strong, as a stream of castle residents were brought up from the ancient dungeon.

The first out into the fresh air, was Jimmy, and Mrs. Gardner, borne up the treacherous stone staircase on stretchers. Jimmy lifted up a weak hand as he passed them and they both returned his greeting.

"Such a brave boy," Pru said.

"Yes," replied Hooper.

There was silence from the pit below them, and then a scuffle and shouting. Hooper tried to stand but Pru restrained him and he sat back on the grass. Two figures appeared in the doorway, a burly policeman and a struggling Sampson, his hands cuffed together.

"I am your superior officer. Let me go!" he yelled.

"Yes sir," said the police constable, firmly clasping Sampson's shoulders and leading him to the police van. "Now then, sir, in you get," said the policeman.

Hooper smiled a weak smile. "Who would have thought it Pru," he said.

"No, you wouldn't. So, it was he who killed Stacey and Woodley and then he kidnapped Jimmy and Mrs. Gardener to cover it up?"

"Looks that way," agreed Hooper.

"But why kill Stacey and Woodley?"

"I don't know. Greed maybe? He wanted a slice of the family business and Stacey wasn't playing. Woodley may have been involved or more likely he knew something that could have exposed Sampson's involvement in the murder."

"He's mad, isn't he?"

Hooper nodded. "I fear so although whether that will be the verdict of the court I don't know."

Hooper and Pru sat and waited, the stench of vomit permeating the air around them. Pru could sense that Hooper was recovering; he was fidgeting, anxious to stand up, but Pru restrained with a gentle push.

"Let them manage, Herb," she said.

Hooper stayed sitting on the grass as another figure appeared in the doorway. He was tall, broad shoulders almost obscured the constable behind him. He walked out quietly, no handcuffs, just the constable holding his arm. He walked past the two reclining figures and paused slightly. He gave them a resigned smile and walked on. He climbed into the barred police van without assistance and sat down.

Hooper shook his head. "Pru," he said, "I remember the day that man told me to go on the streets and find Stacey's killer."

"Why was Wilkinson involved?"

"Money probably," said Herb. "I bet he'll say the violence was all down to Sampson and he knew nothing about it. Sheer luck they were all in the castle having a council of war when you locked the door or it would have been difficult to prove his involvement.'

Pru nodded and nudged him. He looked towards the door; the desk sergeant was emerging. "All the rats out of the hole now?" Hooper asked.

Pru smiled and squeezed his hand. "Look again," she said.

Intrigued, he leaned forward, and there, following the docile sergeant was Yates. Hooper almost bounced to his feet unrestrained, this time Pru let him go. She struggled to her feet to follow him. Suddenly, the smiling Yates put up his hand, the flat palm bringing Hooper to a halt.

"Charlie?" asked Hooper. "I thought you had gone home."

"I was paying a farewell visit to the station when Pru's call came in. Herb, you stink. Go home and take a long bath." Charlie Yates laughed. "I'll see you when I've finished with these guys."

Hooper nodded and gave him a salute as Yates and the sergeant passed through the iron gate and into the police van.

"Come on," said Pru, linking her arm through his, "I don't care how smelly you are. Let's go to my place. You can soak in my old bath as long as you like. I'll even add some scented bath salts."

Chapter 14

Hooper pulled himself to his feet; the pine scented bath water rolling from him. He climbed over the rolled top of the cast iron bath that Pru had found in a scrap yard, and picked up a towel. Downstairs he could hear the whirr of a washing machine as his vomit covered clothes were sloshed around. He wondered if Pru had put pine in there too.

He dressed and went out on to the landing. The smell of fresh ground coffee assaulted his nose. He stood for a moment and took a deep breath. It was nice to be looked after. He walked down the stairs. At the bottom, several cardboard boxes were standing by the hallstand. Hooper went into the kitchen and sat down.

"What are in the boxes?" he asked.

Pru continued to pour the coffee. "I'm starting to pack Herb. I'm moving back to Prune House."

Hooper didn't reply. Pru brought the coffee mugs over to the table and looked down on him. "I have to Herb," she put a mug in front of him.

Hooper picked up the mug she had set before him. "You don't have to do anything," he said.

Pru pulled a chair towards her and sat down. A silence settled between them.

"I can't neglect it," she said, and then, "It's the same with the estate. Now daddy isn't there, it has to be looked after."

Hooper raised his eyes to the pretty girl sitting by his side. Wealthy, out of his league. He smiled weakly. Suddenly the front doorbell pealed out 'They'll be coming round the mountains'. Pru stood up, walked over to the front door and opened it.

"Charlie!" she almost shouted in relief. "Come in. Herb, look who's here. That's not taken long Charlie."

Charlie Yates laughed, his infectious laugh ringing through the hall. "No, they're all banged up ready for a hearing in the morning."

Hooper came into the hall, his hand outstretched.

Yates pretended to sniff the air. "What's this? Only pine I can smell." The two friends embraced. "And fresh ground coffee."

"I'll get another mug," said Pru walking past them.

"Charlie what brought you back here?" Hooper asked.

Yates raised an eyebrow and looked at Hooper and smiled. "Pru," he called, "shall I tell him?"

"He'll kill me if you do," a voice shouted from the kitchen, over the sound of clinking mugs and gushing water.

"Oh, I think it's worth the risk."

"Well?" demanded Hooper.

"Pru thought you were a little under the weather and could do with a bit of support."

"Oh, she did, did she?"

Pru came into the dining room from the kitchen, a tray of steaming mugs and full supporting cafetière rocking precariously on it. Yates took it from her.

"Now don't lose your cool Herb," Yates said, putting the tray on the table and setting a mug in front of Hooper. "Black coffee and a lot of sugar will set you up for the day."

"Are you trying to butter me up Charlie? What are two up to?"

Yates sat down beside his friend and picked up his mug. Pru walked to the other side of the table and sat down, her elbows on the table nursing her mug in her hands. They both looked at Hooper saying nothing.

"You're ganging up on me."

"When did you have your last pint?" Yates said.

"I'm having my next and probably several of them as soon as I've finished this coffee." He picked up the mug and drained it in one gulp.

"Are you coming Charlie?" he said, with his eyes on Pru, and starting to rise from his chair.

"Sit down Herb." said Yates. "That's just the point."

"The point. What do you mean?"

"Promotion, Herb. Now that lot is getting what's due to them, this place is wide open for the right man."

Hooper looked at Yates and then at Pru and back again and said nothing.

"Don't you like that thought, Herb. Promotion?" asked Pru.

"Promotion? Where to?"

"The top job will be up for grabs," said Yates.

"Chief Constable, you must be joking."

Yates leaned back in his chair and said, "For the right man."

"For the right man, what does that mean?"

Yates stood up, he leaned forward and stretched out his hand, and, as if clasping a pint glass lifted it to his mouth. Hooper watched him and said nothing. Yates sat back down.

There was a long pause and then Hooper said, "And there was me thinking I wasn't the right class to get that far. I didn't come from the right social background. Basingham elementary school hardly stretches to Chief Constable Charlie."

"Oh Herb," sighed Pru.

Yates sipped his coffee and scrutinised Hooper over the rim of his mug. Lowering his mug he said softly, "Herb, what rank are you?"

Hooper looked at Yates with a puzzled look on his face. "That's a stupid question; you know what rank I am."

"Humour me, Herb, what is your rank?"

"DCI, theoretically suspended."

"Do you expect to get reinstated?"

"I don't see why not."

"Do you think your education at Basingham elementary school and Grammar school will stop that from happening?"

Hooper swirled the dregs of his mug around like a fortune teller studying tea leaves. His face was studious. "No, I don't expect so."

"Then why do you think it will stop you from getting the top job?"

Hooper didn't reply and a silence dropped across the table. There was a loud knocking on the door. Pru stood up and went to answer it. She came back with a padded envelope in her hand.

Pru picked up a knife lying on the table and slit it open; the two men sat and watched. Poking inside she extracted a small, sealed plastic envelope and held it up for them to see.

"What's that?" said Hooper.

"Remember I said we ought to get those blue stones evaluated?" Hooper nodded.

"I sent them off to a London jeweller and asked if they could do it; they've just returned them."

"What did they say?"

Pru poked in the packet again and brought out a letter. She unfolded it and began to read. A smile began to spread across her face.

"Well?" asked Hooper.

"Our friend James won't be as rich as he thinks he is," she said.

Hooper and Yates said together, "Why?"

Pru looked at them in turn and said, "This is another of my father's little scams. These stones are not diamonds but a mixture of zircon and man-made zircon, and zircon is the nearest stone to diamond there is."

"So to the uninitiated they could be passed off as diamonds?"

"Yes, and I expect that is what daddy was doing. Perhaps not at the full diamond price, but a lot more than the Zircon price."

"Another nice little earner for Zeke Prune," said Yates. "I wonder if there were real diamonds as well and if so what he has done with them?"

"And that's a thought. I wonder where he is?" said Hooper.

Pru put the letter down on the table and sat down, "More coffee?" she asked, adding, "Nowhere you'll expect to find him."

Pru filled the mugs. "This seems to be getting cold, I'll make some more."

"OK Herb, back to promotion. I made it, why can't you?"

"You know what the selection committee is like, always looking for some new highly polished guy with all the right connections."

"You brush up OK," said Pru, bringing in a fresh cafetière, "and you have the advantage of knowing most of them."

"Yes, but they're snobby, you know that."

Pru sat down again and pushed the coffee pot into the middle of the table. "Herb, you can't let that attitude deter you."

"There is one thing though," Yates said.

Herb and Pru looked at him questioningly.

"Nobody minds a copper having drink Herb, but they don't want him coming into work sozzled."

"What are you suggesting Charlie?" Hooper asked.

Yates drank his coffee and refilled his mug from the fresh pot. "A little holiday," said Yates.

"Holiday, what does that mean?"

"Come on Herb, you know what it means; rehab, drying out. Call it what you like, but you have to get off the booze."

Hooper looked across at Pru. She shrugged her shoulders and then nodded. "Although it's nothing to do with me Herb, I've handed in my notice. It's your career."

Hooper sat back in his chair, his shoulders sagging, staring at the coffee mugs on the table. Suddenly, he sat up, "Right," he said, "If that's what it takes that's what I'll do."

"Good man," cried Yates. "I knew I could depend on you."

Pru poured herself some hot coffee and smiled.